# *The*
# BABE RUTH
# *Deception*

**Books by David O. Stewart**

*Fiction*

THE LINCOLN DECEPTION*

THE WILSON DECEPTION*

THE BABE RUTH DECEPTION*

*Non-Fiction*

THE SUMMER OF 1787: THE MEN WHO INVENTED THE CONSTITUTION

IMPEACHED: THE TRIAL OF PRESIDENT ANDREW JOHNSON AND THE FIGHT FOR LINCOLN'S LEGACY

AMERICAN EMPEROR: AARON BURR'S CHALLENGE TO JEFFERSON'S AMERICA

MADISON'S GIFT: FIVE PARTNERSHIPS THAT BUILT AMERICA

***Published by Kensington Publishing Corporation**

# *The* BABE RUTH *Deception*

DAVID O. STEWART

KENSINGTON BOOKS
www.kensingtonbooks.com

KENSINGTON BOOKS are published by

Kensington Publishing Corp.
119 West 40th Street
New York, NY 10018



All Kensington titles, imprints and distributed lines are available at special quantity discounts for bulk purchases for sales promotion, premiums, fund-raising, educational or institutional use. Special book excerpts or customized printings can also be created to fit specific needs. For details, write or phone the office of the Kensington Special Sales Manager: Kensington Publishing Corp., 119 West 40th Street, New York, NY, 10018. Attn. Special Sales Department. Phone: 1-800-221-2647.



Library of Congress Card Catalogue Number: 2016945051

ISBN-13: 978-1-4967-0200-5
ISBN-10: 1-4967-0200-X
First Kensington Hardcover Edition: October 2016

eISBN-13: 978-1-4967-0201-2
eISBN-10: 1-4967-0201-8
First Kensington Electronic Edition: October 2016

10 9 8 7 6 5 4 3 2 1

Printed in the United States of America

*To Nancy*

# *The* BABE RUTH *Deception*

# Chapter 1

Eliza clutched the door handle for safety as the big Packard swerved down the snaky riverside road. Her free hand held her hat on. "For the love of Mike," she yelled into the wind, "slow down!"

Despite her shout, the grin stayed on the Babe's broad face. He kept the throttle wide open.

"She sure can fly," he called back, blue eyes locked on the road. "Going slow in this baby would be a crime!"

Then he oversteered on a wide curve. The Packard tilted up on its right tires, a movement that brought Eliza's stomach up, too. The car launched into the roadside ditch, slamming into the far bank.

Eliza's scream cut off when she banged against the door, then lifted up. Her hip scraped painfully over the windshield and she tumbled awkwardly onto the car's long snout. She landed hard on a shoulder on the lip of the ditch. Her splayed hands partly broke her fall.

Quiet fell. The engine had quit. Eliza lay still and panted, her heart racing, pain starting to replace terror. Moving her arms gingerly, she started an inventory. Her arms worked. Then her head. It was clear, though it felt jagged inside and oddly remote from the scene. She pushed herself onto her side. The hip—Jesus, it hurt. She sat up. She flexed her right leg. Then moved her right arm and shoulder. That hurt. She decided not to move any more for a while. Could have been worse. Probably should have been.

She had known it was dangerous to climb in with the Babe for the ride to the Hudson River ferry. It wasn't only his love for speed, though there was certainly that. It was also that he was a lousy driver, which didn't make a lot of sense. Great athletes should be great drivers. The magical coordination and timing that allowed him to hammer home runs over distant fences should mean he piloted cars with precision and skill. But it didn't. Since they'd started filming Babe's movie that summer, he had averaged a crash every few days. He also got pulled over for speeding sometimes but never got tickets. He just smiled, signed autographs for the cops, and moved on.

Eliza heard him groan. A car door opened and slammed shut. Uneven steps approached. "You okay?" he asked, his voice gravelly. He hawked and spat to the side.

She tilted her head so she could look all the way up at him. She was used to large men. Her husband Jamie was as tall as Babe. But no one gave off a sense of power like Babe did. "I suppose," she said. She winced. Her shoulder and hip weren't good, but they weren't bad enough to talk about. She didn't ask how he was. He always walked away from his wrecks.

She was tempted to ask why. Why drive so fast on a twisty road like New York's notorious Route 3? But there was no point. The Babe did what the Babe did. Getting angry was a waste of time, like losing your temper at a thunderstorm.

He helped her to her feet. A shooting pain suggested something really could be wrong with the shoulder. She shrugged it, then moved it back and forth. She'd have Jamie look at it.

Sometimes it helped having a doctor in the family.

Babe patted the Packard's hood, then smiled. "Isn't she a honey? Twelve cylinders." A lock of brown hair spilled over his forehead. His eyes were luminous, framed by the thick mascara he hadn't taken the time to remove while rushing from the movie set.

"Jeez," Babe said. "We've gotta hustle. I've got to get to the ballpark." He waved at a small boy who had appeared a few yards off. Babe's crash was bound to become one of this hick town's legends, the most exciting local event since the soldiers came home from the Great War the year before.

"Hey, kid," the Babe said, putting a big grin on his wide face. "You live around here?"

The boy, wide-eyed, nodded.

"That's fine, kid. Now, listen. I'm Babe Ruth"—the boy nodded again—"and I've got to get to the Polo Grounds for today's game." The boy continued to stare. The power of speech had fled. "Honest, kid, that's the truth. I wouldn't kid you." He struck a muscleman pose, a fist curled over each shoulder. "Does your pa or someone around here have a car they might run us down the ferry in?"

"I pull for the Giants," the boy said.

"Don't worry, kid, we're playing the Indians today. How's about that car?"

The boy ran off at top speed.

"You're just going to leave this one?" Eliza said.

Babe shrugged. The world would pick up after him. It always did.

Sitting in the clubhouse after the game, Babe noticed the mascara. Somebody might've told him. After weeks of filming every morning before the games, his teammates no longer mocked his movie makeup.

He had no energy to wash it off now. He felt dead inside.

Which was lots better than Ray Chapman had to feel after getting drilled by that submarine spitball thrown by Carl Mays. That asshole Mays hadn't even noticed that he hit the poor bastard. After the ball bounced off Chapman's head, Mays fielded it cleanly and threw to first base. Chapman stood for a second, then he was down, blood coming out of his ear. What an asshole.

Babe leaned back against his locker, his uniform unsoiled. The clubhouse was quiet, guys showering and dressing and getting the hell out. Nobody much liked Chapman's odds.

Babe sighed and let the fatigue in. The whole damned day had been a bust. First the dawn trip upriver to the movie set. Babe hadn't made it to bed the night before, which wasn't totally unusual but wasn't so great two nights in a row. He could do with a couple hours of shut-eye.

Then there was getting made up, standing around, getting made up again, waiting while they monkeyed with the lights, standing around some more, having that pansy director tell him what to do and how to walk and how to look. Which didn't matter because the Babe was going to do and walk and look how he was. That's the way it was going to be.

The only good part of the day had been the drive back on Route 3, letting that Packard engine open up and roar. He even enjoyed having Eliza Fraser along with him. She was sort of an old broad, had something to do with the money behind the movie, but she'd kept her looks, wasn't all dried up. He'd heard maybe she'd been an actress back before there were movies. You could see how she might have been, the way she walked and stood, like she knew people were watching.

Running off the road was bad luck. They shouldn't make roads with curves like that. Still, he got to the park by the fifth inning, only the first thing he saw then was Ray Chapman getting his and Mays fielding the ball off his head. Damn, the sound the ball made.

Huggins had refused to put him in the game, making a big deal about being late. Huggins knew damned well that Babe was always on time, always, except when he couldn't be. If the road hadn't been so twisty, he would've made it easy. He actually didn't mind not playing. He hadn't felt much like playing after Chapman got hit. Nobody had. That's probably why the Yanks blew the game, 4–3. That was bad luck. The squad needed every win this time of the season.

After years of the Yanks being lousy, Ruth and his home-run swing had arrived over the winter. That changed everything. Now, in mid-August, the team was hard on the heels of the first-place Clevelands, riding the Babe's forty-two home runs, already more than anyone had ever hit in one season, and he wasn't done. Which was why every American man, even kids like that hayseed by the side of the road, knew his name. Plus it was an easy name to remember.

"Hey, big fella, how ya doin'?" Babe didn't have to raise his head to take in Abe Attell. The man was a squirt even if he had been a world champion. Featherweight or something. Attell looked like an ad for lemonade in the summer, straw boater tilted back on his head, white suit, blue shirt.

"If it ain't the Little Hebrew," Babe said. "Hope you had your money on the Indians today."

"What, me bet against the great Babe Ruth?" Attell's mouth impersonated a smile. His prizefighter's nose bent one way and then another. "You know I couldn't do that."

Babe shook the man's small paw, which was stronger than you might expect, then rose to shed his uniform. The other man glanced around the deserted clubhouse. Even the sportswriters, those bloodsuckers, had scrammed. Probably at the hospital watching the poor bastard die.

"So, Babe," Attell started. Babe kept undressing. "Ah, there's some news coming you oughta know about. You know, ahead of time."

Babe, standing in his altogether, scratched a spot between his nose and eye. He cursed when the finger came away with black makeup. When he got back from washing his face, Attell was waiting, one foot up on a bench.

"So, you see, there's this grand jury in Chicago. It's gonna hear evidence about the World Series last year. You know, the White Sox and Cincinnati?"

"No kidding."

"Yeah, no kidding." Attell pushed his straw boater forward and rubbed the back of his head, then slid the hat back where it had been. "Story's going around that some of the Chicagos threw the Series, you know, for cash."

Babe grunted an acknowledgment. He'd heard about gambling on that Series, which the White Sox managed to lose even though they seemed a good bit better. Which didn't prove a lot. There were lots of reasons a team played better or worse than you figured. "Ah, you always hear talk like that. What do I care? I wasn't in that Series."

"Well, there's a couple of things. First, I thought you oughta know, telling all my friends since they may be looking at me for some of this." That hardly qualified as a surprise, not with an operator like the Little Hebrew, considering his type of business and his type of friends. Come to think of it, Babe wasn't nuts about being called one of his friends. Attell kept talking. "So I want you to know it won't make any difference to the financing for your movie."

Babe stopped buttoning the crisp new shirt he'd brought for his evening appointments, which would begin at the Butterfly Club on Fifty-sixth Street. He grimaced, then cocked a hip and refocused on Attell. "What're you saying? You're in on the movie?"

Attell chuckled and grabbed the Babe's bicep. "'Course I am, Babe. I wouldn't miss a chance to back America's biggest hero, no matter what cockamamie thing you're doing. I put the money in through that Broadway dame. You know the one?"

"Eliza Fraser?"

"Yeah, that's the one. Knows her stuff, for a broad."

"How do you know her?"

"Ah, it's through a guy, one both you and I know. The boss, y'know, he likes the shows, all the bright lights. Knows lots of those Broadway types."

"Okay." Babe resumed dressing, stepping into trousers of a pearl gray chalk-stripe. He liked the double-breasted look. It made him look even bigger.

Attell, pulling on an ear, started again. "There's a second thing. You may hear some talk, you know, around that grand jury."

Babe kept his attention on buttoning his fly. He was looking forward to getting some help unbuttoning it, maybe real soon. He'd have a couple of steaks first; that'd be just the ticket. Jeez, he could eat a horse. He needed to ditch this guy.

"You see, Babe, they may start asking about the Series the year before, you know, 1918, the one you won with the Red Sox?"

Babe paused and fixed Attell with a level gaze. The little man repeated himself. Then Babe stepped up close and looked down his shirt front at this nasty little weasel. He dropped his voice low. "What's that to me? Like you said, the Red Sox won. Couldn't've been any payoffs to us, right?"

Attell stepped back and showed Babe the palms of his hands. "That's what I says to the boss. I says, hey, the Babe's good on this one, couldn't be a problem. But the boss, you know, he says I should pass the word, make sure the Babe don't get surprised by anyone, say, someone coming around and asking questions. The boss, you know, he's real careful. That's why he wanted me to mention that other thing, too, make sure you remember it."

The ballplayer's left hand shot out and grabbed a fistful of Attell's shirtfront. He lifted the smaller man up on his toes until the crooked nose was inches from Ruth's big pie face. The fans loved that mug, round like the moon when it broke into a smile, but the fans never saw this expression, blue eyes blazing, jaws grinding. "Don't push your luck, you lousy kike," he said in a low voice.

"Whoa, whoa, whoa. I don't mean nothing bad. I'm your friend here. Every time your name comes up, Babe, I defend you. But the boss, like I said, he's real careful."

Babe dropped Attell back onto his feet. He took a clean collar and necktie out of the locker and started toward a wall of mirrors that hung over a line of sinks. He had few pleasant memories of that 1918 World Series. It was nothing but fighting, starting with the fight over whether there would even be a World Series. Who needed ball games when our boys were dying in France to save democracy? Then there was the fight with the government over whether ballplayers should be drafted to help out with all that dying. And then fighting with the other players over whether to go out on strike for a decent payday. Then there was fighting with the fans who jeered that the ballplayers were disloyal ingrates, ought to all go enlist in the army. The gamblers, they'd been the worst, frantic for action, what with the racetracks shut down for the war. Those creeps packed the team clubhouses to the gills, scrounging for inside tips, making friends, passing out favors. Then the Series—that had to be the least fun anyone ever had winning a championship. And then there was the other thing. Stupid. He'd been set up, sure, but it was still stupid, especially since it landed him way too deep with Abie Attell and his boss, Arnold Rothstein.

As Babe set to work on his tie, Attell walked up behind him. "Okay, I'll be moving along. Take care of yourself."

Babe's eyes followed Attell's retreating image in the mirror.

The small man bounced on the balls of his feet, like he was getting ready to box a few rounds. Or maybe just had. Bastard, Babe thought. Feeding on the Babe's carcass. All of 'em. That's all they did.

Porterhouse, he thought next. That would pick up his mood. Two of 'em.

# *Chapter 2*

Jamie Fraser, with Eliza on his arm, took a deep breath of brisk September air. Chinese lanterns bordered the rooftop patio of Madison Square Garden. Flaming torches lit the buffet tables, spreading a faint aroma of paraffin. White-gloved waiters offered trays with glasses of champagne. Jamie lifted two and handed one to his wife. He knew that set of her jaw. It wasn't ever good.

"Twenty minutes, Jamie. Please keep track. Then we flee." She pounded down the champagne in two quick swallows. She reached around a woman in blue for another.

"You're overreacting. It wasn't that bad." They and nearly fifteen hundred other New Yorkers had just left the Garden's theater downstairs after viewing the premiere of *Headin' Home*, the new feature film starring the great Babe Ruth.

After a more moderate swallow of champagne, she shook her head. "It was only bad if you like a plausible plot and actual characters. For those who prefer shopworn clichés served up by a blend of no-talent hambones and stiffs, *Headin' Home* is perfect." She finished the second glass and looked around for a waiter. "I suspect that audiences will be 'headin' home' soon after the opening credits."

"Come on, now. You knew this wasn't going to be an artistic triumph. The idea was to cash in on Ruth—give baseball fans around the country a close-up look at the new hero. No one's expecting Chekhov."

Eliza wheeled on him, hazel eyes flashing. "If you think it's helpful to remind me of my own idiocy, I can go home in a taxi."

In their early days together, Jamie had delighted in his wife's high spirits. Like a proud mustang, he had thought. These days the word that came to mind was *difficult*. Increasingly, he found himself paddling dazedly in her wake, surprised by some unforeseen eruption. What was his crime this morning? Ah, yes, taking too long with the news section of the *Herald.* And that was after she had already looked through two other newspapers. Lock him up and throw away the key! Of course, she'd never been easy, which he had liked. Imagine that.

Eliza issued a dramatic sigh and slipped a gloved hand into the crook of his elbow. "All right, dear. Let's face the music before I drink enough to tell everyone what I really think. It's actually good champagne. Remarkable in view of our supposed Prohibition laws."

"We should find out who their bootlegger is."

As they began to circulate, Fraser kept away from the edges of the roof. He also took care not to look up at the sky. He never knew what would trigger his vertigo. Even thinking about being on the roof could do it, trigger fantasies of plunging through space. He minded the current fashion to dismiss any fear of heights as a "phobia," a sign of mental disorder. Avoiding high places was simple common sense. Any species without a healthy fear of heights was courting extinction. At least, that's how Fraser saw it.

Eliza greeted actors, critics, newsmen, socialites. Her smile was bright, her words warm but never cloying. She laughed her social laugh, the one with brittle undertones that used to grate on Fraser, but he'd gotten used to it. No one would guess that she despised the movie. When she introduced Jamie, she pumped him up. He was always "*Doctor* James Fraser, of the Rockefeller Institute uptown." He smiled genially and muttered affable words, secure in the knowledge that no one in her world cared a fig about some dreary medical researcher. Their only concern was the fervent wish that he never say anything about science, medicine, or illness, so he never did.

Sometimes Eliza found it too much trouble to introduce him, which left him free to stare at the crowd. He enjoyed watching her operate. He also liked that she was wearing the gray pearls, the ones he bought in Paris. He liked her in those pearls.

Fraser noted a young man as tall as he was, about twenty feet away, looking equally detached from the social scrum. With a start, he realized it was the Babe, dark hair flopping onto his forehead. There was something elemental, even brutish, about his size, the way he stood, yet that disappeared when he smiled. The movie screen flattened him out, concealed the force of his presence.

Pressure on Fraser's arm meant that Eliza was weary of her current conversational partner. Fraser leaned down. "That's him, over there," he said into her ear.

She raised her head. "Ah, yes. Fresh from his dramatic triumph!"

"He doesn't look all that triumphant."

"Fitting."

"Introduce me."

Eliza looked up. "Really?"

"Is there anyone else here you'd rather speak with?"

"Just when I think you're not paying attention, it turns out you are." She squared her shoulders. "Prepare yourself for monosyllables and a bit of unfiltered leering."

He smiled. "Your appeal spans the generations."

She patted his cheek. "You can have a sting, dear. I'm aware that my appeal to Mr. Ruth is that I am female, which is the sole quality required to earn his single-minded attention."

"He'll take us up to twenty minutes and then we can go home."

"It's a deal."

The big man enveloped her in a bear hug. He waved over a waiter as Eliza disengaged and introduced her husband.

"A grand movie, Mr. Ruth," Fraser said. "How did you enjoy making it?"

"Call me Babe," the ballplayer said, snatching a glass from a tray. "Everyone does." He stared over the crowd.

"How'd you find the movie-making?"

"Huh?" Babe looked back at Fraser. "Ah, it was sorta silly. I'm not really much like the guy in the movie—he's all shy and modest. But your wife, that fruitcake director, they all said that's what people want." He finished his glass and looked for another. "I liked kissing the girls," he said over his shoulder.

Eliza shot Fraser one of her "see?" looks.

"Do you think you'll make another?" Fraser asked.

"Only if they pay me." Ruth reached over a small man's head to snare another glass and toasted Jamie. "Here's lead in your pencil." After swallowing, Ruth noticed that Eliza had arched an eyebrow. "Oh, jeez," he said. "Sorry, ma'am."

Eliza laughed, not her social laugh. "You're really not at all like that fellow in the movie."

Ruth smiled happily and killed the rest of the champagne. "Shit," he said as his scan of the room focused on a far quadrant, "would you look at him."

"Who?" Fraser twisted around to follow the ballplayer's gaze.

"The goddamned Little Hebrew, Abie Attell." Ruth reached into his suit jacket and brought out a silver flask. He offered it to Eliza and Jamie, who declined, then he took a long swallow. "Tell me something," he said to Eliza. "Why was it a secret that Attell was backing the movie?"

"Didn't anyone tell you?" She was cool. Butter wouldn't melt.

"Not a word."

"It wasn't a secret, not that I knew about."

Ruth's face was grim. "It was from me."

Eliza turned to Fraser. "Dear?"

"Ah, yes," Fraser answered. He turned to Ruth, who was working on his flask again. "Babe, I'm afraid it's our turn to be headin' home."

Ruth put the flask away and focused on Eliza. "Say, you live up at the Ansonia, like me. D'you have your car here? I could do with a lift. I got some places to go to."

Babe's eyes danced when the valet stepped out of Fraser's brand new Stutz Bearcat, scarlet body with a black roof. "Doc," he called as he walked around the long front end, "you've got great taste in cars as well as dames." He grinned at the car's tall front grille, its headlamps as big as melons. "She's a beaut."

Waiting for Eliza to clamber into the rear seat, Fraser answered, "The car's nice, too."

"How fast can you get it up to?"

Fraser nodded at the police officer listening in from the curb. "I don't really remember, Babe. I always take it easy here in town."

Fraser set off at a modest rate, pausing at every intersection. Manhattan traffic was becoming ever more treacherous, forcing drivers to stutter uncertainly through a maze of cars, horse-drawn wagons, bicycles, and those afoot. Babe hunched forward in his seat, taking swigs from his flask and drinking in the sights Fifth Avenue offered on Saturday night. He was absorbing New York through his pores.

"Getting out of Boston, moving down here," he said to no one in particular, "it was like getting out of school." He looked over at Fraser. "Most towns, you know, you gotta go find what's happening. There's usually something going on, even in the dumpiest places, but you gotta go find it, starting with finding the people who can show you where it is. It's like a damned treasure hunt. Here, it's just right out there. Casinos, speakeasies, whatever you want. Half the speaks haven't even taken down their signs as saloons."

"You like getting out at night?" Fraser asked.

Babe laughed and sat back. "Why not? Gonna be dead a long time."

"Babe," Eliza said, leaning forward from the darkness of the backseat. "Why does it bother you to have Abe Attell behind the movie?"

"Abie? Damned little chipmunk's always got an angle. See, also, there's talk he's gonna get indicted out in Chicago, for fixing the Series last year. Helen—she's my wife—she thinks maybe I shouldn't be seen with guys like him right now. You know, makes a bad impression." He took another pull on his flask.

"Sure," Fraser said, "but your team wasn't even in that series. It was Chicago and Cincinnati, right? What could it matter to you whether Attell gets charged?"

"I sure as hell was in the Series the year before, 1918. Remember? The Red Sox beat the Cubs."

The traffic tower at Forty-second Street, the city's first stoplight, brought them to a halt. Fraser, bathed in red glow, tapped the steering wheel impatiently while waiting to turn left. He planned to take Broadway uptown. "But you said they're not looking at that Series, the one in 1918."

Babe snorted. "Bet your sweet life they will."

"Why?"

"D'you follow that Series?" He smiled over at Fraser as his skin suddenly shone green. Fraser worked the shift lever.

"No, I was in France, at an army hospital."

Ruth started to giggle, an odd sound from such a large figure. "You hadda see it." He giggled again. "This guy Flack, I pick him off base twice in the same game. Like a sleepwalker, he was. Then I come up to bat and his own pitcher waves him out deep—you know, I hit the ball pretty far. Most of the time, anyway. But Flack just stares back at him. He stands there, doesn't move a muscle. So I hit the ball over his head and win the game."

"You're saying that the game was rigged, Flack was paid off?"

Babe shrugged. "I don't the hell know. The Cubs won a couple of games, so it's not like they just lay down and died. But a couple of times, during the games, jeez, I'm telling you. One time a ball hits the outfielder in the glove, he doesn't move two feet to get it. Hits him right in the damned glove and it pops out. Guys in the dugout start joking that we should just hit the ball right at 'em, let 'em drop it, throw it away. Easier than trying to get a hit."

Fraser turned onto Broadway. The lights of the wide avenue stretched before them like low-hanging stars. Babe drank again, sipping now. "And if there's anything rotten went on," he said, "you can bet your bottom dollar that Abie Attell was in the thick of it. Hell, him and his boss, that guy Rothstein, they've got some ballplayers on weekly salaries, just in case they need some game to go one way or another."

When they reached Fifty-seventh Street, Babe sat up. He looked around the car and barked out, "Pull over here." He was halfway out the door before Fraser could stop the car. "Thanks for the lift," he said, then stood on the sidewalk, a tall figure in a suit that fell just so from his broad shoulders. With a purpose, he set off down the cross street.

"So much for poor wifey, sitting home alone," Eliza said from the rear seat.

"Babe's not really a homebody?"

"Not *his* home."

Fifteen blocks later, they turned the Stutz over to the doorman. For Fraser, entering the Ansonia's imperial lobby was an experience that never grew old. A large ceramic urn perched on a marble table worthy of St. Peter's in Rome. Tonight the urn exploded with blue gladiolas, orange hibiscus, and ivory calla lilies. Lobby noises echoed across checkerboard marble floors that alternated with plush carpeting. Overstuffed furniture awaited distinguished backsides.

They could never afford such a premier address on Jamie's salary at Rockefeller. But Eliza, a leading theatrical agent, could handle the rent on her own. And lobby encounters with their neighbors—sports figures like the Babe and heavyweight champ Jack Dempsey, musicians like the opera tenor Caruso—were good for her business. It didn't hurt that every floor held a kitchen with staff who would prepare meals for tenants. Neither Eliza nor Jamie was much of a hand at the stove.

The lobby was quiet. The Ansonia's friskier residents were still at post-theater suppers or nightclub shows, while the more staid folks had hunkered down for the night. The elevator operator knew they were going to the third floor. His presence made Jamie choke back the question until he was fumbling the key into their door lock. "How deep are you into these people—Abie Attell, Arnold Rothstein?"

Eliza placed her bag on the hall table and flicked on the lights. When he closed the door, she stepped into his arms, her face against his shoulder, facing away. "Maybe the better question," Jamie said, "is how deep are they into you?"

"I don't know."

"Really?"

She sighed and stepped back to look up into his eyes. "If that terrible movie makes any money, which it shouldn't if there's a God in heaven, everything will be fine. Money fixes everything."

"And if it doesn't?"

"I don't know. I've never been in business with people like this before."

"How'd it happen?"

"How does any bad decision happen? I got talked into this movie in the first place, even though I don't know much about films or anything at all about baseball." She stepped over to the mahogany coffee table in the parlor and took a cigarette from a silver box. She lit it and inhaled deeply. "You liked the idea, remember?"

"Sure, anything with Babe Ruth seems like a sure winner, but when was the last time you listened to my opinion about business?"

Eliza flounced onto the couch. She accepted Fraser's offer of a nightcap. He poured them each two fingers of bourbon, good stuff that the Ansonia staff helped him find despite the legal ban on such beverages. He sat next to her.

"All I can say is it seemed like a good idea at the time," she said. "In June, just before we started to film, one of the partners backed out. George Reiniger—you remember him?"

Fraser shrugged a no. Neither of them spent a lot of time on the other's professional life.

"Well, George showed up with a substitute who could cover his fifty thousand for the project. We jumped at it. We needed to get going so we could cash in on Babe's big year, first year in New York, all the home runs. We had to get the movie out before the season ended."

"Well, Babe's holding up his end, still hitting homers," Jamie said. "He broke his own record weeks ago." He felt warm now, expansive. The bourbon tasted like dessert.

"Well, that turned out to be Abe Attell." She finished her cigarette and stubbed it out in an ashtray that advertised a hit show from several years past. "We'd spent most of the money by the time I understood who he is."

"So it was probably Rothstein money."

She finished her drink. "Whoever's it was, it spent like everybody else's. I'm sorry about this . . . connection. I should be smarter than that. But I'm hoping it'll go away. Can't figure out what else to do—no one's going to buy Attell out now, not for that dog of a movie."

"So the problem is if someone gets mad about losing his money?"

"Yeah, who would mind that?" She moaned softly as she stood, picking up the shoes she had kicked off. "What do you think: Eliza Fraser, moll for the mob?" She tried a rueful smile. It was more ghastly than winning.

"I thought being colorful was good in the theater world."

"Colorful, yes. Even downright raffish. But not actually criminal. That's overdoing it." Eliza finished her bourbon, then trailed a finger down his cheek. "Don't drink too much, dear."

He saluted her with his glass. "Be there in a few."

Over his second, which he intended to be his last, Fraser's mind snagged on Eliza's use of the term *criminal*. That word, and the idea behind it, was not a casual matter to her. Through no fault of hers, she was indelibly connected to a man many would call an arch-criminal. Hell, that's what everyone would call him. It was the great secret of her life, one not even their daughter Violet knew. As long as he'd known her, her deepest fear was falling into that category. This Babe Ruth business was definitely under her skin. He wasn't sure if it should be, or if she was just being skittish.

Lately he'd been remembering his first wife, Ginny, dead so long. It seemed like things were a lot simpler with her, but maybe it was just that they'd been younger and young people are simpler. He smiled. No, that wasn't right. Eliza was definitely more complicated. A lot more complicated. He daily confronted how much he didn't understand about her, but one thing he did know. She wouldn't ever ask for help, not from him, and not when she really needed it. But she expected him to help without being asked. He didn't mind that. Except maybe the part about not asking. A third drink, he decided, might be a good idea. Just tonight.

Pouring a short one, he had a thought. He could look up Speed Cook, his old . . . friend. That was the best word, though it really didn't capture it. They had never spent much time together—just a couple of stretches of a few months each. Even those had been twenty years apart. But they were damned interesting stretches. After the Cook family's troubles in Paris last year, troubles that Fraser helped repair, Speed owed him one. At least one.

Fraser stared out the window at the city's lights, making no effort to find a pattern in them. Speed was smart about the world. He had knocked around a lot of places, sometimes in surprising ways. Most important for Eliza's current situation, he'd played professional ball back in the eighties, before the white players drove out the Negroes. Now Speed was promoting Negro baseball teams around New York, also promoting rights for Negroes. He was bound to know gamblers like Abe Attell and the men he worked with. And the one Attell worked for.

Eliza and Speed had gotten off on the wrong foot twenty years ago. That was because of her secret. The thing was, they hadn't found the right foot yet. She probably wouldn't like having her new troubles laid out for Speed. She didn't need to know.

# Chapter 3

It was the middle of the third inning before Fraser, clutching a bag of warm peanuts, climbed the bleachers behind the first-base line. His outing to the Catholic Protectory Oval, the home field for the New York Lincoln Giants, had started badly. An uncertain navigator in the best of circumstances, he had stopped several times for directions to this Bronx outpost. It didn't help that Speed Cook's team, the Atlantic City Bacharach Giants, was visiting the Bronx from its home field in Brooklyn. In Negro baseball, Fraser concluded, geography was a fluid concept.

Settling in on the plank seat, Fraser started on the peanuts and wondered at the design flaw in the ball field before him. The baseball diamond had been imposed on the center of a rectangular piece of land, not nestled in the corner. Rather than have home plate at the tip of the classic pie-slice shape, here home plate bisected the bottom boundary of the field and faced a distorted outfield. Straightaway center field was foreshortened. Both right- and left-field foul lines ended shortly past the infield. Left-center and right-center fields would be graveyards for well-struck balls.

Fraser closed his eyes and let the sun warm his face. He felt his spirit begin to unwind. It was good to be away from the lab, its claustrophobic smells and its formulaic conversations. How was your weekend? Your test results? Plans for next weekend? Nice weather, eh? When the fans around him broke into a cheer, his eyes fluttered open. A batter was trudging back to the dugout, glaring over his shoulder at a dark-skinned, thickly built pitcher for the Bacharach Giants. The first pitch to the next batter smacked into the catcher's mitt with such a pop that Fraser decided the pitcher must be Cannonball Dick Redding. They said he was faster than Walter Johnson.

"Damn, they'll let anyone in here these days."

Fraser swiveled toward that deep voice. Speed Cook stood at the end of the row, smiling broadly. He looked a bit heavier than last time, just as tall and imposing. His hairline was still in retreat, the remaining curls gray. "No trick to it," Fraser said. "Just show up at the ticket booth with two bits." Cook took his hand in a two-handed grip, then sat down next to him. Fraser nodded at the players on the field. "So this is Redding?"

"The Cannonball his own self. Still fast, but not as fast as he used to be."

"True for all of us."

"Bad for pitchers. And for the man who pays him." Cook gripped Fraser by the shoulder and gave a low laugh. "No justice in this world. I get balder and fatter and you get better looking. What's going on in your world?"

They exchanged family news, the innocuous kind. Fraser's daughter was starting at Barnard College that fall. A society-type young man was buzzing around her, someone her mother approved of. Cook's daughter was working at the NAACP for Doctor Du Bois, but Cook had stopped working there, weary of the great man's pretensions. Still, he said, she'd learn a lot. He was proud that his daughter was part of the campaign for Negro rights.

"What about your boy, Joshua?" Fraser asked. "I feel like I got to know him over in France."

Cook took a few peanuts from the bag Fraser offered. As he shelled one, the batter mashed one of Redding's pitches over the left fielder's head, a triple that brought home two runs. Cook groaned and pointed at the pitcher. "See? Not near fast enough."

"Joshua?"

Cook reached for more peanuts. "Not much to say. He hasn't really found his way, not since the war."

"He went through a lot over there."

"Sure, sure. And there's not much for him here, not much that's, you know, worthy."

Fraser nodded.

"He's impatient. You might call it a family trait. Just can't find his place. Maybe another family trait. Tell you what— there's too many people trying to put him *in* his place." The batter struck out, allowing the Bacharach Giants to leave the field.

"What's he trying? What's he want to do? Maybe I could help."

Cook gave Fraser a sardonic look. "That's one more family trait—he doesn't accept help real well, certainly not from old folks." Cook sighed. "Damn fool's spending time with a bunch of damned reds. You know, the things they say sound good to him. Sound good to me, too. Equal rights for colored. Equal opportunity. Share the wealth. No argument about any of it. But the government's coming down hard on those reds. He needs to know better than to be around them." He shook his head. "Can't believe I'm worrying about that boy. He's almost twenty-six years old, but here I am. When I was his age . . ."

Cook didn't finish the sentence. After wiping his hands against each other, he asked, "Jamie, I know you didn't come for the baseball, not when you can watch the Babe over the other side of the river. I even heard talk that Miss Eliza's been doing business with the Babe."

"Wow. Word gets around."

"Anything about the Babe does. That man's the goddamned second coming."

"He's that good?"

Cook smiled. "Better than that. He pitches better than anyone else. He hits better than anyone else. Runs like a deer when he wants to and is strong as an ox. Of course, he's an ignorant lunkhead, but he's a genius about baseball." When Cook reached for the peanuts again, Fraser handed him the bag. Cook smiled out at the field while popping open a shell. "I've seen a lot of ballplayers, but nothing like him. Can't hardly believe he's a white man."

"There's talk about that, isn't there?"

"Usual stuff. Don't see much to it myself. Man's got thick lips is all." Cook smiled over at Fraser. "Not that there aren't plenty of black folks walking around acting like what they know they're not." Cook pointed to home plate. "Watch this guy, Pop Lloyd. He's probably second only to the Babe right now. He doesn't have Ruth's power, but he hits a ton. He's not playing for us this year, but we picked him up for this game. We're listing him as Joe Jenkins."

Lloyd—or Jenkins—stepped into the batter's box. Square-faced, with a grim demeanor, he wasn't as big as the Babe, but his hands seemed to swallow up the bat handle. Fraser thought his hands might be as big as Cook's. The pitcher made Lloyd swing clumsily on a pitch that dove into the dirt. Cook shook his head. "That Cyclone Joe throws a mean spitball. Then he switches over and gives 'em the gas." They watched silently. Three pitches later, the batter rifled a line dive over second base that the shortstop missed with a lunging dive. Cook smacked his hands together with pleasure, then wagged an index finger at his friend. "You remember that—you saw Cyclone Joe take on Pop Lloyd."

When Cook gathered himself to stand up, Fraser quickly said, "Speed—Abe Attell."

Cook gave him a surprised look. "What about him?"

"Well, you mentioned this movie, the one with the Babe in it?"

"Sure. How's it doing?" Cook leaned back.

Fraser made a face. "It's not drawing flies. But here's the thing. Eliza ended up with Attell as one of the investors in the movie."

"Abe Attell? Wouldn't've thought he was her cup of tea. She doesn't even like *me*. Abe would give her fainting spells. How'd they get mixed up?"

"Not on purpose, not on her part. I had no idea. You know, I sit in the lab, see patients, don't really know her business." Cook nodded. "You know about this investigation out in Chicago, about the World Series being fixed?" Cook grunted an acknowledgment. "We picked up the idea that maybe Attell's tied into that business. That wouldn't be great, not for Eliza."

Cook leaned back, his elbows on the bench behind them, and stroked his chin with one hand. "One of the least surprising things you could tell me about Abe Attell is that he was fixing ball games." He nodded down at the field. "Look at those men out on that field. Every one of them's taken money from a gambler. Tough to make a living out of baseball."

"Did you?"

Cook grinned. "Nobody's left can remember that far back. I sure can't."

"So it happens in the big leagues, too?"

"The world's a nasty place."

"Do you think last year's Series was fixed?"

"Got no idea. I can tell you I had a real fine laugh when I saw that Charlie Comiskey, owns the White Sox, is offering twenty thousand dollars for information about fixing games!" Cook snorted. "I played with that old fox, back before time began, and what he doesn't know about fixing games ain't worth knowing."

"No kidding. Comiskey?"

"Comiskey."

"Let me try something out on you, something that worries me. Maybe, you know, there was something going on between the Babe and Attell, and maybe the movie was tied up in it somehow. And maybe it has some connection with that Chicago investigation."

"That's a lot of maybes. How would that work, anyway? The Babe wasn't even in that World Series. It was the White Sox and the Reds."

"I don't know. He was in the World Series the year before, you know, with the Red Sox. This just all seems like a lot of connections. Enough to make me nervous. To make Eliza nervous."

Cook scratched the side of his face. He didn't react when Pop Lloyd stole second, then took third after the catcher's throw bounced into center field. "I tell you what. I'm supposed to be meeting with the Babe tomorrow."

"Really? For what?"

"I want to sign him up to play exhibition games against us in October. He's one hell of a draw, and the thing is, Babe always needs money. We got that in common. I can see what I can find out about him and Attell."

Fraser thought for a minute. This was definitely another coincidence, but that's why he came to see Speed, looking for such a connection. "Yeah," he said, "that'd be great."

Cook sat up and smiled at Fraser. "All right then. You might want to keep Miss Eliza away from that Attell. He's a mean piece of business."

The two of them had been nearly an hour at a small table in Smitty's Five and Dime on Eleventh Avenue, a murky longshoreman's joint that didn't draw race lines. After they'd put away three boilermakers each, Cook gave up on the idea of outdrinking the Babe. Truth be told, Cook wasn't feeling so terrific. Not drunk, not like that, but something hairy and ill tempered had moved in behind his forehead. Ruth showed no effects other than a relentless appetite. He was on his second corned beef sandwich and a mountain of potato salad. Flecks of mayonnaise and mustard dotted his tie and lapels. His table manners were enthusiastic.

Cook took no offense when the Babe was obviously bored by Cook's tales of pro ball back in the eighties. After all, Ruth was reinventing baseball, creating something splashier, more thrilling, his home runs jolting whole ballparks full of people. To Ruth, Cook's stories were like tales of wars fought with stone axes.

Cook had measured himself against the Babe, the way he did with all large men. They were about the same height. Cook carried more weight now, a good deal more, but he had no idea how the man hit the ball so far. It had to be something about timing and leverage. When Cook played ball, a few times he came up against someone so good that he had to accept that the other guy was just better. Not because he'd figured something out, or he practiced harder, or wanted it more. The guy was just better. It still pissed him off.

Cook had no reason to resent Ruth. Signing him up for the barnstorming games had been easy. Cook pointed out that the Yankees were paying him $129 for each game he played. Then he offered $2,000 for six games, more than double what the Yanks were paying. Even if Babe couldn't do the numbers in his head, he knew it was a good offer.

It was a gamble for Cook, but he liked the odds. The other players—white and black—would come a lot cheaper. Cook planned to line up six ballparks, four in the city and two in

New Jersey. Fans would flock to watch the Bacharach Giants square off against Babe Ruth and his All-Stars, a miniature race war played out on the baseball diamond. Whites would come to see the Negroes slapped down, put back in their place. Colored fans would look for vindication, the vicarious thrill of beating white men. And everyone would come to see the Babe clobber a homer, maybe two. Cook would make sure the Bacharach pitchers gave him only pitches that he could belt out of the park. As long as the game didn't trigger a real race war, Cook should do fine, especially on the side bets. Games like these, there wasn't much risk in betting on them.

The Babe belched—low, long, and unrepentant. He smiled and chewed the last of his sandwich. He finished his beer and held up his mug. "Another?"

Cook waved one finger at the bartender. "I'll sit this one out," he said, "if you don't mind."

Babe shrugged. Why would he mind? "Funny how the world goes here in New York. You know that movie I made? That deal was with a broad. Can you beat that? And here I am making a deal with a nigger, and you're sitting there buying the drinks and got the money to do it. I'm telling you, it's something else."

Cook wasn't real interested in the Babe's experience of wonder, but he welcomed the opening to talk about Eliza Fraser's movie. "That movie . . . You know, I heard that Abe Attell was part of it somehow. Leastways, that's the word around."

The Babe smiled benignly at the bartender who delivered his boilermaker. He poured the shot into the beer mug and drank off half of it. His expression darkened and his brow gathered in disgust. "Little Fucking Hebrew."

"Movies have never been Abe's line, not that I knew. He's more into gambling. You know, fixing the World Series, that sort of thing."

The Babe smiled. "I hope those bastards out in Chicago string him up. Little fucking son of a bitch."

"What do you hear about Chicago, the grand jury and all?"

"What do I know?" Ruth wiped his mouth with the back of his free hand. "We weren't even in the Series last year." The Babe's belch this time was more modest, hardly worth the effort.

"Yeah," Cook said, trying to seem casual, "but you were there the year before, when you guys beat the Cubs."

The Babe's eyes stopped scanning the bar and fixed back on Cook. "You saying something?"

Cook shrugged, suddenly wondering if the Babe's routine might be an act. "You hear stuff, maybe it's malarkey, from people who may know something or may not. Some of it's just logic, I guess. With all the trouble around the Series in '18—you know, the players going on strike, fighting over money, the war, the gamblers."

The Babe kept his gaze steady on Cook. "What about the gamblers?"

"Well, there's your business partner, Attell. He must've been hanging around the Series, both teams. And I've heard about that train ride from Chicago to Boston, the overnight train with both teams on it. That's a long time on a train, Chicago to Boston. Hard for guys not to talk to each other, play some cards, have a few laughs, you know? And you've always got those gamblers in your underwear, helping with the cards and the dice, shooting the breeze—you know how it is. I was just thinking, if the players were trying to figure out how to get paid more, well, sometimes gamblers and ballplayers can figure that out, you know? Help each other out. At least that used to happen back in my day."

"I don't remember about that train trip."

Cook smiled. "That's a long ride to forget."

"Sometimes I'm forgetful." The Babe pointed to his half-empty beer mug and smiled. "I drink a lot, you know."

Cook leaned forward on his elbows and smiled. "That's good, Babe. That's real good. Nothing good comes from answering questions like that." Cook knew that was sound advice, advice that most people couldn't follow. Most people talked too goddamned much. Maybe the Babe didn't, which would mean he definitely was smarter than Cook had expected.

# Chapter 4

"Brother Briggs is speaking tonight, up in Harlem. Going to talk about Negro armed resistance. We should go." Cecil Washington's narrow face wore an earnest expression under the flat light at Childs' cafeteria. This branch was downtown, not far from Wall Street. At midmorning, amid the hubbub of the financial center, Childs' was a refuge for the confused and forlorn. A few customers, most unshaven, sat at single tables, quietly bearing the burden of another day of having nowhere better to be. At a table against the back wall, Cecil and Joshua Cook nursed cups of coffee and smoked. Since coming home from the war, they had moved from harsh French cigarettes to Lucky Strikes, but still preferred their coffee hot, strong, and with a heavy dose of cream. Childs' coffee usually failed on the first two counts.

Cecil was an earnest man. As a soldier in Joshua's platoon, that earnestness was worth its weight in gold. No matter what the big talk was now among black folks about their army regiment, how the ferocious Harlem Hellfighters won the war all by themselves, not everyone in it was a two-fisted hero. Cecil though, now, he was. Joshua had counted on him over in

France, counted on him every day, and he was never disappointed. Back home, Cecil had become an earnest black revolutionary. He earnestly believed in the need for Negro armed resistance against their white oppressors. In peacetime, Cecil's earnestness could wear a body out.

"You don't need to go hear that man," Joshua said, stubbing out a butt. He was smoking more than he could afford. He could hear his mother fussing how his clothes stank of tobacco. "I can give you his speech right here, right now. So can you. We need to fight the white masters and get our hind ends back to Africa."

"Don't be like that. Don't give me that I've-seen-it-all routine. Sure, we know Brother Briggs's message, but you need to be refreshed on it, let it steep into you. Feel it deep in your bones. Need that on a regular basis."

"Like going to church on Sunday?" Joshua allowed himself a grin and reached for his cigarettes.

"See!" Cecil pointed a long finger at him. "You're doing it. Making fun of it. We got to stand up for ourselves, stand up for our brothers and sisters. Stand up for the African Blood Brotherhood."

"I don't know, Cecil." He exhaled his first puff, the one that felt best and you paid most attention to. "I need a movement that'll fight for my right to sit down, sit down like all those bosses sit down. That's the movement black folks need. More sitting down."

"Come on, you know Briggs is telling it right. Ain't nothing going to be given us. We need to stand up and seize it. You used to tell me that over in the trenches, told me your daddy told you that your whole life."

"Cecil, you need to think over all this standing up business. Standing up just makes it easier for the government to find you. Then they write your name down, come see you in the middle of the night. If Mr. Briggs doesn't watch out, he's going to get himself a one-way ticket to the pokey, or out of the country, sent away like all those Russian reds got sent away."

Lowering his voice, Cecil increased his intensity. "Joshua, you know there's got to be revolution, just like they had in Russia. Seize the government and take the wealth of the rich for the benefit of the poor. For black folks, ain't no other way. We're never going to get anything that we don't take. Things can't keep going on this way."

"Cecil, we just need to think this thing through." The tobacco was starting to taste as sour as Cecil's dedication to the African Blood Brotherhood. Joshua balanced the cigarette on the rim of the saucer. "You say you want to take the wealth from the rich folks. You really think that's going to bring money to black folks? Haven't you noticed how all those Bolsheviks are white? You think they're going to forget all of a sudden how that skin makes them better than us? We may take the money, but *they're* going to keep it, leave us with nothing except maybe that ticket back to Africa, where nobody in the Cook family has lived for a few hundred years."

Cecil sat back with some force, clucked his tongue and shook his head. "Come on, you can't really think it'd be any worse than it is now. Look at your daddy—smartest colored man I ever met, right? Back in Africa, he'd be a goddamned king. What's he do now? Hustles bets on some broke-down Negro ballplayers who play for nickels and dimes. And he's got to pay off Jewish gangsters just to do that."

Joshua stared through the cafeteria. New customers were working their way down the food line. He was sorry he'd introduced Cecil to his father. Sorry, too, that he'd spoken about his father's business, such as it was. Cecil never knew his own father, so he'd got real impressed with Speed Cook. Too impressed.

"Joshua?"

He raised his eyebrows in answer.

"You sound like you're ready to go into business, turn into a capitalist, maybe with your old man, like he wants you to."

"Hell, he doesn't want me to do that. That's about the only thing we agree on—I should do something better. I don't even like baseball—playing it, watching it, even knowing it exists. My daddy knows that. 'Course, he does want to stop me consorting with dangerous revolutionaries like you." Joshua traced his finger around the rim of his coffee cup. "But you know, I've been thinking. . . ." His voice drifted off and he stared for a minute more.

"Bully for you." Cecil made a face and shook his head. Joshua was his friend, his best friend, but sometimes the man acted like the whole world should stop and wait for him.

"No, listen to me. I've been thinking about this for a while." He pushed the cup aside and leaned forward. "What about bootlegging?" When Cecil made an exasperated sound, Joshua held out a hand. "No, no, hear me out. You know, there's some colored men moving into it now. It's a brand new business, so it's wide open. And there's lots of money just wandering around in it, looking for a place to go. People're drinking more than ever now we got Prohibition. It's like if you said turnips was against the law, suddenly everyone'd want nothing but turnips."

"Bootlegging's against the law."

Joshua laughed. "Some revolutionary you are. I thought you wanted to break *all* the laws, bring down the government!" He drained the room-temperature coffee from his cup. "How about this? Think of bootlegging as a way to undermine the government, American style. It's a revolutionary act that just happens to put dollars into empty pockets like yours and mine."

"You're serious?"

"I think I am. I'm heading over toward lower Broadway, an errand for a couple of bootleggers. They were hanging around the old man's baseball team. It's a little collecting work, some speakeasy."

"Look at that. Capitalism is already making you a criminal. They won't let you make an honest buck."

Joshua smiled. "But Prohibition's such a dumb law."

Joshua cut across Wall Street to get over to Broadway. He saw some black faces here in the heart of American capitalism, but none of them was dressed as well as he was. He owned two suits and they were both sharp. This one was a soft brown, single-button number with a rich chocolate stripe. The vest had lapels. His cream-colored fedora sported a tan silk band. He looked better than most of the rich men he passed. He kept to the north side of the street to stay in the sunlight.

At the corner of Wall and Broad, he paused to take in the imperial offices of J. P. Morgan & Co., the beating heart of the capitalist beast. Though only a few stories high, the squat building radiated the self-importance of an Egyptian pharaoh. Joshua craned his neck. Getting out of a taxi over there, that looked like the blond head of Violet Fraser. He'd met her in France the year before, when her father helped him on that business with the army. He liked her. She seemed like more than just a pretty girl. They had vowed to get together back in America, but they hadn't. No surprise there. He wasn't from her world, not even a little bit.

He caught a second glimpse as she crossed the sidewalk. It was definitely Violet. He thought about calling out, but didn't. She was going into the Morgan bank. She wouldn't want to deal with him right now, even to be seen with him. She probably had a boyfriend in there, some Ivy League man. And Joshua had business.

Halfway down the next block, the sidewalk surged under his feet. Something slapped him down on his face. A roar burst into his ears. The world hung suspended. Time stopped.

When Joshua's mind began to work again, whenever that was, he had trouble understanding the thought that was struggling to be recognized. It hung right near him but he couldn't reach it. Then it was there. After surviving six months dodging German shells, he wasn't about to get blown up on the streets of New York.

Debris was settling around him. Rock and dust. Wood and fabric. Bits that might be flesh. He coughed and squinted, then rolled up on an elbow. He shaded his eyes to look back at the blast site. A crater gaped at the entrance to the Morgan bank. Wagons and cars were twisted heaps. Broken glass lay everywhere. Bodies littered the pavement at terrible angles.

The silence confused him. No sound. He rose onto all fours, his head hanging down. Still silent. He lifted his head, then raised up on his knees. He squeezed his eyes shut and placed his hands over them. He opened the lids. There . . . there were screams. They were far away. He got to his feet, still shaky, and turned toward the Morgan building. He fumbled in his pants pocket for his handkerchief. He put it over his mouth. His palms were raw, scraped when he was knocked down. A woman knelt nearby. She held her hands over her mouth. They were her screams. He could hear them better now. But only them. Wait. A bell was ringing. A fire truck? In the gutter, off to the right. It was a hand. He looked away, willed his feet to move forward. He'd seen worse in France.

He could focus. Others were moving in the same direction he was. Toward the bank. They were calling out but their voices were muffled. He heard coughing. Blood pooled under a horse that had been blown out of his harness. The horse had only three legs. Its eye stared up at the sky, the cart reduced to kindling. An open-top car rested on its side, its fender crumpled and driver gone, who knew where.

Joshua grew steadier. He could hear more. Sirens now. Shouting. The air was still filled with . . . he pushed the thought aside. The front of a building across from Morgan was gone. Girders and struts and wiring stood naked to the world. There was moisture on his lips. He tasted it. Salty. He touched it. Blood was trickling from his nose.

The Morgan entrance was torn open, its heavy doors intact but splayed to the side. A leg in blue serge extended from under one door. Joshua stepped over the corner of the door, over the leg. He peered into the bank. Daylight streamed in from unnatural holes, spotlighting debris in the air. He felt shaky again. His legs froze. He leaned against the thick granite wall that had withstood the blast. He breathed through his handkerchief. A massive chandelier had crashed down on the lobby, pulverizing everything beneath it.

Nothing he saw looked like Violet. There was movement toward the back. The bomb's impact would have been less there. He started forward, reaching out with both hands. He struggled past the chandelier, then beyond upended desks and chairs, chunks of ceiling. He veered around two bodies covered with rubble, stopped to cough. The coughing bent him over. He could hear himself. Bells and sirens, too.

He wasn't sure until he was standing over her. She made no sound. Her hands and arms were free, her eyes wide. One leg was under a heavy desk covered with ceiling plaster. The end of a ceiling beam rested on the desk. He spoke to her, his voice small in his head. She said nothing. Her eyes were scared eyes, but he thought they knew him. His brain was still slow. He didn't see other people nearby. He stopped to calculate, to figure out how the debris would shift when he moved things. He didn't want something new sliding on top of her. He started methodically, removing one piece at a time. His strength started coming back. Then he reached the ceiling beam. It was too big. He looked back to the doorway. Others were climbing inside, arms held out for balance, to ward off the horror. He called out and waved his arms.

A young white man approached. Joshua pointed at the beam,

then at the direction it should go. Once the newcomer understood the job, he shouted to the front of the bank. More men came near. The building was filling up. Joshua crouched down to Violet. He explained what they had to do. Her eyes were wet but she nodded.

Five of them strained. They lifted the beam, pivoted it, then dropped it with a thud. Joshua lifted the side of the desk by himself, fired by the prospect of setting her free. Balancing the desk up on its end, he made sure it was stable, then turned back. Her right leg was turned at a slant. It was black from internal bleeding. He bent down and spoke again, urgently. She shouldn't look down. She nodded but then looked. Her eyes rolled back in her head.

Joshua felt his control slip. "Stretcher!" he screamed. Then screamed again. "For God's sake, where's a stretcher?"

# Chapter 5

Fraser walked quickly from his lab to the Flower Hospital, a ponderous brick structure that resembled a home for ghosts and witches more than a place of healing. Happily, the hospital's human residents included the city's finest orthopedic surgeon. A week after the bombing, Violet and her poor leg still needed the best.

The call came through before he heard about the blast on Wall Street. An unfamiliar voice, distorted by the overloaded telephone lines of that terrible day, said it was Joshua Cook. Violet, the voice said, had been in an accident. She was at Volunteer Hospital near City Hall. Fraser hadn't asked for details. He said he'd be right there, slammed down the phone, ran downstairs, and jumped in his car.

He had learned more from the shouts of street-corner news vendors, already hawking reports of the disaster. Desperate, he'd raged at the people who swarmed the streets, indifferent to the crisis and how they slowed him down. Horse-drawn delivery wagons, messengers on bicycles, old men with long beards and sad mustaches, and young women tired before their time. They were all malevolent obstacles. When he had arrived in New York twenty years before, he marveled that the air held enough oxygen to support so many. He had grown numb to the wonder of it, insulated by the Ansonia and his hard-won respectability.

South of the numbered streets, he'd slowed to a crawl. Vehicles avoiding the bomb site butted up against those coming to aid the injured. He'd abandoned his car a mile from the Volunteer Hospital. Out of breath, sweaty, he found the building was only a clinic for the poor, deluged with mangled bodies from the bombing. His white lab coat worked as a badge of authority in the mayhem. He searched the corridors, ignoring anguished cries that came at him from all directions. He was there as a father, not a doctor.

Joshua saw him first and called his name, waving a hand. The boy didn't look any better than the other victims. Dust and plaster bits made his hair and skin a spectral white. Blood had crusted under his nose. His suit was filthy and torn. Violet lay on a stretcher on the floor. The boy, crouching, held her hand. Her eyes opened when Fraser took Joshua's place.

"Do you have much pain?" he asked.

She nodded.

"It's her leg, sir," Joshua said, and pointed. A rough splint, wrapped with gauze, hung on the outside of her right leg. Fraser's heart sank. Above the knee. Swelling was stretching her blackened skin to the bursting. Internal bleeding. She needed attention now. Better attention than she could get there. He told Joshua to wait.

Fraser dodged down the corridor to a supply room he had passed. He told the nurse on duty that he needed morphine for a patient. She gestured to a shelf and let him through.

When Fraser gave Violet the injection, he spoke to Joshua over his shoulder. "Son, can you carry her with me?"

"Of course. I got her here."

"I mean a long way. It's madness out there."

Joshua stepped behind Violet's head and reached down for the stretcher handles. Fraser told Violet that they had to move to a better hospital. It was the only way. They lifted her and set off. She weighed so little. Fraser called out warnings over his shoulder as he backed through the crowded hallways. Violet's face looked translucent. Her eyes were out of focus.

The air was cooler on the street, easier to breathe. They set her down so Fraser could turn to face the direction they were walking. People made way for them. Fraser headed uptown, vaguely toward where he left the car.

"What do you need, Doc?" A red-faced police officer fell into step next to him.

Fraser shouted that they had to get to Flower Hospital. They needed an ambulance. At the corner of Park Row and Chambers, the cop told them to head north to Pearl; he'd be there with an ambulance. Then he took off. When they reached Pearl, the ambulance was there. Fraser hugged the cop before climbing in after Violet. There was no space for Joshua.

Eliza didn't leave the hospital for the first three days. Now, a week into the siege, they were taking turns, changing off at noon and at midnight. Starting his shift at midday, Fraser stopped to see Doctor Nylander, who was the reason he brought her to Flower. He had served in France with Nylander, who was young enough to know the new techniques. Today Nylander had no news. The thighbone was crushed. Violet had endured two surgeries to ease the swelling and align the remaining fragments. More surgery was possible. Amputation still not out of the question. They were using a Thomas splint, one of the recent innovations, but no one could predict what healing would occur or if infection would set in. When Nylander mentioned amputation, Fraser turned cold. From the war, he knew the emotional price of amputation. It seemed so much worse for a young girl. His beautiful girl, disfigured forever. He could see that leg, dimpled with baby fat, take its first step. He told Nylander not to mention it to Eliza or Violet. Not unless he had to.

Fraser paused outside Violet's room. He tried to wipe away his anxiety over all the wrong turns her injury could take. She would feel his anxiety if he brought it in with him.

Eliza was sitting in the straight-back chair that was the best the hospital had. She had a pillow from home to soften the seat. Both hands held the purse in her lap. She rose as he entered. "Have to fly, dear," she said. "Another of the leads is trying to bail out on that miserable farce at the Orpheum." She kissed Violet on the forehead, her hand cupping their daughter's still, pale face. She smiled. "I think you'll find the patient doing well." She nodded at the window. "Keep that open. The smells in here are horrid. They're hard on her." She gave him a businesslike peck on the lips.

The departure of Eliza, the natural focus of any group, left a silence. Those who remained had to reorient themselves. Fraser asked Violet how she felt, how she slept, her appetite, the sensations in her leg. He inspected the dressing. He made a note to talk to Nylander about weaning her off the morphine. They had used it too much in France.

Finally, Violet pulled up the sheet and protested. "Isn't Doctor Nylander the one who's responsible for me?"

"Don't try that, young lady. I answer to a higher authority. You can't expect me to face your mother without having formed my own medical opinion." Fraser's eye fell on an extravagant new bouquet on a far window ledge.

"A new secret admirer?" he asked with a smile, lowering himself into the punishing chair. He squirmed in an effort to nudge the pillow to a comfortable position. He wasn't looking forward to twelve hours in the chair. The bouquet must be from his colleagues at Rockefeller. No, it would be from one of Eliza's Broadway types. It had that look-at-me quality that theatrical folks bring to everything.

"It's from your old friends, Daddy. The Cooks."

"The Cooks?"

Violet allowed herself a small smile and ooched herself higher on the bed. "I think it's really from Joshua, but he signed it from his whole family."

"Really." Fraser walked over and inspected the bouquet more closely. He read the note. "Do you remember Joshua from that day? What he did?"

She shook her head. "Not till we got to the hospital."

"The first one?"

She nodded. "I was afraid of him at first. He had all that dust and filth on him. Like some terrible creature from another world. And I didn't expect to see a colored man. But he was so kind."

"If ever there was a knight in tattered gabardine, it was Joshua." He nodded at the bouquet. "I suppose we should be sending something to him. I'll talk to your mother about it."

A soft knock came at the door. Fraser opened it to find Joshua Cook. His gray plaid suit, set off with a burgundy pocket handkerchief, clung to his slim figure. He held a fedora in one hand and packages in the other.

After a moment of surprise, Fraser recovered. He offered a hearty handshake along with apologies for not thanking Joshua properly for rescuing Violet. While Violet joined in the thanks, Fraser retrieved a chair from another room. When he returned with an equally spartan scrap of furniture, Violet held a Whitman's Sampler box of chocolates. Next to her lay a book with two high-society figures on the cover. She had raised herself higher on the pillows. Fraser sat on the new chair, across the bed from Joshua.

Fraser declined the offer of a chocolate. The day before, Eliza had mentioned that his old suits, which had sagged off him when he returned from France, looked to be getting snug. He asked about the book.

"It's by a young guy," Joshua said. "He served in France, too. Named Fitzgerald."

Violet, who had new color in her face, handed the book to her father. "Why did you pick it?" she asked Joshua.

"I'm not sure. It's not about the army at all, or really about anything I've ever known. The main character is rich—he just dribbles away his money, like it doesn't matter. The title, *This Side of Paradise,* seems ironic." Joshua put a finger to his chin. "I guess it was the way the character was broken up, and the story was, too. Like modern times. Also, he keeps lying to himself." He grinned, self-conscious. "Anyway, I didn't think it was something they'd have you read at Barnard."

"Oh," Violet said, casting her eyes down quickly, "I won't be going there now, because of this." She gestured to her leg.

"Yes," Fraser broke in. "The college has been very good. No problem with her starting in February."

"What do the doctors say?" Joshua asked. "Will you be ready by then?"

"They don't know." She shrugged. "So neither do I."

"This doctor," Jamie put in, "says there's no reason why she won't be."

"How is it?" Joshua asked. "Does it hurt?"

She nodded, her expression piercing Fraser. "It hurts. It's hard to get comfortable. I can't even get to the sink on my own yet." She got a curious look. "It's funny, that you happened to find me there in the bank."

Joshua smiled shyly and cleared his throat. "It wasn't a complete accident. I was passing by and thought I saw you go in, but I wasn't sure. Then the bomb went off. Somehow I knew it was you, and that I had to get you out." They smiled at each other.

"That was lucky for me."

"What were you doing there?"

Violet took a long breath. "I was to have lunch with a friend who works there. He was going to show me around first."

"Is he okay?"

"Yes." She hesitated. "At least, that's what Father found out." After a pause, she added, "I haven't seen him, though. My friend, I guess he's busy, or recuperating himself."

"Cleaning up that bank'll take a while, though I don't suppose your friend would do that kind of work."

Before the bomb, Eliza was predicting that Violet would marry that young aristocrat with too many last names. But now he—Griff Keswick, that was it—seemed uninterested in sharing any of his names with a young woman certain to be lame for the rest of her life. Fraser decided to break into the exchange.

"Say, Joshua, has that ear been bothering you?" The young man had cotton wadded up in his right ear.

Joshua shook his head. "It's not too bad. Had some ringing in it for a while, but it's less now."

"If you're getting discharge from the ear, you should see someone about it. I'd be happy to take a look at it."

Joshua smiled. "Thanks, Doctor Fraser, but I'm fine."

"So," Fraser said, "what have you been up to, when you're not rescuing my daughter?"

"Oh, different things." Joshua looked at Violet, who had fixed her blue gray eyes on him. He found the color disconcerting, like a pale, high sky. He looked away, dangling his hat on one finger. He twirled it halfway round. "Can't say I've settled on any one thing."

"What sorts of things interest you?"

"Like I said, I'm still not entirely sure."

"How about the baseball business, like your father?"

"Father," Violet broke in, "I'll thank you not to subject my guest to the third degree." She had a smile on her face, but her tone wasn't humorous.

"Hardly the third degree," Fraser objected. "I'm just making conversation."

"Well . . ." Joshua stood and said to Violet, "I'd best be getting on. I don't want to wear you out with all you've been through."

She turned her smile to him and spoke gently. "It's so wonderful you came, and thank you for the gifts. As Father said, we should be giving you gifts. I'm very grateful."

"No, really . . ."

"Well," Violet filled the gap. "I'm not going anywhere, so I hope you'll come to see me some more."

"I'd like that," Joshua said. He nodded to her, then shook hands with Fraser on the way out.

When he reached the sidewalk, Joshua palmed his hat onto his head and tugged the brim into place. He lit up and sucked down the smoke. The thoughts that had swum through his mind for days and weeks came into focus. No more drifting. He wouldn't again flounder like that, unable to explain just what it was he did. He was going to make himself a place in this world. A big place.

A wagon clattered by on Sixty-third Street, pulled by a swaybacked gray. Under a canvas tarp sat several barrels that certainly contained beer. Across the street, a young white man pulled a silver flask from his hip pocket and took a long draw. Yes, Joshua thought. The signs were all around him. He took a contemplative puff.

Everybody, even Doctor Fraser, thought that since he was Speed Cook's boy he'd just naturally go into baseball. He'd never be anything but Speed Cook's boy in that tiny world.

But booze. No one was going to stop Americans from taking a drink when they wanted to, and they'd pay a pretty penny to do it. Bootlegging was the thing. It was new, wide open. He needed to study it, make it his business. Then he needed to start making some real money. Once you get your hands on some money, it doesn't matter how you got it. All those doors open just the same.

# *Chapter 6*

Speed Cook sat on the first-base side at Brooklyn's Ebbets Field. Babe Ruth's All-Stars, a collection of players from several teams, were loosening up for the exhibition game against Cook's Bacharach Giants. When the major leaguers took over the field from the colored players, the men had exchanged some good-natured banter. Maybe not all of it was good-natured. Cook had hustled his players back into their clubhouse, an unknown luxury where they usually played. He reminded them that they were here for a payday, not for payback, so they should forget about evening up the score for anything that had happened five years ago or fifty years ago. If they kept their mouths shut, they could run up the score all they wanted and walk away with money in their pockets. Babe's team had no interest in playing hard, unless someone went and riled them up. So, Cook said, don't do anything, don't say anything that would get them angry. And be sure—he was definite about this—that Babe gets nothing but fat pitches to hit. The older heads nodded.

A week before, the Ebbets Field grass got chewed up during World Series games between the Brooklyn Robins and the

Cleveland Indians, but it was still better than the Catholic Protectory Oval on its best day. Cook felt happy, sitting in this fine ballpark, warm in the autumn sun, waiting for the first pitch. The air carried pungent smells of roasting chestnuts from carts outside, reminding him of the aroma of burning leaves that meant autumn in his boyhood. That aroma was scarce in Manhattan. So were leaves.

Cook couldn't help but envy the Robins this field. When he'd been playing thirty years before, big league parks weren't anything like this. The grandstands here—double-deckered around much of the field—could hold more than twenty thousand fans. The outfield wall shouted messages about Gem safety razors, Lifebuoy soap, Green River whiskey, and Bull Durham tobacco. Walls outside the park recommended tires, candy, and shirts. All products for men—which made sense. Almost all the fans were male. Come to think of it, Robins was a pretty weak name for the Brooklyn club. It didn't command respect like the Giants, or the Senators, or the Tigers, the Indians. Well, the sissy name hadn't kept the Robins out of the World Series.

The crowd today would be smaller than for a Series game, but not by that much. Babe was putting rear ends in the seats. Neither Ebbets Field nor National League fans had seen the game's greatest home-run hitter before. The Babe had been in this park with the Red Sox for the 1916 World Series, but then he was strictly a pitcher. Anyway, he never threw a pitch in Brooklyn then. During batting practice, Cook had enjoyed watching that gorgeous swing. Like poetry, or music. If Cook's pitchers did as he'd told them, there would be at least one Ruthian home run for the fans to tell their grandchildren about.

"Comin' up in the world, Daddy."

Cook grinned up at his son, standing in the aisle in front of him. "Boy, d'you get lost somewhere? Ain't no socialist Abyssinians scheduled here today."

"I got a phone call from some crazy-sounding woman, said my daddy was having a proud day and that if I ever wanted to eat her roast chicken again, I'd get myself over to Brooklyn and share it with him." Cook stood and grabbed Joshua's hand, pulling him into the seat next to him. "You got any idea who that woman was?"

"You know," Cook said, "she can have a mean temper, which I know better than anyone. But underneath it all she's a pretty nice old gal. A man could do a lot worse."

Joshua leaned away from his father and pulled a serious face. "This is a baseball day, right? Not one about finding yourself a good woman."

"Every day's a day for finding a good woman, son. Haven't I taught you anything?"

"Just 'cause you're teaching doesn't mean I'm learning."

They leaned back, elbows on the riser behind them, and gazed out at the field. Cook didn't care for his son's snappy vested suit any more than he liked that smart remark. The blue was too blue, the fit too sleek. Cook didn't mind that his own suit was shapeless from wear, the elbows shiny and a cuff button missing. Sharp clothes on Cook would only make the players think he was making more money than he was. Joshua's suit confirmed the talk Cook was hearing, that the boy was into bootlegging.

Joshua nodded out at the field as he lit a cigarette. "That big one over next to home plate, that's him?"

"Not hard to pick out."

"Is he as thick as the newspapers let on?"

Cook considered the question. "You know, he's ignorant, that's sure. I wouldn't ask him the capital of Egypt. But he's the best damned ballplayer I've ever seen, which means he's figured out some things. Things about baseball, anyway. Did you see his season? He had 54 home runs, 130-some RBIs, batted .376.

Add up all nine of my seasons and I didn't come close to those numbers."

"Different game back then, Daddy."

"You can say that again." He shook his head. The whole business still made him angry. That last season in pro ball, he knew he might be close to being through. It was his hands, a catcher's best asset but also his most vulnerable. That was before they figured out that a bigger glove would provide some protection. Most of his fingers got broken one time or another. Also, some bones in his hands. By the end of a game catching fastballs, curves, spitters, shine balls, whatever the hell the pitcher was dishing up, his hands swelled up to twice normal size. The pain got to be too much. But the bastards didn't drive him out because of his hands. It was for his skin. He was the last one, the last Negro they got rid of. No one would give him a contract. Not one of them. And that was the end of colored ballplayers in the big leagues. He tried to relax his hands. They hurt when he clenched them into fists.

"How's the crowd look to you?" Joshua said.

Cook checked over his shoulder. "Good. Real good. Figure we'll go over fifteen thousand. Should make a few pennies for our trouble." They stood to let some fans shuffle past them.

"Went to see Violet Fraser the other day," Joshua said. "At the hospital."

"How's she doing? That was a bad business."

"Got hurt pretty bad. I don't know about that leg. She's something, though, keeping her spirits up."

"I'm glad you were there that day, that you could help." Cook cleared his throat. "Say, son, was that really just a coincidence, you being there when she was there, on Wall Street?"

"Yeah, it was, Daddy. Fate, eh? Throws us together again."

"You may not want to overdo that fate business, son."

"You want to tell me again how black boys don't go with white girls?"

Cook shrugged. "Well, there's something else I've been meaning to raise with you."

Joshua raised an eyebrow, an unmistakable signal that defenses against paternal advice were fully engaged.

"Don't be like that, now. I've got a right to say some things."

"I always listen, Daddy. It's not about the cigarettes, is it?" Joshua dropped the butt and stamped it out.

Cook took a breath, knowing that his words would fall on deaf ears. "I've been hearing, you know, hearing around, that you're getting mixed up with some bootleggers, some rough customers."

His son looked at him but said nothing.

"You know that's not a good idea, Joshua. It makes your mother worry—"

"Now don't go hiding behind her."

"All right, it makes me worry." Cook leaned toward him. "Listen, why don't you come into this baseball business with me? I tell you what. Negro baseball is going to take off now. I'm not exactly sure why. Maybe it's from the war. People are interested. They like it. It's an exciting game. You know they're organizing a real league out in the Midwest. We can do that here in the East, maybe have our own World Series."

Cook swept a hand around the park. "Look around you, at those people paying good money to watch this game. Our players are as good as the ones in the white leagues, maybe better whenever the Babe stops passing for white."

Joshua smiled. "Daddy, this kind of crowd, you know it's here for Ruth, not for these no-account traveling men you put out on the field."

"Sure, sure, our crowds are smaller, but they're growing, and it's a lot less dangerous than bootlegging. There's mean folks running that liquor. You know that's true."

Joshua leaned toward his father and spoke softly. "I know I

killed more men in France than any of those so-called mean folks ever has."

"That was different."

Joshua waited a second. He decided not to ask how his father would know what it was like on the front line in France. He stood into the aisle. "Gotta go," was all he said. He placed his hat on and started down the steps.

"Come to dinner on Sunday," Cook called after him. "Your mother's expecting you."

Joshua waved without turning his head. Then he was gone. Cook tried to concentrate on the game. It was only the top of the second inning. So much for watching the game with his son. The pain flared in his left hand, the one he'd caught most of the pitches with. He tucked it under the other bicep and waited for the warmth and pressure to help. The hands were getting worse. So what? There wasn't anything was going to make them better.

The Babe was out in right field, hands on his knees, watching the duel between pitcher and batter. A foul tip careened off the catcher's forearm. The game paused while the catcher stood up and ate the pain, flexing his arm but never rubbing it, not giving in to it. Out in right field, the Babe toed the ground and walked in a tight semicircle. He hunched and relaxed his shoulders, then crouched down for the next pitch. Not for the first time, Cook thought how he should have played outfield. Old outfielders didn't have hands like his.

By the sixth inning, the Bacharachs had a solid 6–2 lead. Cannonball Dick Redding was turning the major leaguers into pussycats, though that presented the problem Cook was worrying about. The Babe hadn't hit his homer yet.

It was mostly Ruth's own damned fault. The right-field fences at Ebbets Field were nice and close, and Cannonball had served up some juicy grapefruits. But the Babe's timing was off. Maybe he'd had a late night, maybe a few in a row. He popped up in the first, then lined out to the right fielder. He was the third batter this inning. Now was the time to hit one out. Cook had no interest in sweating this out until the ninth inning, when the Babe would be overanxious and the fans would be grumbling. Before the Bacharachs took the field, Cook stepped down to the fence next to their dugout. He told Cannonball he had but one job this inning—to groove a homer for the Babe. There didn't need to be men on base, but the ball had to land on the far side of the outfield fence.

Back at his seat, Cook found Abe Attell waiting. The little man's checkered, snap-brim cap set him apart in a sea of fedoras and bowlers. He also was the only white man on the Bacharachs' side of the field. He nodded affably as Cook resumed his seat.

"I heard," Attell said, "that your boys're going to win."

Cook snorted. "A little bird tell you?"

"A big one." Attell nodded toward home plate. "The Babe himself. Though I think the big fellow thought he'd have at least one homer by now. So did a lot of us, actually."

"Not to worry. The fans'll have something to remember."

"That's terif. Then I should have a good day, too."

They watched one of the All-Stars whiff at three Redding pitches. There was something majestic about how hard the man was trying to avoid hitting the ball. Cook winced inside. It was one thing to know the game was fixed. It figured that the All-Stars wouldn't be all that interested in winning this game. What did they care? Cook had figured on that. He'd put some money down on the Bacharachs this afternoon. But it was something else for some clown to show the world he was trying to lose.

"You seem pretty relaxed," Cook said, "for a man just got indicted in Chicago for fixing the World Series."

"That business with the White Sox last year?"

Cook smiled. "The papers are calling them the Black Sox."

Attell laughed softly. "Do you *schvartzes* take offense at the name?" Cook didn't respond. Looking back out at the field, Attell shrugged. "That indictment, it's bubkis. It's under control. Mr. Rothstein, you know, he knows a lot of people in Chicago."

The second batter struck out, too. At least he took the trouble to foul off two pitches before fanning. The crowd came alive as Babe strode to the plate. The fans started to stand to get a better look. His bat looked as thick as a table leg.

"So," Attell nodded out at the Babe, "one of the things we don't know is why the Babe and you are suddenly such good friends."

"What're you talking about? We made a business deal for these games. Straight-up deal. Not a lot of friendship involved."

The sound startled both of them. More than a firecracker but less than a bomb. A sound that reached into your bones. That's how Cook described it to Aurelia when he got home. Like a gunshot. Cook saw only the end of the swing, the Babe corkscrewed around, his bat curled behind the wrong shoulder while he watched the ball's flight. Cook and Attell stood and shouted with everyone else. A Ruth home run was an act of nature. In nine years playing pro ball, Cook never saw one like it, partly because the baseballs were so lousy then. This ball cleared the right-field wall by fifty feet; it might have hit some car driving by. Every fan whooped. Most of them asked the man in the next seat if he'd ever seen *that* before. Cook watched the big man trot around the bases, taking his time, giving the fans a show. Then Cook caught Cannonball's eye out on the pitcher's mound. He nodded. Everything was fine. Cannonball could concentrate on winning the game now.

Back in their seats, Attell turned to Cook and spoke in a low voice. "Listen, you're a smart guy. We like you. We know we can do business with you. You just need to know that Mr. Rothstein takes a special interest in the Babe. It usually doesn't pay to get between Mr. Rothstein and anything he's got a special interest in." The small man patted Cook's arm, tipped his cap, and took off.

That took care of any elation Cook felt over the home run. He wanted nothing to do with Attell or his boss, Arnold Rothstein. And he didn't think the Babe should have anything to do with them, either.

Ruth had signed a second barnstorming deal that would kick in after the games with the Bacharachs. He would go to Cuba, where they were supposed to be crazy about baseball, and hit homers there. In a foreign country, the Babe should be able to stay away from Rothstein and Attell, and away from grand juries and subpoenas.

Cook scratched his head, wondering to himself why he was worrying about the Babe. The man was a national hero playing a kids' game, making as much in a month as Cook made in a year. The world was that man's oyster.

# Chapter 7

"Put 'em away." Cecil's voice hissed through the dark night.

Joshua stuffed the cigarettes back into his peacoat. "I know, I know," he whispered back. "Just keeping my hands busy."

Cecil leaned against the shed at the beginning of the dock. The planks creaked when he shifted his weight. They were in Bay Ridge, in Brooklyn, a place Joshua had needed a map to find. When he checked out this dock two nights before, it took him a subway trip, two bus rides, and a half-hour's walk.

Cecil gave Joshua a sly look. "Come on, Sarge, you know this is for keeps."

Joshua grunted. That's what he used to tell the men in France, after reminding them to clean their weapons, strap on their helmets, take cover. He reminded them every goddamned time. No exceptions, no moments of feeling lucky, no begging off or not giving a rat's ass anymore, figuring it would be easier to get wounded and go home. None of that not caring anymore. He couldn't let them not care because that might get them all killed. Cecil was right. Tonight was for keeps, too.

Joshua bunched his shoulders and jammed his hands in his

pockets. "Cold bastard," he muttered. A few lights sparkled across the Narrows from Staten Island, which didn't seem very far away. In the moonless night, clouds pressing down on the land, Joshua could barely make out the shapes of two large ships tied up to their left. Patches of mist drifted over the water, diffusing a low glow from the human lights on land. A bootlegger's night.

Cecil leaned toward him. "You sure this is the place?"

Joshua knew it was a dig, not an actual question. The smugglers' boat was late, but that wasn't any shock. Smugglers didn't run on a timetable. Anything could gum up the works. Engine trouble. Fog. A squabble over price. Confusion about which liquor supply ship was the right one. Six or eight supply ships might be loitering out in international waters, past the three-mile limit, waiting for the speedy rumrunners to show up. Even the coast guard might have stuck their big noses in the deal, though the word was that the coasties didn't bother Halloran's boats. Joshua had heard there was an arrangement.

Two white guys stood out at the business end of the dock, over the water, stamping their feet and blowing on their hands. When they drove up in their truck two hours before, Cecil and Joshua were already crouched behind the shed. They could have taken these two guys, but then they would have had to do something with them until the liquor boat showed up. Tying them up wasn't a great option and Joshua wasn't eager to kill over booze. Anyway, neither of these geniuses thought to look behind the shed. He smirked. Hard to get good help these days.

Joshua figured there'd be two more guys on the boat, the skipper and a guy to haul the cargo. That was the crew when he watched them come in the other night. That would make it two against four, but he and Cecil would surprise them, have that edge. Also, when Joshua watched them the other night, they looked soft. They weren't careful, not nearly careful enough. The krauts would've eaten these guys for breakfast.

Wearing dark clothes, pistols in their waistbands, he and Cecil watched and listened. It was a quiet neighborhood. A few foghorns in the bay. Some damned bell that never stopped clanging. Twice they heard a car engine. Not much else.

In France, on the line, he had clung to the night. Daylight showed the horrors. Mud everywhere—on clothes, seeping into skin, caked on guns, sucking boots down. Men scratching. Bodies all around, some alive, some sick, some asleep, some dead. And the eyes. So many dead eyes. Night was better, at least when there wasn't any fighting. It cloaked the horrors, leaving only the monsters of his imagination, and his imagination couldn't come up with anything to compare with what lay around him. For months after the war, those images stayed stuck in his brain, but they were fading now, at least a bit. Joshua mostly wasn't afraid of sleeping any more, not the way Cecil was. Joshua wondered if there was something wrong with him, if he'd been emptied out, numbed to the horror. He thought about Violet and smiled, then pushed her out of his mind.

Joshua checked his pistol again. It was the Mauser he took from a dead kraut officer. The crazy thing was that after the army let him out of prison, after his record got cleared, they gave him the gun back. Like it had been his. Damned US Army didn't know where half its soldiers were during any battle, but they'd kept track of this stolen pistol, delivered it to him in a cloth sack with a pack of cigarettes, the lighter he carried when he was arrested, and two letters from his mother.

Their plan wasn't airtight, but that didn't bother him. With houses around them, gunplay wasn't a great idea, so they had left a couple of oars out on the dock. Those would be the weapons. Unless they had to use guns. They would see what was what, improvise. Also fuzzy was how to get the liquor from here to where Cecil left their rented boat. The war taught Joshua to mistrust detailed plans. Nothing worked out like you planned. Check out the ground and understand what it offered. Think about the options. Trust yourself. Then get on with it. They weren't up against the German High Command tonight.

A throaty engine gurgle came over the water. The other night, Joshua had been impressed with the bootleggers' boat, its V12 Liberty plane engines. He half expected it to take off and fly. He touched Cecil's arm. With the engine noise as cover, he started out on the dock. On his toes, staying low. Cecil right behind.

The skipper cut the engine to glide the last three hundred yards. Joshua and Cecil froze. They weren't quite to the dock's T intersection. The oars lay a few feet in front of them, left of the T. The two onshore bootleggers stood to the right of the T, looking only at the arriving speedboat. Joshua slowed his breathing. The boat slid out of the mist, a man in the front dangling a rope end. The boat swung alongside the dock. The crewman threw the rope to one of the shore crew, then turned to the back of the boat.

Cecil's hand pushed him as Joshua rose and reached for an oar. He sprang forward and swung. He hit his man across the shoulders, launching him into the water with a startled shout that the water swallowed. Cecil ran by, wielding his oar like a jousting lance. He caught the other man as he turned and reached into his coat for a weapon. An *oof*, another splash.

Joshua was swinging the oar at the crewman on the boat. The man dodged the blow but lost his balance. Wearing a surprised look, he fell awkwardly into the drink. Joshua dropped the oar and jumped into the boat, pulling out his pistol. The skipper was reaching for the boat's throttle. Joshua fired a shot in his direction, aiming high. The skipper raised both hands. The struggling men churned the water around them. A clotted shout: "Can't. Swim." The man was in the wrong line of work. Joshua waggled the gun. "Off! Off!" he shouted.

Before the skipper could move, Cecil clouted him with the oar. Cecil dropped the oar, climbed into the boat, and heaved the skipper over the side. "The rope," he yelled. Joshua unwrapped the bowline. Cecil fired the engine and swung them away from shore. A thump on the right side of the hull. Must have been a bootlegger.

Heading toward the East River, Cecil hugged the shoreline. He kept the engine at midspeed, trying not to be noticed. This early on a January morning, a small boat in New York harbor was probably running booze. Joshua rifled the boat's storage compartments until he found a container of oil. He carried it back next to Cecil.

They came around a long pier with tugs tied up on either side. A spotlight glared from the Brooklyn shore. An amplified voice came through a megaphone, but the words sloshed into each other. Cecil gunned the engine. The bow pushed high as the propeller bit into the water. The cargo, piled around them, held down their speed. A coast guard cutter was casting off, pointed right at them.

When Joshua regained his balance, he hauled the oil can out onto the boat's back ledge. Looking away to shield his eyes, he poured oil on the hot twin engines. Acrid smoke billowed up and mingled with the mist already in the air. Cecil slowed the engine to a purr and turned them toward New Jersey. He cut across the path of a tug that was plowing along from that direction. Then he spun the boat around and hit the gas. They dove into the shadow of the tug and clung to it, lurking on its Manhattan side.

When they passed under the Brooklyn Bridge, Cecil dropped his speed further and eased them over toward Brooklyn. They scanned the waterfront for the coast guard. Joshua looked at Cecil and shrugged. Cecil turned them around again, back toward where they'd left their rented boat. They went slowly, as quietly as a powerboat could, staying just beyond the reach of the lights from shore. This was the worst part. They probably couldn't shake the coast guard a second time, not with dawn coming on. Joshua's heart hammered against his ribs.

Their rental was a tired-looking workboat, ropes and tackle strewn across its deck. They tied up next to it. Both of them carried the whiskey bottles into the workboat's hold. They changed into overalls and denim jackets and took off again. Joshua felt calmer. Their disguise was good. He could hear the city start to wake up. The waterfront, too. A sliver of sky lightened over Long Island. Thirty minutes more.

At the dock in Greenpoint, they humped the sacks of booze into the grubby warehouse Joshua had rented with the last money he had on earth. When the final sack was in, the two men shared a smile, then laughed and slapped each other on the back. They hadn't spoken since they left the bootleggers splashing in the water.

"Those boys," Cecil said, "they didn't know what hit 'em."

"No idea at all." Joshua led the way to the small office in the corner of the warehouse. A bare bulb hung over a table with three spindly chairs. He opened the bottles of beer he'd left there, handing one to Cecil. "Not so different from France. Ambush, surprise, deception. Get in and get out." He swallowed some beer. "The big difference is that these guys are dumber."

Cecil shook his head after taking a long draw on his bottle. "There's some other differences, Sarge."

"Yeah?"

"Yeah. Like no bayonets. No hand grenades. No artillery. No gas. And no killing, not yet."

"Nothing we can't handle."

Cecil shook his head again. "Another difference, you know, is that we're on the other side from the government."

"Say what? You mean the government was on *our* side over in France? Do tell." Joshua tilted his head back and smirked at Cecil, who smiled back. "That's a hundred fifty sacks, six bottles to the sack, near a thousand bottles."

"It looked like bonded stuff."

"Absolutely, straight from Scotland. We sell 'em at two bucks apiece. That's close to two thousand dollars, most of which we take home free and clear."

"No taxes."

"Not a dime."

They finished their beers and headed out. Joshua knew it wouldn't be quite that easy. They'd have to peddle the hooch to neighborhood bars and speakeasies. That was donkey work, a mug's game. Some would be slow to pay. They'd have to reward a few cops for looking the other way. Maybe the cops' bosses, too. Maybe the bosses' bosses. But they'd clear a lot, then use that money to buy a seat at a bigger table. Joshua was aiming at the wholesale end of the business. He wanted to be the guy who paid hungry stiffs like him to run those boats out to the supply ships, then paid other hungry stiffs to sell it around. The return would be better, the risks fewer.

# Chapter 8

The skirt reached. Violet sighed her relief. It was going to be bad enough using a crutch at a chic nightclub. If people also could see her shriveled lower leg, she would just die. So long as she stood up straight, the leg brace on her upper leg didn't bulge out, not unless you were looking for it. The colors in the dress were bright enough that few eyes should stray down toward the floor. High heels were out of the question. She could get by with black, medium heels.

She heard the front door open. She had told her mother to leave the latch off as she left. "Joan?" Joan Battaglia answered, her voice uncertain. "In here," Violet called. A small squeal from the doorway announced her friend's approval of the blue and green print dress with the swishy skirt.

"Aren't you going to turn heads tonight," Joan said. She leaned over to look past Violet's shoulder at their images in the mirror. "Those colors are wonderful for you. And what an apartment this is." She gazed up at the high ceiling and turned slowly in place.

"Oh, Joan, it's like any home. Come on, now. You promised

to help with the makeup," Violet said. "I've gotten so pale. I look like a ghost."

"Are you sure that isn't a good thing tonight?"

Violet gave Joan's arm a light swat. They had both been new at the clinic, the one where Violet was learning to walk again and where Joan had her first job as a nurse. Weak from lying in bed so long, depressed at the deafening silence from Griff Keswick and by her continuing debility, Violet was grateful for Joan's gentleness. Other nurses seemed to hector their patients through exercises. They were abrupt, their voices harsh. Violet responded to Joan's quiet encouragement. They became friends. Without Joan, she never could have considered tonight's adventure.

Joan pulled a chair to the dressing table and began to brush Violet's hair. "It's such a beautiful shade," she said. "Anything would be better than my mousy brown."

Violet, comparing two sets of earrings, decided on the simpler ones. "But yours is so thick," she protested. "I'd give anything to have hair with so much body. It's lush!" Violet stretched her arms out and twisted in mock pleasure. Joan smiled and placed her hands on Violet's shoulders. Violet felt the tears threaten. She grabbed one of Joan's hands. "Oh, I'm such a fool. He's going to take one look at me and this ridiculous leg and wish he was anywhere else in the world."

"He, of all people, knows about your poor leg. And *he* asked *you*." Joan gave Violet's shoulders a squeeze, then resumed her brushing. "The wonder of it is how brave you've been, going through all those exercises, and now tonight. I could never be so brave. And daring."

"Now, you remember the movie we're supposed to be seeing, in case my mother asks?"

"Really, Violet. I don't know why you didn't tell your parents the truth. It's just one night. They seem like fine people, not strict-from-the-old-country like mine."

"Please, Joan. The movie?"

"*Male and Female,* over at the Odeon." She put down the hairbrush and smoothed Violet's hair with her hand. "Fitting title?" Violet grinned. "And we'll see the nine-thirty show that won't be over until almost midnight, and then we'll stop for coffee and pie at the diner on Sixty-eighth Street. All right?"

"Do you remember the plot?"

"Yes! Do you?"

"Of course. Some claptrap about spoiled rich people being helpless. Whatever could they have in mind?"

Joan smiled but said nothing. She stood and stepped back from the dressing table. "Now, stand up and show me how you're going to move through that nightclub like a queen."

Their taxi dropped Joan off at her home on Tenth Avenue, then headed uptown to the address Violet gave the driver. She wiped her palms on the insides of her coat pockets, then moved the crutch to an angle that would make it easier to get out of the taxi. She was excited, nervous, scared. She had never been to Harlem. She certainly had never been out with a Negro before. Or several Negroes. Or any Negroes. No. That wasn't right. She and her mother and father had been with the Cook family in Paris, several times. Even with Joshua. So this really wasn't her first time.

But, no, it definitely was her first time for this. This was a date. A date with a man, close to her age, who might have romantic ideas. Until she met Joshua, she hadn't ever thought about romance with a Negro. She hadn't thought about it when they first met, not so she could remember. But she liked him, right from the beginning. She liked his confident, steady way. He seemed smart, but didn't have to show it off. He did like nice clothes, more than most men do. She noticed that when he came to the hospital. He looked good in them. Could she kiss a Negro? Be intimate with one? That was stupid. It wasn't some

Negro she was thinking about. It was Joshua. She knew Joshua. She liked him. What else did she have to know?

Anyway, she had to get out of that apartment, out of her narrow little life. Her life as a cripple. That's how people thought of her. Maybe her parents didn't, and she hoped Joshua didn't, but everyone else did. She could see it in their faces as she crutched past. A few looked sympathetic, most impatient. Children stared when she and Joan left the clinic and slowly circled the block. That was certainly what Griff Keswick saw that one time he came by the hospital. That's what she was. That's what she'd always be. All right, then. Cripples could go out on the town, too.

Joshua, elegant in a camel-hair coat, was on the sidewalk when Violet's taxi pulled up. He opened the door and bent over, his smile wide. "You came." Looking up, she took a deep breath. He gripped her arm as she maneuvered out of the taxi.

From the sidewalk, little suggested that a nightclub sizzled in the building before them. No lighted sign announced fun within. No doormen stood in livery. Inside, Violet had to climb a flight of wobbly stairs one at a time, something she'd been practicing with Joan that week. With her coat still on, the stairway was warm. The steps seemed to take the whole evening, but Joshua's smile remained in place. He supported her elbow.

He knocked twice on a door marked R & G IMPORTING. The door opened a crack. He said, "Ginger." They passed into a hum of voices and movement, music in the distance. After checking their coats and complimenting her dress, he offered his arm, his dark double-breasted suit immaculate. As they walked forward, she tottered when the tip of her crutch came down on a shoe. The man whose shoe it was looked over, surprise on his dark face. "Sorry," she said. He turned away without a word. Joshua steadied her with his free hand. Then his smile returned and they started again.

The floor captain was small and slender, with a thin mustache and marcelled hair. That might be his natural wave, Violet decided. He welcomed them to The Big House. "Good evening," Joshua answered. "Cook. Table for two." On the far side of the room, an orchestra of colored musicians played with a jazzy tempo, but not too much. Their white tuxedoes were blinding. A small dance floor was empty. The captain led them to a table in the second semicircle that looked out on the dancers, whenever they might show up. It was a good table but not a flashy one. After some confusion over what to do with Violet's crutch, which she would not relinquish, the captain slid it under the table so it wouldn't trip other customers. Violet closed her eyes briefly. She gathered herself.

"Next time," Joshua said, "it'll be easier."

She smiled and looked at him. "I'm sorry. You're very patient."

"Are you kidding? There isn't a man in this place who wouldn't kill to change places with me right now."

She laughed. It was a lovely lie.

While he ordered champagne and oysters, she began to look around. Candles flickered on tables covered with sparkling linen. Several tables had only white people. Several had only colored. A few, like theirs, had both. The staff was all colored—that seemed to be the rule. Everyone spoke with heads close together, or in loud voices, competing with the music that cushioned them against the world outside.

"I wasn't sure you'd come." Joshua leaned close.

"I wasn't either. It wasn't easy getting out. My mother took forever getting ready for her evening."

"No, I meant I wasn't sure you'd come up to Harlem. To see me."

She smiled and put her hand on his. "I knew what you meant. Since I'm here, there's not much to say about it." She looked around again. "I'm so glad to be out. To have a little bit of freedom. And to be in this exciting place." She smiled again. "And with you."

Their talk came easy, just as it had in the hospital room, and before that in France. He talked about the army. Not about the war or the fighting, but the army's rigid rules and how the soldiers got around them when they could. She talked about growing up in New York, tromping around backstages with her mother, extravagant theatrical characters, about her work with Joan. During a lull, when they were on the last of the champagne, she gazed out at the few couples on the dance floor. A woman was singing about her broken heart, though the uptempo rhythm contradicted the words. The song was like ragtime, which Violet knew, but different. More relaxed, less thought out. She swayed slightly.

"You look like you want to dance," Joshua said. "Do you think you can?"

"I'd love to. But no." She finished her champagne. "I wish I could."

"Maybe we can dance sitting right here." He pulled his chair closer and put his right arm around her shoulder. He turned and reached his left hand across to take hers, looking into her eyes and smiling. He was very close. Feeling his pulse through his hand, her own heart seemed to stop. She cast her eyes down and felt herself flush. They swayed in rhythm until the music ended.

Joshua, sitting back, dropped his head to look into her face. "Thank you for the dance, Miss Fraser. Are you ready for a cocktail?" She nodded. He ordered old-fashioneds.

"Your special rye, Mr. Cook?" the waiter asked.

"By all means," Joshua answered. "It's a special night."

Violet looked the question at him. His special rye? He smiled broadly and shrugged. "I have some involvement in supplying the beverages here."

Violet clapped her hands together and looked at him. He nodded. "You're a bootlegger?" she asked.

"I prefer it the way I said it." He gave her a sideways smile.

Her eyes were wide but a grin danced at the corners of her mouth. "So that's where the money comes from!" He nodded again. "You've been mysterious, so I was wondering. This all seems so extravagant." She looked around again. "So, Mr. Cook, not only have you led me into this den of iniquity—"

"Which was fully disclosed ahead of time—"

"—but, as a bootlegger, you are directly threatening the moral foundations of our nation."

Joshua looked away and pulled on an ear, then met her smile. "I believe I have already stated my occupation. As for moral foundation, it turns out that our nation is extremely thirsty, a dire situation I try to help with."

She turned her shoulders toward him. "Tell me about your adventures, all the thrilling things you do while I'm lying on my back with Joan bending my leg into horrible angles. Or while I stumble down the street with poor Joan telling me to slow down, slow down, get into a rhythm."

"No stories unless you save the last dance for me."

"I'm not sure I can. You'll have to elbow aside all the men who have been pestering me all night."

"They're too intimidated to approach such a magnificent woman."

"And you?"

"Beverage suppliers don't intimidate easy. Speaking of which, I haven't received an answer to my request for the last dance."

The waiter arrived with their drinks.

The rest of the night was a swirl. Their waiter announced curfew just before 2 AM, when they did have the last dance, never rising from the table. Then it was down the alley next door for a nightcap at The Big House Annex, an after-hours dive where the tables stood between empty coal bins. Hanging steam pipes threatened decapitation for men as tall as Joshua. After the champagne and cocktails, Violet felt downright spry on her crutch. Nothing to it. She laughed when Joshua pointed out that in the Annex the drinks were cheaper for Negroes than for whites, but he had to pay the higher price because he was with her. She liked that.

On their way home, he drove to the Hudson River piers and killed the engine. The moonlight cast a conical glow across the water, the light shimmering as small waves beat by. After hours of talking, they talked some more. He had plans, large ones. He wasn't going to stop with what he was doing. Bootlegging wasn't a career. It was a way to get somewhere. When he fell quiet, Violet said she didn't think she would ever walk right again. She knew she'd never run again. A tear formed in the corner of her eye.

"I know," he said. "It's a terrible thing. But there's lots worse." He leaned over and kissed her. Even though they'd been in with all those coal bins, he still smelled good.

# Chapter 9

This guy—what the hell was his name?—he was driving Babe nuts. He was lingering over his putt on the eighteenth green like it was a crate of nitroglycerin, had to be handled just so. Babe didn't spend a lot of time lining up his putts. He looked at the green, the ball, the cup. Hit the ball into the cup, right? He got impatient with these old biddies who stare at the ground for two, three minutes, like some message was painted between the blades of grass and they could figure it out if only they looked long enough. Then they walk to the other side of the hole—see, there he goes—to check out how the grass is growing over there. Is it really greener? Christ. If you need to go through that rigamarole, maybe golf ain't your game. Think about chess, you know?

Then Spencer, who wrote for the *Tribune,* missed his putt, just like they all knew he would. Babe handed his cigar to his caddy. He stepped to the ball. About a twelve-footer. Looked at it. Looked at it again. Swung. Solid tap of putter on ball. Then the warm, hollow sound of the ball rattling into the cup.

After the handshakes, the payment of twenty dollars to the

team of Ruth and Meusel, Ruth gave his share to the caddy along with his putter. He retrieved his cigar and pulled a jacket from his golf bag. "Next time," Babe called to the sportswriters who were aimed at the club bar, "we play for real money."

The afternoon shadows stretched toward the parking lot. That's where Babe was headed. Back to the hotel for a shower and fresh duds, then out to a country place that served the best fried chicken around, then on to where a different type of chicken was on offer, definitely not fried but extremely fresh.

He zipped up the jacket. The air was cool. Shreveport in February wasn't such a bargain for spring training. Warmer than New York, sure, but the Yankees' mornings on the ball field were on the frosty side. Frosty like that damned manager. That little Huggins—Babe snorted at the thought of the runt who had made them practice bunting for two hours that morning. Everyone but Babe, of course. Nobody came to the park to see Babe Ruth bunt, and he had better things to do than practice something he'd be goddamned if he'd ever do in a game. Huggins had been steamed about Babe not taking his turn, but what could he do about it? Babe was a hell of a lot more important to the Yankees than Miller fucking Huggins was.

"Hey, big fella."

Abe Attell was leaning against Babe's car, a tan Buick on loan from a local dealer who asked in return only a bunch of photos of Babe behind the wheel. Attell wore a bold plaid suit and straw boater, like it was the middle of summer. He must've figured he was in the South, have to wear summer clothes. Jesus, this guy was all Babe needed now.

"If it ain't the Little Hebrew in the flesh." The caddy held the door for Babe, having stashed his left-handed clubs in the trunk.

"Ride back to the hotel with you?"

"Sure. Hop in." How the hell'd the guy get out here, walk?

Babe felt better when the car was moving at a respectable

clip. This one had some pep. He grinned into the wind, the February sky still light even though it was nearly suppertime. Spring, the new baseball season, were on the horizon even if Abe Attell was in the next seat.

"So, Babe," Attell called. He was trying to light a cigar behind cupped hands, his head ducked below the windshield. He gave up on the cigar and threw the match away. "I heard you were lucky to get out of Cuba. They took all your money, that's what I hear."

"Damned spics. They run crooked games. I don't mind the house having an edge. Sure, that's how it goes. Everybody's got an angle. But they oughta give you some kind of shot at winning."

"How much they get you for?"

Babe nodded his head. "I'm all right." He gestured toward the dashboard. "Like the car?"

"Sure, Babe, it's a sweetheart." Attell picked a piece of tobacco off his tongue and flicked it out the window. "You look like you're in pretty good shape."

Ruth slapped his flank. "Best ever. Did workouts up in New York, when I got back from those thieves down in Cuba. This doc in my building told me about 'em. They were a lot of work, but I did 'em. I think it'll pay off." After a silence, he added, "You remember the guy, his wife was one of the producers for that movie."

"Don't remind me of that movie. Worst deal I've been in for a long time."

The Babe downshifted through a curve, mashed down on the accelerator to swing out of it. The transmission wasn't as smooth as a Packard or a Cadillac, but the motor had guts. He threw his cigar, not even half smoked, out the window. "What is it, Abe? You came down to the sunny South just to see what shape I'm in? I'll save your time. I'll hit even more homers this year. Okay?"

"Ah, you know, I like to see how all the players look, make

up my own mind. Who's taking care of himself. Who isn't. What kids may have the goods to make a difference. It helps with my business."

"Stop beating around the bush. You better not be thinking you're going to shove me around or anything."

Attell looked over. "Babe, you and me know the score. No need for that sort of talk, am I right? I just wanted to make sure you understood about those confessions, the ones the White Sox guys were supposed to have given when they got arrested for fixing the Series."

"Uh-huh." Babe downshifted again as they entered the town. What there was of it. Down here they stashed all the fun outside town, in country places where no one could see you were eating good food and drinking hard and enjoying someone else's company. It was like they were ashamed of having a good time. "I heard those confessions were bad."

"Did you hear about what happened to them?"

"Tell me. What happened to them?"

"Don't you take the papers?"

"People tell me what I need to know."

"Those confessions, and like you say they were pretty bad, turns out they disappeared. Poof." He puffed his cheeks out and blew away imaginary papers.

"No fooling."

"What'd I tell you before? That there's nothing to worry about, if only people are smart. If only they don't go around blabbing about things they don't really know or understand. Hey!" Attell was pointing to the side of the main street they were on. "Set me down there. There's a guy I need to see."

Babe eased the Buick to the curb. Attell turned and stuck his hand out for a shake. "I'm telling you, Babe. Chicago's a great town. A reasonable town. They understand that people have to make a living. And you need to remember to trust your friends, Babe. That's the key to the whole thing. You got to trust your friends." With a two-finger salute at the brim of his boater, Attell stepped out. He didn't look back.

Babe relaxed as he waited for a trolley to clatter by, then pulled out behind it. Trust Abe Attell—that was a laugh. He wouldn't trust that guy as far as he could throw him. He trusted him once and look where it got him. Permanently behind the eight ball.

Inside the lobby of the Arlington Hotel, Babe stopped for messages. The desk clerk pointed to a large man seated near the front windows. He was folding his newspaper and rising. He looked like law. Working the bar at his old man's joint back in Baltimore, Babe got pretty good at sniffing out the law. Of course, lawmen tend not to hide what they are. More like they announce it, how they walk and how they stand. Like their problems are your problems and you'd better start worrying about them.

The man approached Babe and said, "The name's John Slaughter, Mr. Ruth. I wonder if we might have a word."

This couldn't be good. No one called him Mr. Ruth except if he was bringing trouble. "I'm pressed for time, kid. How about an autograph?"

Slaughter was almost as tall as Babe but older, a bit thicker. He moved like there was serious muscle underneath his wrinkled suit. He smiled and took off his derby. "We really need to talk. Won't take long." He indicated the passageway to the right of the front desk, then led the way.

They went down a flight of stairs, then through a thick door into a tunnel lit by overhead bulbs. "What the hell?" Babe said. His voice echoed in the narrow space.

"Just in here," Slaughter said over his shoulder, pushing open another door as though there was no question that Babe would follow. "You'll be glad we did."

Feeling stupid, Babe entered. The room looked ordinary

enough. A few chairs, a table in the middle. A window near the ceiling looked out on the sidewalk at calf-level.

"So," Slaughter said as he sat down, waving at another chair for Babe. "I represent the office of the commissioner of baseball, Judge Kenesaw Mountain Landis."

Babe nodded but didn't sit. He wasn't liking anything about this.

"You know the judge is in charge now."

Babe nodded again. He was thinking about leaving, but didn't want it to look like he was afraid. Which he was.

"And you know the judge. He's been brought in to deal, first off, with this White Sox situation, them throwing the Series in 1919."

Slaughter was giving him the straight look, right in the eye. The one that was supposed to make you tell him everything. Babe nodded.

"You got anything to say about that?"

"I never played for the White Sox. What would I have to say?"

"What do you know about it?"

"People talk, you know. I don't know what's true or not. Not my problem." Babe pulled his watch out and looked at it. "I've got someplace I need to be, pretty soon now. Need to shower and change. Okay?"

Slaughter held up his hand. "What about Abe Attell?"

"What about him?"

"He's here in Shreveport, you know. And he's under indictment in Chicago for fixing the Series. Not a guy that a star player like you should be hanging out with."

That's right, Babe thought. I'm a damned star and who the hell are you? But he said only, "Thanks. Glad to have your view." He turned to go.

"One other thing, Mr. Ruth. What about the 1918 Series? That's one you did play in."

"What about it?" Babe leaned forward with his fists on the table. Slaughter took his time, showing he wasn't impressed.

"The judge, he's been wondering how long this game-fixing business may have been going on. Seems like maybe a long time. That's what Eddie Cicotte says. You know him, Cicotte?"

Babe shrugged. "Just on the field. Pretty good pitcher."

"Yup. For the White Sox." Slaughter paused to stress that point. "Cicotte says we should be looking at the 1918 Series. You played in that one."

Babe shrugged. He started to say something. He thought better of it.

"So we've got questions about some of the guys in that Series, that one you played in. About Max Flack. You remember him? And Phil Douglas. And, yeah . . ." Slaughter rubbed his forehead, like his fingertips were drawing information out of his head, "Charlie Hollocher, the Cubs shortstop. The way he played out of position so much?"

Babe grinned and shook his head. "You think I'm looking where the shortstops play? I don't hit the ball to shortstops. I hit it way past them. Shortstops could be sitting down eating peanuts for all I care. Anyway, in that Series I was still pitching. Only played in two games."

"You were there."

"Thousands of people were there, at every game. Maybe they were watching that shortstop, what's his name. You should ask them."

"Tell me how it was, Mr. Ruth. Tell me about that train ride from Chicago to Boston and what went on during that ride. And what Abe Attell was doing on that train and who he was doing it with."

Babe put his grin back on. "I can't help you, kid. I've been on hundreds of train rides. They all mix together, you know? Seems like you'd do better talking to guys on the Cubs, not me.

I gotta take a shower, then I'm meeting someone. You know, someone you want to smell good for."

"Your choice, Mr. Ruth. But remember—I came and asked you, politely. You chose not to say anything."

Babe left without shaking the man's hand. He climbed up to the hotel lobby and then up to his room. When he was cleaned up, feeling good, he had an idea. On his way out, he stopped at the front desk. He wrote out a telegram to Speed Cook.

# *Chapter 10*

Cook made himself ignore the opulence of the Ansonia lobby. Rich folks. Some time back he decided to give up worrying about them, wanting to be them. It only made him hot and he got hot too easy. At least that's what other people seemed to think, especially Aurelia. So he set out to change what he wanted. He'd want to look after himself, his people. That would do. The rich folks could take care of themselves. They always had.

The elevator doors opened and Babe strode out in a red satin dressing gown. The green and white diamonds of his pajamas brought a low whistle from Cook.

"Morning, kid," Babe said. "Lemme grab the papers." He stalked over to the front desk, nodding at those surprised to encounter this mountainous legend in his sleepwear. When he returned to Cook, he held out the *Daily News,* opened to a half-page photo of him in full swing.

"Don't you love this?" he said to Cook. "They *show* you the damned news, don't screw around with a bunch of poetry and gas. Yesterday the season starts, so you can go to the game in their pictures."

Cook noted a headline predicting the Yanks would be in the World Series by the end of the season. "They're expecting great things from you guys."

"We got a hell of a team." In the elevator, Babe didn't have to tell the operator which floor. "This kid Hoyt, the pitcher we got from the Red Sox? He's a good one. Mays is still a son of a bitch. The hitters are all afraid he's gonna kill 'em, and the bastard just might. And Meusel and me'll keep the runs coming across. Who's better than us?"

Despite Cook's policy of not paying attention to the ways of rich folks, the Ruth apartment was hard to ignore. Its scale matched the size and reputation of the young man who lived there, while its wood paneling and leather expressed his bank balance. Cook had to remind himself that the Babe was a year younger than his son Joshua, still a babe really, but also a national hero with New York City at his feet.

An eight-sided poker table dominated the parlor. Poker chips and several decks of cards mingled on the green felt with dirty glasses and overflowing ashtrays. On a divan, a middle-aged man snored, his collar open and askew, his tie drawn down, his mouth gaping. The Babe kicked the sole of the man's shoe. "Mac, hey, Mac! Time to get a move on. Game's been over for an hour." The man groaned and rolled on his side, almost sliding off the couch. Babe reached down and shook his shoulder. "Gotta go, Mac. Want a cab?" The man sat up slowly, rubbing his face with both hands.

Babe raised a window and gave a token wave against the tobacco stink. "Someone'll come straighten up. Helen's up at our place outside Boston. You know, that's where she's from. She's not so crazy about New York. Want some coffee? Had breakfast?"

"Coffee would be great," Cook said. The man on the couch was shuffling toward the door. Babe ignored him. He walked to a small table that held a telephone and a glass cylinder. "Watch this," he said over his shoulder. He jotted something on a slip of paper, placed it in the cylinder, which he closed, then inserted it in a port cut into the wall. When he closed the port hatch, he pressed a button, which loosed a whoosh. Babe grinned. "Love that thing. Helen calls it the pneumonia cylinder. They'll bring the food and coffee in a few minutes."

The sound of the front door closing signaled that the card-player was gone. The Babe gestured to two easy chairs next to the room's windows. "Let's take a load off, eh?" When they were settled, Babe asked what Cook had found out.

Cook raised a finger and cocked his head. He walked quickly out to the foyer and confirmed that the man was gone. When he returned, the Babe said, "You're pretty cautious."

"That's how I got to be so old."

"That old rummy, what's his name? Pretty harmless."

"People can surprise you. They surprise me, anyway."

"So, what do you know?"

"Before we do this, I've got a question. And I want to say that I'm glad to do this job, there's no problem there. But I need to know why'd you hire me? You don't really know me."

"When we met, I could see a couple of things. First off, you ain't much of a drinker, not more than you can handle, which is good. And you seem straight. Near as I can tell. And the Frasers, the doc and his wife, they like you. That's in your favor. I know they're straight."

Cook shook his head. "That's all nice, Babe, but it's not half enough."

Babe leaned forward, his elbows on the arms of the chair. "How about this? If you screw up, it won't come back on me." Cook gave him a puzzled look. "Think about it. Half the people in the country, maybe more, think I'm a jig. You've heard what they yell from the stands. Nobody thinks about how I got blue eyes, right?"

Cook nodded. Cook hadn't actually heard the racial taunts, but everyone knew about them. Where Cook sat, in the colored seats, the fans took a quiet pride in the general view that Ruth had to be at least part Negro. There were colored folks who had light eyes.

"So I figure," Babe went on, "no one would expect me, of all people, to hire a jig for something this—you know—this sensitive. I figure if something goes wrong or you get in a jam somehow, I just say I don't know you from Adam and it won't come back on me." Cook nodded as though the Babe was making sense. It sounded screwy, but maybe that's how the guy thought. "So," the Babe said, "what do you know?"

Cook took a second to organize his thoughts. "This guy Slaughter, the one who approached you in Shreveport? He's been talking to a bunch of guys, grabbing them unawares, like he did with you." The Babe nodded. "He's been real interested in that train ride from Chicago to Boston during the 1918 Series, after the first three games. When the players from both teams were together for so long. He knows there was lots of fraternizing between them."

"Fraternizing? Hell, we were all just bitching. You know, about not getting paid right. When times get tough, you don't see the owners taking any losses. They sure don't say, okay there's a war on, no one wants to go to the ball games, we just won't make so much money this year. No, sirree. They figure out how to pay *us* less so *they* all make just as much."

Cook wasn't real moved by Babe's complaining. The man was less than half Cook's age and was pulling down thirty thousand a year for playing ball. Even if he had made a lot less in 1918, he hadn't been over in France getting shot at like Joshua was. There were lots of soldiers who would have played baseball for free rather than spend that summer fighting Germans.

"Is that what guys like Harry Hooper will say?"

"Hoop? Why ask about him?"

"He was the leader, right? Took charge of that players' rebellion. And he's a friend of yours."

"Hoop's a good guy, though he got hung out to dry pretty bad. I tried to tell him it wasn't going to get us anywhere, but he didn't listen. He'd got all heated up over how unfair it all was."

"Well, listen, Babe, the problem here probably isn't Harry Hooper. It's the Cubs. They've been getting sort of a juicy reputation for this sort of thing. You know Cicotte said the White Sox got the idea for throwing the Series from the Cubs. And that grand jury out in Chicago started out by looking at whether the Cubs threw some regular season game against the Phillies. And then you add in the Cubs who played so bad in the Series—Max Flack, Phil Douglas."

"Hell, that don't mean it was fixed. Everyone plays bad sometime. Especially in the Series. Especially some bush-leaguer like Flack who's got no business being in the Series in the first place."

"You pick Flack off base twice in the same game, plus he misplays a routine fly ball into a triple." Cook leans forward. "And what about Phil Douglas—he can't toss the ball to the first-baseman from twenty feet away?"

"Nerves'll get you. Anyway, Douglas was probably half in the bag when he took the mound that day. Tell you the truth, sometimes he pitches better half in the bag." Babe leaned forward. "Anyway, we *won* the Series. If anybody threw it, it wasn't us. So how do I end up with any kind of a problem here?"

At that moment a white-jacketed, white-gloved waiter stuck his head around from the vestibule. "Mr. Ruth? Where shall we set it up?"

"In here. The grub's for me."

The waiter entered. A second man pushed a cart that was covered with platters and a large pot of coffee. The two men carried over a table from the side of the room. When Babe stood, Cook copied him. The waiters placed the table between the chairs they had been using. With a flourish, one threw a creamy white cloth over the table, distributed place settings, and arranged the platters in a semicircle around the Babe's side.

After the waiters poured coffee and retreated, Babe began lifting the silver domes off the platters. A mound of scrambled eggs gleamed on one; nearly a pound of crisp bacon was stacked on another; a third held enough fried potatoes to end an Irish famine. The Babe started by slathering a biscuit with butter and jam. With his mouth full, he used his free hand to offer Cook his choice of the food. Cook shook his head and watched Babe pitch in.

"Go ahead," Babe said indistinctly around a mouthful of biscuit, pointing at Cook with his fork.

"Okay, your question was why would anyone suspect you about the 1918 Series? A few things seem to be on Slaughter's mind. First, he's interested in you and Flack, this bush-leaguer. Apparently you two had some escapade back in Baltimore. You were with the Orioles and he was with the Federal League team."

The Babe swallowed some coffee, then some more. "Flack's a guy can't hold his liquor. They should have a special Prohibition law applies just to him, Max Q. Flack. So a couple times, I run into him when I'm out and about, when he's pretty damaged, and I help the guy get home. Shoot me."

"One of those times Jack Dunn had to get it hushed up?"

Babe shrugged and scooped up some potatoes with a large spoon. "Jack's a square guy."

Cook put down his cup and sat back. He wanted to leave the Babe a little room on this one. "So one theory I've heard, not from Slaughter yet but I've heard it more than one place, is that you helped your friend Attell talk to your friend Flack about fixing the Series."

"Abe Attell sure don't need anyone to introduce him to ballplayers, and he ain't no friend of mine."

"There's another thing. I'm hearing that Attell's been loaning you money. The amounts I'm hearing about make it sound like Attell's not just a friend. More like family."

The Babe concentrated on the food. He had the eggs down by about half. The potatoes a bit more. Only a couple of bacon slices still survived. He picked up a biscuit and sliced it lengthwise. He deliberately buttered each half, then smeared jam on each. He looked up at Cook when he bit into one of the halves. While he chewed, he shrugged, then swallowed. "That's private business."

Cook spread his hands apart. "If a jig like me can find out about it, then so can John Slaughter and so can Judge Landis." The Babe concentrated on making the biscuit disappear. After about thirty seconds, Cook started again. "Look, I know Attell was on that train ride from Chicago to Boston. So Slaughter knows, too. I know you owed Attell money. So Slaughter knows that, too. I know that the gamblers were swarming over the Series, what with all the racetracks closed, which meant there was nothing they had to bet on, coast to coast, except the World Series. You guys were the only game in town. In any town. And Slaughter knows that, too." Cook stopped and took a couple of swallows of coffee. "So you need to tell me about it. If I don't know what really went on, I can't figure out what might put you in the clear."

The Babe kept eating. He slid the last potatoes into his mouth, then wiped up with his napkin and sat back.

"Nothing happened."

"Did you see Flack? On the train?"

"Sure I saw Flack. I saw all of 'em. Attell, too. Would've had to jump off the train not to see 'em, all of 'em."

"Okay." Cook knew there was more. Otherwise this whole conversation wouldn't be happening. Babe was afraid for himself, of course, but Cook knew the risk went far beyond him. Baseball couldn't stand a second scandal after the Black Sox. Not a second World Series fixed, especially one that tarnished its greatest star, wrapped him up with underworld gamblers who rigged the whole system. America might just find itself another pastime.

"Is there any actual *thing*," Cook asked, "like a piece of paper or a gift or something, that might tie you to Attell or Flack or any of the others—you know, any of the Cubs, or any gamblers? Something that Slaughter might find."

The Babe looked over Cook's shoulder for another silent moment. "Maybe," he said. "Maybe this one thing. But it's got nothing to do with baseball or the Series. Not directly."

# Chapter 11

Eliza disliked the Marlowe, a theater that had decayed too quickly. The lobby carpet was frayed at the edges. Paint had flaked off the flowers carved into the ceiling molding. The air was weighted with stale cologne and dust long undisturbed, plus a hint of mice concealed in unexpected numbers. Eliza felt the implied judgment of such neglect, that the objects neglected—the building and the lives lived inside it—didn't matter. Nothing survived that judgment.

This theater could have been much more. Barton Marlowe was a canny old pirate. He made his pile in the two-fisted business of shipping fruit from Central America. Once rich, he set out to buy respectability and glamour by building this theater within a block of Times Square. He might have pulled it off if he hadn't choked on a fish bone at a downtown restaurant. Young Bart, his son and a man destined always to be called Young Bart, lacked his father's nerve, his drive, and his charm. When the loans on the theater came due, Young Bart didn't have the gizzard to face down a roomful of bankers that his father would have laughed at. Young Bart inherited the Marlowe name and the Marlowe Theater. Neither would outlive him.

"Well, look what the cat dragged in!" Eliza smiled at the sight of her cousin Wilfred. His silver hair slicked back, Wilfred was dapper in cutaway evening clothes, preening next to a handsome young man. Eliza never could recall their names. Not that it mattered. There would be another soon.

After greetings, Wilfred asked what brought Eliza to the plebian rural melodrama that was premiering that evening. "Personally," he added, bouncing on his toes, "I'm expecting to nap *outrageously* during each act! I've asked Herbert to disturb me only in the event of *loud* snoring. Anything less can only enhance the performance."

"Oh, the director's an old friend. I promised I'd come. I'm hoping to slip off after intermission, after gushing over the brilliance of the show."

"Dear Eliza." Wilfred dropped his voice to a conspiratorial level. "Wouldn't it be ever so much easier if we could simply offer our praise now and skedaddle, thereby salvaging our entire evening to our preferred pleasures?" Wilfred chuckled and raised a meaningful eyebrow toward the smiling Herbert. In anything more than the smallest doses, Wilfred made Eliza's teeth ache. He was, however, family.

Abruptly, Wilfred suggested that Herbert find their seats, then guided Eliza toward a quiet corner. As other theatergoers swept past, Wilfred returned to his confidential tone.

"Dear Eliza, I've been absolutely wracked with the most exquisite indecision over whether to tell you this."

Eliza waved at a friend and began to pull her gloves off, finger by finger. Confidences from Wilfred usually carried the whiff of scandal. The old reprobate gloried in his own scandals, flaunting his boyfriends with no restraint. Eliza resolved to propel her cousin's story as quickly as possible. "Wilfred, I do need to get on."

"Oh, you want to hear this." Eliza experienced a small flip in her stomach. Their family had secrets. Big ones. Stepping between Eliza and a group walking by, Wilfred began to describe a recent late-night outing to a black-and-tan club in Harlem. "The kind," he said with sparkling eyes, "where all the handsomest darkies dress up in their Sunday best and dance to that evil jazz music that corrupts us innocent white folk."

"Wilfred." Eliza's tone signaled diminishing patience.

"I'm getting there, my dear."

A tall couple stopped to congratulate Wilfred on a new role he had landed in a comedy that would open that summer. When they left, Eliza asked why he took the part. "You know that Jesperson hasn't written an amusing line in ten years. He'll throw in some smutty references, have the actresses smoke cigarettes and cross their legs, and hope that the sensation of it all will sell tickets."

"Dear Eliza," Wilfred said reproachfully. "We gentlemen of a certain age can't afford to be too fussy about our roles."

Duly chastised, Eliza offered her own congratulations and turned to go. Wilfred put a restraining hand on her forearm. "That night at the black-and-tan? I ran into Violet, with a very handsome young Negro."

Eliza froze. "What do you mean?"

"My words were quite clear, Eliza. Don't play the ingenue with me."

"Did you know him? Tell me."

"I didn't know him, but she introduced us, didn't bat an eyelash. They seemed to be having the gayest sort of evening. Though not actually dancing, of course. Poor dear."

"Stop it, Wilfred. Who was it?"

"His name was . . . I think it was Joshua. Is that the lad that Jamie helped save from catastrophe last year in France?"

Eliza lost the power of speech for a moment, then recovered. "You're sure you got the name right?"

Wilfred didn't dignify the question with a response. "You know, my dear, he was spreading a lot of money around, and my, was he dressed beautifully. Of course, he has the figure for it."

"When was this?"

"Perhaps three weeks ago. Perhaps a month."

"And you didn't tell me?"

"Later in the evening, Violet stopped by my table and swore me to secrecy. That's why I have dwelt in such exquisite indecision. When I saw you here tonight, it was a great relief, the prospect of banishing that agony from my thoughts."

Through the melodrama's first act, Eliza paid no attention to it at all. The actors might have been speaking Danish for all she cared. When the house lights came up for intermission, she found the director at the lobby bar, flashed her best smile and raved about the script, the sets, the divine experience. Two minutes later, she was hailing a cab.

Eliza arrived in the apartment like a brisk wind. She covered the distance from the front door to the sitting room in the time it took Fraser to look up from his newspaper. His bourbon glass sat empty. The sight of her determined face made him grateful that he had delayed the decision to refill it. Whiskey-delayed responses would only trigger waspish comments. He sat up and pulled his feet off the hassock.

"Where is that girl?" Eliza demanded.

"Violet? She went out."

"Out where? With who?"

"She went to a show with that nurse from the clinic. Joan, that's her name. You know how they've become thick as thieves."

"Hmmph." Eliza sat on the couch facing him. The storm clouds plainly were about to burst.

Fraser sought shelter in remembered details. "They went to that musical, the one you said was overrated."

"Like hell they did." Eliza took a cigarette from the metal box on the coffee table and lifted the heavy lighter next to it. Fraser placed his paper on the hassock and waited. The lighter required four tries to ignite. Eliza took a deep drag and sat back. "I ran into Wilfred at the theater tonight, before the show."

"How is the old dear?"

With a quick roll of her eyes, Eliza made it clear that Wilfred had not stopped being garrulous, well-meaning, and tiresome. She took a contemplative pull on her cigarette. Fraser imagined the glow of its tip as a third eye at the bottom of her face. He blinked to clear the image.

"He was brimming over with news." She stubbed out the cigarette and pointed at his empty glass with her other hand. "Give me one of those."

Oh my, Fraser thought. Not some charming story about dotty, exasperating Uncle Wilfred. Fraser might as well freshen his own drink. When he delivered hers, Eliza took a healthy swallow.

"Violet is involved," she said, "romantically involved, that is, with that Joshua Cook. Your friend's son."

Fraser set his drink down, far more violently than he had intended. He breathed a curse he rarely used. "What are you saying?"

"What do you think I'm saying?" Eliza's eyes were bright and her cheeks flushed. "They're seeing each other. They're sweethearts, lovers, flames, valentines, whatever cloying, nauseating term you wish to use. And it's disgusting, and it's been going on right under our noses."

"And you had no idea?"

"For Christ's sake, Jamie. Don't you think I would've mentioned it? And what about you? Did you have any idea? Of course you didn't."

"You're her mother."

"You're her father." She had stood. Her face was inches from his, heat coming off it in waves. "Just—just—just look what you've done, you and that Speed Cook of yours. You brought those people into our lives and now they've ruined everything. Ruined."

"You're blaming me for this?" He stepped away.

"Jamie, there are lines in the world for reasons, thick bright lines. People need lines. You can't just act like they're not there. Like they don't matter."

The words in his head fell over each other. What she was saying was wrong, but what did that matter? What mattered was Violet. He walked to an open window that looked out over Broadway. He had to make sense of this, not just give in to anger. He drew several deep breaths. He couldn't believe this. Two delivery wagons wobbled down the street, the hollow clop of hooves on pavement carrying up to the window. A few voices reached him. A limousine roared uptown, noisily shifting gears as it gained speed. Fraser wondered if it was going to Harlem.

When he turned back, Eliza was seated again, one hand shading her eyes. "So," he said, clipping his words. "Wilfred knows this? He actually *knows* it? It's not some inference based on gossip picked up from one of his boyfriends?"

"Jamie," Eliza scolded. "That's beneath you."

"Give me the whole story, what Wilfred said."

After she was through, Fraser asked, "He's sure it was Violet?"

"He's known her all her life, Jamie. Anyway, there aren't that many beautiful blond cripples. Not even in New York City."

"She's not a cripple, she limps." Fraser hadn't meant to shout.

Eliza looked away. Since September, he was always the one to say that Violet would be fine. She'd walk again. She'd dance at her wedding. Time and hard work, that was the ticket. Eliza couldn't do that. She had to brace for the worst, to say the worst out loud so maybe it would lose its power. The more harshly she said it, the less power it would have. She hated how it sounded but she kept doing it; she needed to do it to keep her expectations from outrunning what her daughter could manage. She knew it hurt him, but she couldn't help that. "Have it your way," she said.

"How long?"

"How am I supposed to know? Really, Jamie. I had no idea this was going on, and you—you wouldn't ever notice anything outside your sacred laboratory, where you're curing the sick and the halt and the lame."

Fraser let it pass.

"Jamie, this is serious. She's not a child."

"Yes. Yes, I know. When was this, when Wilfred saw them?"

"Weeks ago. Violet swore him to secrecy and the damned fool felt honor-bound to respect his pledge. What a time to discover his honor. When he saw me tonight he decided he couldn't keep the secret any longer."

Fraser was pacing behind the chairs that faced the couch. "Please stop," she said. "I'm on edge enough without having you on sentry duty."

Fraser sat. He crossed his legs. His top foot began to jiggle. The newspaper on the hassock mocked him, a meaningless artifact of how simple his world had been twenty minutes before, when he had read quietly about other people's problems. He drank off the second bourbon.

"How could she?" he said. "And not say anything to us?"

Eliza looked sad. "Not telling us is the easy part to understand. Look at us, how we're acting. Would you tell us?"

"I don't know. I don't know what to say."

"I don't even know how she could feel that way about him."

"I don't know that, either." He stood and started to pace again, jamming his hands in his pockets. "What do we do? How do we keep her from throwing her life away on this infatuation? He's a fine fellow in some ways, I know that. But really—they've got nothing in common, and what could her life be like with him? The world isn't ready for this sort of thing. It can only end terribly."

"Wilfred said he made a big show of spending a lot of money."

"Really? The last time I saw Speed, he said Joshua couldn't find decent work." He made a face. "I wonder if he's a bootlegger. It's the only way to go from unemployed to rich in a few months. He couldn't make that kind of money working with his father. Christ, that would be perfect. A criminal, to boot." Fraser rubbed his hands together. They were cold. "So, did Wilfred at least try to talk her out of it?"

"He probably thinks that's the responsibility of Violet's parents."

"A responsibility that can't be discharged when Wilfred ensures that we sit here for weeks in ignorance."

He saw that Eliza wasn't listening. She had a faraway look and spoke in a quiet voice. "She simply has no idea what she's doing. She can't." Eliza looked over at Fraser.

"It's that terrible bombing, her leg," he said, standing still for a moment. "It's made her desperate. She thinks she's damaged goods and will never be worthy. I saw it overseas. The wounded soldiers, the worst of them, they just felt like they were . . . less. It was so hard for them to get any kind of confidence back."

Eliza said nothing. He began to pace again. He stopped and ran a hand down his jaw. "Maybe you and she could take a trip to Europe, get away from all this. Let time do its work. She's got to get over this."

"Do you propose to kidnap her?"

"Why the hell not?"

"She's of age. And you'd never do it, anyway."

"Eliza, she's our little girl. I've got to do something, something other than physical violence. Whose side are you on?"

"Ours. Yours and mine and Violet's." She inhaled sharply. "When was the last time you saw your friend Speed?"

"Back in December." Pacing again, he swung his arm down at an imaginary obstacle. "That dreadful basketball game in Harlem he was staging. What a ridiculous sport. Bouncing a ball up and down a room, back and forth, back and forth."

"Did he let on about anything like this?"

"God, no. I would have told you. And he would've told me if he knew."

"Are you sure? Violet would be quite a catch for the Cook clan—it would complete the trip up from slavery."

Fraser shook his head. "I don't know. I really don't know. I wonder if Speed'll have the same reaction we do."

"What, precisely, is that reaction?"

"I'd say that's pretty obvious."

"No, Jamie. After the rage, the disbelief, the fear." He stopped and looked at her. She was more collected. "We need to know what each of us is thinking."

His pacing resumed. "That if they persist in this . . . this . . . this dalliance, they'll become the targets of hateful people who'll want to hurt them. Yes, have it your way, that there are lines in the world. That this single ill-considered decision will ruin their lives, shrink Violet's world forever. . . . What she can do, where she can go, who she can know. Shrink it beyond what it's already shrunk to with her leg. And that's if the romance is successful. The world just isn't ready for a Negro and a white girl to be married. I don't care who they are. Look how they hounded Jack Johnson, that Negro fighter!" He stopped again and spoke to the window. "And I'm sure as hell not ready for it."

Eliza, lids drooping over eyes growing moist, said softly, "You're right. This is all from that wretched bomb. She thinks this Negro is the best she can do now that she's a—now that she limps." Again, she shaded her eyes with a hand. "Lord, Jamie, will we ever be done with the Cooks?"

He sat down. The silence stretched between them. Suddenly he felt exhausted. "We need to think about what we're going to do. She said she'd be out late, that we shouldn't wait up."

Eliza stood and walked to his chair. She took his hands. "You go to bed. I'll talk to her."

"I'm supposed to trot off and go to sleep? Like it's just any night?"

"Let me do this. I've had longer to get used to this idea. It'll be easier for her if it's just one of us. It won't seem like we're ganging up on her."

"I'm her father. I have to do something."

"It'll be easier for her to talk to me than to her father. You know how she idolizes you."

Fraser stood and they embraced absently. He took his glass to the cabinet and poured himself two fingers worth, then a third. After a swallow he turned to Eliza. "Do you think she loves him?"

Eliza's face fell into a vacant-looking fatigue. "She must think she does. Maybe she does. Not that it matters." They stayed in silence for several moments, lost in their thoughts.

"You know, Joshua probably saved Violet's life that day," Fraser said. "She may still see him as her savior, now her savior a second time when she feels so damaged, after that bastard Keswick left her high and dry. But this will bring so much more trouble than good."

Eliza put a hand along his cheek. "Her father, you know, fell in love with someone who brought a fair amount of trouble with her."

He bowed his head so their foreheads touched. "Don't," he murmured, watching her eyes. It sneaked up on him, how much he felt, how he wanted to protect her. Not that he ever could. Or that she needed it. "You need to tell her that this must end. No romance with Joshua Cook. If you won't tell her that, then I'm staying."

She kissed his lips. "Go to bed, Jamie."

# Chapter 12

Spiffed up for a night in Harlem, Joshua parked next to the Brooklyn warehouse. After stepping away from the car, he turned to admire it in the dusky light. It was only a Ford. In his business, it was better not to be too flashy. But it was *his* car. The old man had never owned one. At the rate he was going, he never would.

Joshua turned to the warehouse. *His* warehouse. He liked every part of that, too. Even better than the car, to tell the truth. It felt substantial. As did tonight's expected load of rum. There was a new supplier out past the three-mile limit, a guy who operated out of the Bahamas and claimed to carry premium rum. They were planning to lift some of his product from some dopes out on Long Island's south shore. Joshua used his key on the side door.

"Evening, Mr. Cook." The watchman called over from his desk at the main entrance. He gave a salute at the brim of his cap. Cecil had insisted they hire a guard, though Joshua couldn't figure out why. This worn-out relic wasn't going to shoot it out with any cops who were suddenly seized with a passion for enforcing Prohibition. Nor was he going to confront competitors who might want to steal from Joshua. A lone guard would have to be crazy to try either. Joshua shrugged mentally. Maybe he kept the neighborhood kids away. Not that he'd ever seen any kids in the neighborhood.

Cecil, wearing workman's clothes, sat in the office at the sorry-looking table, its gouges glinting with the colors it previously was painted. Cecil leaned back and grinned. "If it ain't the playboy of the western world!"

Joshua threw his gloves on the table. He gave his partner a level look.

Cecil whacked the table with his open palm and smacked his lips. "Sure do likes me some of the white meat, boss. Sho' 'nuf, you knows I do."

Joshua stared a while longer. "I might expect that kind of horseshit from ignorant street niggers or from crackers, but not from you. Don't keep on like that—you know what's good for you."

Cecil sprang from his chair. Joshua didn't flinch. "So what's that, what's good for me, boss? Is it good for me to be hooked up with some high-yaller big shot who's lost his head over a white girl? 'Cause I'm here to tell you that doesn't feel so good." Cecil stepped closer and pointed a finger at Joshua. "Don't you get it? Nobody likes you sashaying around with Miss Princess Blondie. The Jew boys don't like it. The greasers don't like it. The mick cops sure as hell don't like it. And I'm the guy who gets to hear about how no one likes it, and let me tell you, I'm hearing it a lot. And, you know what? I don't like it either."

Joshua forced a smile to his lips and nodded his head. "Okay. Now I've heard it. Again." He gripped Cecil's elbow with his left hand. Cecil turned back to his seat. "What happened? Why this now?"

"You know that bastard Hanlon, over at the Greenpoint precinct house?"

"Sure. Gave him his envelope, what, two days back."

"He dropped in, maybe an hour ago. Had that giant guy with him, the one with the lazy eye?"

"Yeah. Dumb as he looks, which ain't easy."

"Hanlon said he was up at the Plantation Club the other night, saw you there. With your little friend."

Joshua smiled and took the chair across from Cecil. "Damnation. Never occurred to me that paying off the cops would make them so uppity. A police sergeant like Hanlon could never afford that joint without our money."

"No fooling. Listen, you got to know that girl's bad for business. If having her on your arm makes the cops stop taking our money, then we got no business at all."

Joshua pursed his lips and leaned back. "I know it. But if that's the price, I'll pay it. You want me to buy you out, get away from this, say the word. I'll figure out a way." They both knew that the only way Joshua could buy Cecil out was to go to the shylocks. That wasn't a real way. He'd never dig out, would probably end up working for someone else. That meant the only actual way for both of them was for Cecil to stick around.

Cecil took a quick breath and sat forward. "Not yet. But maybe soon."

Joshua nodded, noticing how quick his heart rate was. He worked to keep his tone even. "Anything else on your mind?"

"Everything, my friend. Goddamned everything." Cecil reached over to a small side table where a hot plate held a scarred coffee pot. He poured the brown liquid into a saucerless cup.

"You drink from that? Cup looks putrid."

"Looks better than any I used in France."

While Cecil sipped, Joshua went over and poured one, too.

He sniffed a bottle of cream, decided against it. Back in his seat, he winced when he took a sip. "Okay. Shoot."

"Way I see it, we got three big problems. First, we can't keep hijacking other people's liquor. It's too damned dangerous. And we're making enemies."

"Nobody knows it's us doing the hijacking."

"Yet. They don't know yet. Just a matter of time, brother." Joshua nodded. "Okay, second. The reason we keep hijacking other people's liquor is that no one'll sell decent hooch to us at a fair price, because we're the coons. Not to mention the romantic attachments some of us have formed and rammed down other people's throats, which other people don't care for one bit."

"Right."

"Right." Cecil took a breath. "Finally, I ran into one of the fellows from Brother Briggs's operation."

"Haven't they gone back to Africa yet?"

"Worse than that. He said there's a new investigator on that Wall Street bombing case. The one where you saved the princess? This new guy, he's looking into the Brotherhood, trying to connect it to the bombing. He's thinking it was a Negro protest."

"What do we care? That damned bomb almost blew me to kingdom come."

"Don't you get it? That's the biggest problem you've got. Lots of bombers blow themselves up. Pretty common, actually. They may even know you were there, playing knight in shining armor and all. So then they figure you set the bomb but were too nigger-stupid to get out of the way."

"I never gave my name to anyone."

"Yeah? How many people helped you pull that girl out? They all know there was a colored man there. The hospital's got records that it took care of a blond girl, her name, that she was hurt in the bombing. You went to see her there. Probably signed the guest book. Only colored man who ever walked through that hospital without a mop in his hands." Cecil held his hands out. "Who knows what they figure out. What someone might say."

Joshua sipped more coffee. He put the cup aside. He nodded his head once and looked up. "Okay, Cece. You're right. We need a new plan. It so happens I've been thinking that way. Nothing final. Just some ideas."

When Joshua had finished describing his plan, Cecil shook his head. Then he grinned. "D'you think all this up yourself?"

"I've been listening, thinking, looking around."

"How come I'm the one goes to Canada while you go to Europe?"

Joshua shrugged. "I've already been talking to some folks, trying to figure out some contacts. In England mostly. Also, I'll admit it, it's Violet. If we're going to make a go of it, together, we need to get the hell out of the US of A. *Far* out of it. You're dead right about that."

"Near as I remember, there's white people over in Europe, too."

Joshua stared down at his hands. "Sure, but it's not as bad. Not near as bad as here. You were there." He gave his friend a smirk. "You remember when we went on leave?"

"I remember. Those mam'selles were okay."

"And Canada's not so bad. Maybe a little cold, but if we do this right, you can go down to Cuba every winter." Joshua noticed that his friend wore a faraway look. He decided to stop talking. This was big. It needed thinking through, getting used to. Cecil needed time. He was worth waiting for.

"It'd mean leaving everything we know," Cecil said. "Really, not being American anymore. You ready for that?"

Joshua put on a disbelieving look. "For a revolutionary, you're pretty damned sentimental. Okay, I'd have to leave a country that threw me in jail for risking my life against the Germans? A country that doesn't want me to vote, to have any rights at all? A country that'll want to kill me because of the woman I love?" He shook his head. "Brother Cecil, don't get between me and the door."

"You wouldn't see your family much. Hardly at all. That's no big deal for me. No family to miss. But your ma. Your daddy. Your sister. You ready to walk away?"

"None of them's gonna want me to be with Violet, either. So I've got to choose. I can make that choice. It ain't hard."

Joshua waited for Cecil some more. When his partner began again, his tone was firmer. "The idea, the goal, that's all great. We go where what we do is legal. We buy the booze cheap, sell it to people we know, and let them take the chances. That's solid. But you know there's a big problem."

"I do."

"That's the bankroll we need to start. The way you want to get that is completely crazy. Get you locked up in any nut ward in the city."

"Well, with what we've been making, we don't have even a third of what we need. And you're right, we're on borrowed time with this operation. Not going to be lucky forever. This plan's expensive. So we got to go get the money."

"You mean, steal it."

"Yeah."

"Are you that tough?"

"You know, in France, we learned that when there's only one way out, hell, there's only one way out. So that's what you do. No use fretting over it."

"Is she worth all this?"

Joshua smiled. "Absolutely." Forgetting, he took a sip of coffee. Still terrible, now cold. "So, you in?"

Cecil looked down, then spoke. "Two conditions. At least, two I can think of now."

Joshua nodded.

"Before going after this, I don't want us taking any other chances. No more little jobs. That's just running more risk that doesn't get us where we're trying to go."

"Okay."

"And if we're going to put it all on black and spin the wheel like this, we only do it once, no matter how it comes out."

Joshua held out his right hand. "Partner, you've got yourself a deal."

# Chapter 13

Starting the walk down Broadway to her office, Eliza could think only of Violet. She had been gone for two days. Eliza could hear every word they had said to each other. And didn't say. Eliza had been a fool. She thought she could manage the situation, that she had calmed down. She expected Violet to be emotional, to cry and profess undying love for young Mr. Cook. Eliza would be understanding and loving, but firm and clear. There would be no nonsense about it. She couldn't, she wouldn't, let Violet throw away her life, not on some bootlegger, not on someone so completely different. It didn't matter how charming he was or how sure Violet thought she was. So she shooed Jamie off to bed and sat down in Violet's room to wait. She waited. And waited.

It was almost dawn when she started awake. Violet was in the room, leaning on her cane. She didn't need the crutch now. Her black shoes dangled by their straps from her free hand. Violet seemed surprised but not fazed.

"I know where you've been," Eliza said, "and who you've been with."

Violet tossed her cane on the bed. She limped to her closet and took out her bathrobe and nightgown. "Really, Mother," she said, "it's late."

It was the flatness of her daughter's voice. The lack of concern, even of interest. That threw Eliza off balance, kept her from reasoning with Violet, kept her from presenting the logic of the situation—that what Violet was doing just couldn't keep on. Instead, she snapped, "You simply can't do this, Violet. You can't."

"Oh, Mother. Do we really have to have all this out now?"

"When were you going to tell us about this young man?"

" 'This young man.' " Violet gazed levelly at her mother as she gathered up her dress to pull over her head. "He has a name, and you know it. He's Joshua. You remember Joshua, don't you? In France? And then how he pulled me out of the bank after the bomb went off and got me to the hospital? You know, I'd expect a mother to remember the name of a man who saved her child."

Violet was so comfortable with his name. It was no effort for her to say it, to talk about him in this familiar way. It was too real, not just some scandalous story retailed by Wilfred in a theater lobby.

"Violet," Eliza said, thinking she was under control, fooled by the steadiness of her own voice. "Don't you understand what a terrible mistake this all is? You can't be serious. You can't do this."

Violet's eyes flashed. "I can't?" She pulled her dress back on and shimmied it over her body, then lurched back to the closet. She pulled out a suitcase and threw it on the bed. She limped to her dresser, the anger in her movements threatening her balance.

Eliza looked on as Violet opened a drawer and pulled out underclothes. She threw them into the suitcase. Eliza felt frozen. This couldn't happen, not over a Negro bootlegger. She rushed over and took Violet's arms. "Stop it. Just stop it. This is a terrible mistake. You just can't see it right now." Violet, her eyes cold, stared back. "You're tired, dear. I'm tired. You were right. It's late. Let's get some sleep and talk about it in the morning."

"There's nothing to talk about." Violet pulled away and opened another dresser drawer.

Eliza pushed the drawer back in. "Violet, I started this badly, but we must talk. Really, we must. Your father and I, we care only about you, about your welfare, your safety. This romance, whatever it is, it can't end well. It can't and it won't. We can't stand to see you hurt. We're worried only for you. You're too young. You don't understand. You don't appreciate what you're doing. How people will react to it. People aren't ready for something like you and Joshua. They're not. It could be horrible. It *will* be horrible." Then she stopped, frozen again by Violet's self-possession.

"Are you done?"

"Oh, dear. I've barely begun, but I can't get you to hear me. You must listen." She grabbed her daughter's arms again.

"No, Mother. I mustn't and I won't. Not about this." Violet broke free and hobbled back to the suitcase with an armful of blouses. She flung them in, stopping to stuff in a few stray sleeves.

"Violet. I'll make tea." Violet was back at the closet, pulling skirts from hangers. "You can't go. Where would you go?"

"Where do you think?"

"Violet, just give me one chance to talk about this. I'm a woman, dear. I've been in love. You can ignore whatever I say, but at least hear me out. You're still just a girl."

Violet clicked shut the latches on the suitcase and straightened. "I've seen nothing in your romantic life," she said, "that I care to learn from, except maybe to marry a fine man. You did that. And so will I."

That was when Eliza came closest to crying, but she didn't.

Without thinking, she said, "How can you be so sure? What do you know about him?"

Violet sat on the bed and assumed a gentle tone. A patronizing tone. She loved Joshua. She would make her life with him. Her father would understand.

Eliza still couldn't unscramble how it ended. She recalled being at the front door. Jamie came rushing out of their bedroom in his pajamas. His face was terrible. "Violet, what's happening?" he said.

Violet cracked just a little. She hugged him. Her eyes were moist when she turned and gave Eliza a dutiful embrace. And she was gone. Eliza remembered standing before the window over Broadway, staring at a western sky that slowly brightened with reflected sunrise. She didn't let the tears come then either. She had to understand how everything got reversed. Instead of stopping Violet from this awful mistake, she had driven her deeper into it. She wanted to shriek over her irrelevance. Her world was shattering and it didn't care what she thought. She had no say. How could her child, the child of her heart, care about her so little? What could they do?

Jamie stormed at first, that goddamned pacing. He didn't shout any more. He sputtered. He slapped one fist into the other palm. The anger wasn't like him, but what was anyone like in a situation like this? She made herself not hear his words. She knew he didn't mean any of it, except the part about how she had failed. She had sent him to bed so she could handle Violet. She was her mother. She knew about these things. Of course he was angry. He finally sat down, his face bright red, his cheeks wet, kneading his hands together.

She knelt and put her head on his hands. She still had no words. It was her fault. Violet looked like her father and she laughed like her father, but inside . . . inside she was just as hard as her mother. How could Eliza not have known that?

She led Jamie to the kitchen. She made tea. She burned the

toast. Jamie scraped off the char and ate it dry. He denied it when she said that Violet wasn't coming back. By the time he finished his toast, and then hers, he had stopped denying it.

They agreed to start looking for Violet right away, but not anything official. No police. If Violet was with Joshua, she would be in danger, but not the sort of danger the police could help with. Who knew what a bunch of ignorant policemen would do? They might start arresting people. Eliza would start with Violet's old school friends, and that Joan from the clinic, who must know about everything.

Jamie started with the Harlem nightclub where Wilfred had met the young couple. He asked the entire staff, then the people who worked at nearby nightclubs, all black-and-tans, catering to those thrilled by race mixing. By nightfall, he admitted that when he asked the coloreds where Joshua was, he got the feeling they wouldn't tell him even if they knew. If they knew Joshua, if they knew Violet, they would know that Jamie was The Father, the denier of romance, the oppressor.

"Where else do you look," Jamie wondered, "for a bootlegger?"

"Joshua's father," she said.

"I don't want to see him."

"I know. But you have to."

He sighed. He agreed.

Eliza was standing in front of that tired building on Eighth Avenue, between Fifty-second and Fifty-third. Her office. She couldn't remember the walk from the Ansonia, the streets crossed, the carts and cars evaded, the people ignored. The home of Fraser Productions was on the second floor. It bore a distinct resemblance, she realized, to the Marlowe Theater. Not in the best neighborhood. Affordable rent. Still presentable, but on the downward slide. She felt edgy, anxious. She thought she might explode.

The airless stairwell exaggerated the moist heat of late June.

She climbed to the second floor, her blouse plastered to her upper arms, her skirt to her thighs. It wasn't even ten in the morning. On the landing, she paused to unstick her clothes. Her receptionist looked up when she entered the anteroom, quickly shifted her eyes to the left. Speed Cook rose from one of the two visitor chairs. He extended his hand. Unthinking, Eliza took it. Then quickly pulled hers back.

"If you're looking for Jamie, Mr. Cook," she said, "he doesn't often come by here. Let me give you his address. He'll be glad to talk with you."

Cook held his bowler hat by the brim, with both hands. "I thought we got past 'Mr. Cook' over in France." She didn't answer. "And I'm here to see you, not Jamie. It's a business matter. Won't be but a few moments."

"Is it about . . . ?" Eliza caught herself. The receptionist. The girl didn't need to hear about Violet, which would only lead to more gossip. She composed her face and gestured for Cook to enter her office.

Armored behind her large desk, Eliza waited while Cook placed his hat on the edge of the desk, then sat. When he sat forward, she heard a knee pop.

"I'm here on a confidential matter," he said.

Her heart began to flutter. He must have news about Violet. Maybe Jamie had been right all along. Maybe he wasn't so bad. Maybe he was. "Yes?"

"Yes." Cook cleared his throat. "I'm acting for Mr. Babe Ruth on this matter." Eliza couldn't keep the disbelief from her face. "Yes, I know it's surprising that he should retain me, but he did, for his own reasons." Eliza saw his lips move but couldn't listen. The world made no sense. He stopped talking and looked at her.

"What did you say?" she asked.

"I know it's surprising. It's because of this fellow Abe Attell, and the movie that you produced with Mr. Ruth and Mr. Attell last summer, *Headin' Home*."

Eliza wanted to scream. When she finally spoke, she couldn't be bothered keeping the tension out of her voice. "You're here about *Headin' Home*?"

"Yes, ma'am. My concern is with the financing side, which I know is what you do." Cook was oblivious to her agitation. "Now, Babe, well, he's not the savviest businessman, as you know. He's told me that part of the financing involved a debt he owed to Abe Attell and his gambling partners. Particularly Arnold Rothstein."

"My God, you came here to talk to me about Babe Ruth and Arnold Rothstein?"

"Yes, and your movie." She seemed to want him to speak more quickly, so he sped up. "See, with the investigation going on now out in Chicago—you know, into the connections between ballplayers and gamblers and all—we're concerned about this debt Babe had, which was supposed to be resolved, but hasn't been, and which might not look so good if it came to light. Actually, it's really important. It could even determine whether organized baseball survives, because the Babe, he's become the key to the whole thing. Believe me, I wouldn't be here if I could figure out another way—"

When Eliza stood, her chair slid back and banged into the shelves behind her desk. She felt every hair on her head bristle. "Mr. Cook, where is my daughter?"

"Excuse me?"

The man was an idiot. "My daughter, Violet. You've met her."

"Yes, yes, I remember. She brought the cognac for those police in Paris. Saved my bacon that day, for sure." He furrowed his forehead. "I was sorry to hear of her injuries, but Jamie said she was recovering, last I saw him. That's some time back, of course." He shifted his eyes, realization creeping in. "Has she gone somewhere? Is she missing?"

"How can you do that? Talk like nothing's happened? You know perfectly well that she's been seeing your son for months, and I don't know what all else has been going on, and now we haven't seen her for more than a day and we're crazy with worry."

A severe look fell over Cook's face. "Why would you think she's with Joshua?"

"Mr. Cook, they've been together for weeks and months now. She deceived us about it until very, very recently."

"He wouldn't do that. Joshua wouldn't do that." Cook had sat back in the chair. He spoke quietly, but with force.

"Why not?"

"His mother and I raised him to be smarter than that. That boy's got a college degree."

Cook's face, creased and dark and alarmed, told her. He hadn't known. Eliza's righteousness began to slip away. The chair springs creaked when she sat. "Yes, well, I can tell you only that Violet thinks she's in love with him."

"She said that?"

"Yes. And she couldn't act the way she has if she didn't think so. At least I don't think she could."

"And you don't know where she is?"

Eliza nodded. She hated how much she wanted to be comforted, just to collapse. She wouldn't. Not in front of this man. "I tried to talk to her about it, but I couldn't get through."

Cook shook his head, spoke angrily. "Sweet Jesus. After everything, all we went through for him in Paris, I'll thrash that boy if he's fixing to throw it all away like this. The war, that goddamned war. It changed him. Some things, he doesn't register them like he should. He doesn't respect risk, not like he should. Jesus. They'll kill him."

Eliza had spent no time worrying about why Joshua took after Violet. Violet would be a prize for any young man, especially a Negro. But now she could see that Violet wasn't the only one taking chances. "Look, Mr. Cook, Jamie and I agree that this . . . connection, well, it's not safe. It's reckless and crazy. Frankly, we find it terrifying. Do you, do you see it that way, too?"

"'Course I do. Make no mistake. Joshua's the one they'll hurt. That's how it always is."

"Are you in touch with your son?"

"Not lately. Aurelia and I, well, we haven't been liking some of the things he's been doing."

"You mean the bootlegging?"

Cook looked up, surprised. "Why, yes, and . . ."

"You knew nothing about Violet?"

Cook grimaced. "We heard he was running around with a white girl. Aurelia took that hard. She spoke her mind to him about it. He just laughed her off, like he does, then he stopped coming around. But we didn't know who. I would've gone to Jamie if I'd known. I would have."

"Can you get in touch with Joshua?"

"Don't you worry about that."

Eliza took a few breaths. "I know, Mr. Cook, that we've never gotten along."

"Yes."

"For my husband's sake, because of whatever you two have shared, I've made an effort, very likely a poor one. But I have certainly never intended to share your grandchildren. That can't happen."

"Let's not get ahead of ourselves here."

"In my experience that's not getting ahead of ourselves. We're dealing with two young people who believe they're in love."

Cook slouched in his chair. Eliza tried to put some force in her voice. "We have to know that Violet's safe. Can you please help us know that? Then we can figure out what to do about this situation."

"Yes, yes, of course." Cook stood to leave. "Tell me one thing. Did Jamie try to get in touch with me about this business?"

"He's looking for you now."

He reached for his hat. "From now on, Mrs. Fraser, it might be best for him and me to talk about this, instead of you and me. He knows how to get ahold of me."

"Of course." When Cook reached the door, she called his name. He looked back. "About that movie, with the Babe." She looked over his shoulder to focus her thoughts on this other subject. "As far as I know, that Attell creature invested fifty thousand dollars. He was to get a large piece of the profits, and there weren't any other conditions or agreements. Not that I knew about. I never heard about any debt owed by Babe."

"Did the movie make money?"

Eliza frowned. "A complete flop. It didn't matter how popular Babe was. Nearly cleaned everyone out."

"Attell, too?"

She nodded.

"Jamie'll hear from me."

# Chapter 14

"A cop came by about twenty minutes ago." The words sliced out from the shadows through the steam-furnace air that pressed down on the Greenpoint waterfront.

Joshua almost jumped out of his shoes. Then he realized. "Daddy? That you?"

His father stepped into the light. "This cop, he checks the door and jiggles the handle, like he's making sure it's locked up tight." There was irritation in his tone.

"Just looking after a local business."

"How much does that cost—for a local business?"

Joshua smiled. "What can I do for you?"

"You can tell me what the hell you're thinking—taking up with Violet Fraser." Cook had sweat running down his torso, drops beaded on his face, from doing nothing more strenuous than leaning against the warehouse.

Joshua kept the smile on. He knew how to get his father's goat. "Daddy, how long've you been waiting in this heat?"

"As long as I needed to. Answer my question."

Joshua put the door key back in his pocket. He'd had this

conversation in his mind a hundred times. Might as well have it for real. "Okay. Let's walk out on the pier. It's even hotter inside. Smells bad, too." He pointed the way.

At the end of the building, Joshua led them to a concrete pier. Both men carried their suit coats and had their neckties loosened. Joshua wore a straw boater with a red band.

At the waterside, Joshua asked, "Does Ma know?"

"Of course."

"And?"

"You already know what she thinks. And I agree. Maybe something happened to you in the war. Maybe we just never saw it when you were growing up. But, son, you're living like you don't want to keep living. We're scared to death for you, and you've got to stop it. I can't stand by and watch. This bootlegging, this running around with the Fraser girl—"

"It's not 'running around,' Daddy. It's a lot more than that."

"Goddammit, son, the world's full of white women. As long as you've got this death wish, why'd you have to go and pick the one whose father's my friend, the man who helped save your sorry ass not two years ago? The one white man we actually owe something to?" He put a heavy hand on Joshua's shoulder. "Didn't that occur to you? Didn't it matter to you?"

Joshua didn't trust his voice. All those rehearsed arguments, they hadn't started like this. "Yeah, it matters, Daddy. But, no, no it doesn't. Doesn't make a lick of difference. I didn't plan this. Violet didn't plan this. I didn't pick her. It just happened. It happened to both of us and it's the most important thing in the world. Nothing you can say or do's going to change that." He waited for his father to answer, but there was only silence. In the humid night, auras glowed around the lights of Manhattan, their reflections zigzagging across the water. The air felt thicker every time Joshua breathed. "Nobody's trying to hurt you and Ma, or Doctor Fraser and Mrs. Fraser. But it's everything. That won't change."

"Don't you understand, son?" Cook's eyes glistened. His voice was soft, softer than Joshua could remember it. "They'll kill you. They'll kill you and they'll feel good about it. Doctor Du Bois keeps this chart in his office. How many colored men're lynched all around the country. Lots of them, most of them, did lots less than this. Most get killed just for being in the wrong place at the wrong time. Don't you know that? Haven't I told you, told you a hundred times?"

"I know it."

"What about Violet? Have you explained it to her? Because she can't really know it, not with who she is and where she's from. Did you ask her if she wants to be a widow? Does she want to be the ofay wife? Does she want to have every man, white and black, think she's cheap, no-account, easy pickings. And every woman, white and black, agreeing? Is that what you want for her, for the woman you say you love, who you say is the world to you?"

"Daddy, I've got a plan."

"The only plan that's going to work is to break this off. You both go your own ways. I'm not telling you what to do, as much as I want to, as much as I want to drag you home by the scruff of your silly neck. I can't do that any more than I can put you under my arm and keep you safe. Which I also want to do. You're a man. Son, I'm telling you about the consequences. A man faces up to them. A man doesn't put the people he loves in danger."

"I'm going to make it work."

Cook stamped his foot and shook his head. A strangled noise came out. He looked across the water and tried to pick his words. He still kept his voice low. "You can't. I know this. The one thing I know is what this nasty, stinking world can do. I'm sorry you can't, that she can't, but you just can't."

Joshua took a deep breath. "I'm not going to let that nasty, stinking world take her from me. I won't. That's not how I was raised."

Cook was out of things to say. He hadn't expected to change Joshua's mind. The boy was pigheaded, which he came by honest. All that was left was to watch the two of them head over the cliff. "Listen, son, the Frasers need to know about their daughter, that she's safe."

"Of course she's safe."

"Is she with you?"

"She's safe."

"Jesus, you can't just be a lone wolf on this sort of thing, go crashing around in ways that are gonna hurt everyone who cares about you, who cares about Violet. It's not just you that you're doing this to."

Joshua said nothing. Cook had expected to get to this dead end. He couldn't remember the last time he persuaded Joshua of something. And he had thought about what to do when he got to this point, though he never told Aurelia. She would never forgive him for the next thing he was going to say. "If you won't listen to reason and give this up, what can I do? How can I help?"

Joshua's head snapped up. That was never part of his imagined rehearsals of this conversation. The old man's eyes bore into him. He seemed to mean it. Joshua almost wanted to tell his father about the plan, even get some advice on how to make it work. But he knew he couldn't. It was a trap, even if his father didn't mean it to be. If he told the old man the truth, they'd spend hours going over the holes in the plan, and there were lots of those. Joshua might even end up agreeing with his father, agreeing it was all too risky, then giving up on it. Giving up Violet. He wasn't going to do that.

Cook thought he could feel indecision. "Just getting old doesn't make me stupid, son. I can help."

Joshua shook his head. "I've always trusted you, Daddy.

This is the time you have to trust me." He took a step back to the warehouse and looked back for his father, who followed. At the warehouse door, Joshua nodded at Cook, then went inside alone.

Passing through quiet streets to the subway station, Cook couldn't remember feeling so bad. He thought about chances he'd taken over the years, fights he'd been in. Two men he'd killed, men he hadn't known but had to kill. Others he'd hurt. Times he got hurt. What had any of it got him? What had it got anybody? Now here his boy was, taking the same kinds of chances, or worse ones, in a world that wasn't any better than it ever was.

Abe Attell pushed past a hippy waitress toward the back of Lefty's deli on Broadway, just up from Times Square. He was headed to the boss's private booth, which was also his unofficial office. Rothstein liked the constant uproar of Lefty's, dishes clattering onto tables, forks and spoons hitting the floor with tuneful notes, voices calling, whispering, cracking wise, rising with emotion. He claimed he could think better there. Rothstein always took the last booth on the left, facing the front entrance but next to the back door. That was where he studied the racing forms, hatched his schemes, gave his instructions, and received progress reports. Engulfed by the din of the deli, Rothstein mostly listened. He wanted to hear all the gossip—the good and the bad—but he also listened for what wasn't said. He always heard that, too.

Rothstein was eating cheesecake, no toppings, like every morning. Lefty's finest, taken straight, coffee chaser. Though it was early, the heat from the kitchen overpowered the lazy ceiling fans. No matter. Rothstein looked cool in blue seersucker, a style that gamblers across the city were starting to copy. Everyone knew that when it came to most things, AR had the straight dope, the inside skinny. So they figured he knew about suits, too.

Attell nodded at the two bodyguards lounging near AR's booth. They never ate on the job, so every day AR threw an extra ten bucks at the deli manager, making up for them not ordering anything. AR was listening to Sid Wechsler, a loser who hung around the track at Aqueduct scrounging for tips, fixed horses, or races that could be rigged at a good price. When Wechsler saw Attell next to the booth, he grabbed his hat in midsentence and pulled out. Attell slid into his place. He waved at a brunette waitress with a pixie look. She was new. He took a second look, thinking he'd like to sprinkle some magic dust on her. Giving her a grin, Attell ordered a cheese Danish and a coffee.

When she left, Attell turned the smile on AR. "Great news from Chicago, eh, boss?" The papers were reporting the jury verdict in the trial of the eight ballplayers—members of the White Sox who were now called the Black Sox. All eight were acquitted. Not guilty.

AR ran a hand over his close-cropped hair. He took a breath that flared the nostrils of his meaty nose. "Ah, that crazy commissioner'll throw them out of the game, anyway. Too bad. They seem like okay guys."

"Sure, Landis'll toss them out, but that ain't our problem. They can be replaced. There's thousands of kids out there want to play big league baseball, right?"

With a rattle, the waitress dumped the plated Danish on their table. Annoyance crossed AR's face. Quick as a snake, Attell grabbed the girl's thin wrist. "Darling," he said. "We ain't animals here."

"Sorr-ee," she said. "I didn't know I was serving the king of England."

When she left, Attell asked if he should get her fired. Rothstein shook his head. "Abie, you like 'em like that, a chip on their shoulder. You'd miss her if she was gone."

"I never saw her before."

"I got eyes. I can see. You'd miss her." He pointed a finger at Attell. "What I need from you is to hear that they're done with all this digging into gambling on baseball. Kaput. Over. Yesterday's news." He leaned closer and dropped his voice. "Especially I need to hear that Landis ain't going into the 1918 Series."

The waitress returned with Attell's coffee and set it down gently. "I'm real sorry about before," she said, then retreated hastily. She must have asked who the guys were in this booth.

While Attell fixed his coffee with milk and sugar, AR picked up again. "Listen, one rigged Series is a shame. A few bad apples. The judge tosses them out on their keisters, score one for the American way, and they got what's coming to them. The Babe hits some long shots and makes everyone forget about it. But two rigged Series in row? And one has the Babe in it? That's a fucking epidemic, the whole game's an infection. I don't even want to think about it."

"So what's our leverage?" Attell asked around his first bite of the pastry. "This guy Landis, he's hard to get to. That's the word. Our friends can't help us with him, not like with the courts in Chicago."

AR's expression was a cross between a grin and a grimace. It was as cheerful as he ever looked, but that look usually meant something bad was going to happen to someone else. "What's the biggest thing in baseball—other than this Black Sox thing?"

"Babe. The big fella."

"Exactly. He's the one can stop this. Just has to pass the word. He was in that 1918 Series and baseball can't afford to have Babe Ruth scuffed up, not by something like this. He's the engine who's got to pull the game out of the sewer. He'll pass the word if we ask him to. He knows he's got to."

"Sure, boss, but Landis is supposed to be a real prick, not the kind of guy who's gonna care what some chump of a ballplayer tells him."

"I'll spell it out for you. Just once, so listen. Babe goes to the

Yanks' owner, Colonel Ruppert. Ruppert's rich, a society swell. Like Landis, his shit doesn't stink. But he's also desperate. His beer business is in the dumper with Prohibition. Christ, his brewery's making fucking apple butter." Attell laughed dutifully. "Plus he spent all that dough to get Babe down here to play for the Yankees, which he's looking to build a whole new stadium for, get the hell out of the Polo Grounds. No, Ruppert can't afford to watch his baseball business turn sour, too. So if Babe tells him what needs to happen, then Ruppert tells Landis and everything's jake. Like Tinker to Evers to Chance, only it's Ruth to Ruppert to Landis."

Attell was impressed. It was a long speech for the boss. This was important to him. Also, it made sense. Attell picked up AR's idea. "So, if Babe goes off on this mission of mercy, we promise him that he can have that thing back, the one that we got because of the girl, the young one? That'd be plenty of reason for that big baboon."

Rothstein nodded. He let his gaze wander over Attell's shoulder. Attell swallowed some coffee so he could think, then went on. "There's another thing, too. This ain't necessarily the big fella's strong suit, know what I mean? Pretty complicated for him. Christ knows what he'd end up saying to Ruppert. Might even confess to doing something he didn't do, or something he did do."

Rothstein shifted his gaze back to Attell. "I got to figure everything out for you?"

Attell got an idea. "Tell you what, boss. There's that jig the Babe hired when the Black Sox thing first blew up and Landis started sniffing around. This guy, he's a pretty sharp character. You know, for a jig. He promotes some Negro teams. Doesn't mind when we run some action on their games. He's been known to run some himself. I bet he could ride shotgun on the Babe, make sure he gets it done right, so long as we make it worth his while."

"You got something on the coon?"

"Not a lot. I heard his kid is running booze. One of those ex-soldier boys. Word is he does some hijacking."

Rothstein raised an eyebrow.

"You're right," Attell said, nodding his head. "That's dangerous work. We've probably got friends who wouldn't mind knowing how to shut him down. Hell, we wouldn't mind shutting him down." Attell finished his coffee and set the cup down. "Okay, boss. I'm on top of it. No sweat. "

Rothstein pulled a roll of bills from his pants pocket and threw a ten and a twenty on the table. They both slid out of the booth. One of the bodyguards handed Rothstein his hat. Attell picked up his own.

"When we leaving for Saratoga, boss?"

"A couple days. Still lining stuff up."

"Big stuff?"

Rothstein shrugged.

When they got out on Broadway, Attell said he'd left something inside, he had to go back. AR nodded. "You're missing that skinny dame already, aren't you?"

Attell grinned and gave the boss a wave. He went back to look for the waitress. She'd probably never met anyone who'd been champion of the world.

# *Chapter 15*

Ruth had already doubled once when he came to the plate in the sixth inning. Cook sat forward in the left-field bleachers.

The Yanks' field, the Polo Grounds, was no conventional shape for baseball. Center field was huge, where fly balls went to die, and it sloped downward from the infield. The distance down the foul lines was under three hundred feet, pop-fly range for a hitter like the Babe, while foul territory was generous. The bleachers allotted to Negro fans were far from home plate but allowed Cook to do some missionary work with his neighbors, talking up the Bacharach Giants' games up in the Bronx. He handed out some free passes.

Cook didn't root for any white team, not after they drove him out of their game. He cordially wished that they'd all rot in hell. But he did take special pleasure seeing the Detroit Tigers get beat. Their star, Ty Cobb, was a serious nigger hater. Today, unfortunately, the Tigers held a 4–1 lead over the second-place Yanks, who were straining to catch Cleveland at the top of the American League. And that bastard Cobb had just hit a home run. The Tigers' pitcher didn't look interested in giving up the lead. At least Speed could watch the Babe at the plate. The man's swing was so smooth but still packed such a wallop.

Babe looked at two pitches out of the strike zone. The man next to Cook confided, "That pitcher, he's afraid of that *terr-rr-rrrible* bat."

"He oughta be," Cook said. "That big guy eats pitchers for breakfast." They both laughed. Cook offered his half-empty bag of Cracker Jacks to his neighbor.

The sun felt warm. The breeze off the river was freshening as the early August afternoon approached evening. Cook couldn't help admire the grass and the smooth ground of the outfield. He remembered again the choppy fields when he played, what, twenty-five years ago? Hell, it was thirty-five years. Where does it all go?

Cook still enjoyed the bleacher camaraderie, strangers sharing their knowledge of the game and the players, seminar-style. If anyone misses a play, the others fill him in, adding commentary, maybe some history about the players involved. One fan notes a runner taking a big lead. Another points out an infielder creeping in, smelling a bunt. A third suggests that the pitcher looks to be slipping something on the ball from the bill of his cap—watch how he does right there, see? Even though Cook knew more about the game than the others did, he never dominated the exchanges. He liked to listen. He usually learned something.

His seminar mates had already chewed over Commissioner Landis's decision to throw the Black Sox out of the game despite the jury's verdict. The judgment in the bleachers: throw the bums out. When fans have to cough up two bits for a seat at the ballpark, the least the players can do is actually try to win the game. Cook agreed. Anyway, the consensus emerged, who the hell believes a jury in Chicago?

"Those people out there," one man said, "they tell you the rain stopped? You take your umbrella anyways."

"And then," chimed in another amid the laughter, "you check your wallet, make sure it's still there."

Cook wished he could share such moments with Joshua, but the boy never did take to the game, not from the first. Maybe Cook had come on too strong about it. Now, between Violet Fraser and the bootlegging, that was the least of their problems. It wasn't like they were passing a lot of friendly hours together. Or any. But Cook couldn't hold back the wish. Missing something that never was there. A damned stupid thing to miss.

The smack of wood on baseball broke Cook's reverie. Leonard's fastball had strayed too close to that terrible bat. Cook's eye picked up the line drive as it cleared the second baseman's leap, then bounced joyously between outfielders and caromed off the right-field wall. The big man, surprisingly fleet, steamed into second base with an easy double.

Cook's neighbors roared their pleasure. The colored sections at the Polo Grounds always cheered a little harder for Ruth. After all, he might be one of them.

"If he'd got under that another eighth of an inch," Cook's closest neighbor said, "that was a home run." He turned to Cook. "Think he'll break last year's record?"

"Yeah, yeah, I do." Cook pointed at the large runner taking his lead off second base. "I bet he'll hit sixty. There's nothing that man can't do on the ball field. He's only been hitting full-time for, what, less than three years? Wait till he gets some practice!"

The whole section enjoyed Cook's suggestion that the Babe was going to get better. They basked in the glow that they were watching a man who was the best. No argument. Just the best. Maybe the best ever.

At the end of the game, Jamie Fraser was waiting when Cook emerged at the bottom of the Negro bleachers. "Aurelia told me I could find you here. You've been hard to track down."

Fraser's voice was sharp. This wasn't a social call. Since learning that his son's blond doxy was Violet Fraser, not a doxy at all, Cook had shied from having this conversation. But it had to happen. He put his hands in his pockets. He didn't know how a handshake might strike Fraser right now.

"Been a busy time."

"Yeah, I see." Fraser gave a sarcastic nod toward the playing field.

"I'm here on business. Listen, I don't like this situation any more than you do."

"Don't give me that. If we were talking about *my* son and *your* daughter, you'd feel a lot different. We need to talk."

Cook sighed. "I've got to stop in the clubhouse. Then we can talk, all right?" He pointed to the other side of the stadium. "Wait for me out on Eighth Avenue. Ten minutes."

"And have you give me the slip? Not after the trouble it took to find you."

"So that's how it is? Sure. Sure. You come on with me." He started walking without looking back.

Cook passed onto the field and across to the clubhouse, feeling Fraser on his shoulder but not talking to him. He asked the two guards on the door to let Fraser through, too, another guest of the Babe. Inside the hallway, he paused to adjust to the dim light. Through a doorway, he could make out some men leaning over a card game. Others were toweling off and dressing. A team official in shirtsleeves began to challenge Cook, but Ruth's voice came across the room. "Hey, kid, he's okay!"

Cook made his way across the room, Fraser a half step behind. "Hey, kid," the Babe said, chewing on an unlit cigar. "What's the good word?" He focused on Fraser. "Say, don't I know you?"

"Yeah, I live at the Ansonia, too. We talked about your workouts last winter, remember? Also, my wife, Eliza, produced your movie, *Headin' Home.*"

Babe groaned. "Don't remind me. How's she doing?" Babe

stood to draw on his trousers. "Nice girl, but I'm telling you, that's the last deal I do with a broad. I didn't exactly get paid." He looked reproachfully at Fraser.

"Neither did we." The news didn't seem to mollify the ballplayer.

"Babe," Cook broke in, "I've been talking to the guy you mentioned, you know, the Little Hebrew?"

"Yeah?"

"Yeah. I've got an idea for how we can get what we need. I want to lay it out. Someplace private."

Ruth pulled his suspenders up over his broad shoulders. In his shirtsleeves, in a room full of professional athletes, he stood out as a remarkable physical specimen. "There's a mick bar over on 155th," he said, "away from the river. It's a little noisy, but we can talk there. I got places to go tonight, so it can't be long."

"Anything we need to know to get in?"

"Nah. O'Brien's been there forever, no one's moving him. . . ." He shrugged.

The bar was easy to find. A placard over the door proudly advertised alcoholic beverages available within. Prohibition hadn't yet reached this neighborhood.

Postgame revelers shouted over schooners of beer, hats perched on their heads at all angles. Drawings of prizefighters on the wall celebrated the pugilistic lifestyle. The customers were uniformly male, just like the ballpark crowd.

Cook and Fraser found a table on the side, across from the bar. "Babe won't show for a while, signing autographs and chewing the fat with the fans," Cook said. "So say what you came to say."

Fraser pulled a piece of paper from his jacket pocket. "So we get this note from you this morning. It says that Joshua says that Violet's all right."

Cook nodded.

"That's it? That's all we get?"

Cook nodded again. "You got what I got."

"What kind of crap is that? We need to find our daughter and talk to her. Talk some sense to her. Where the hell are they?"

"Want a beer?"

"No, dammit, I don't want a beer. I want some answers. Eliza expects that I'm punching you in the nose right now and, I'll tell you, it's starting to seem like a good idea."

"If it'll help, I'll say you did."

"Don't get cute. Where's Violet?"

Cook shook his head. "Jamie, I don't know where she is. I tracked Joshua down through his business. He can't move that, at least not yet. I told your wife that I'd talk to him and I did. He says it's love, they're going to make their lives together. Gonna sing sweet songs in the sunshine, God help us. Doesn't mean we can change it." He looked around. "Look, I need a beer. You?"

Fraser made a face.

Cook stepped to the bar and bought a draft. While he was lowering into his chair, Fraser asked, "So what did you tell him, about singing sweet songs in the sunshine?"

"I told him fat chance. No one's gonna let them be. Their lives'll be hell. It damn well could get him killed, get Violet hurt. You know that. I know that. Now I said it to him."

"So what're you going to do?"

"What can I do?"

"You've got to do something!"

"Joshua's twenty-five years old. Since he got back from France—since you and I *got* him back from France—he's done one thing after another that's crazy or wrong or both. The damnedest thing is he still hears me out when I tell him what he's doing wrong, but it's like he's listening to the town fool. Tolerant, not arguing. Then he does just the same as he meant to do, what I just finished telling him *not* to do. And no, Jamie,

I don't know where he lives." Cook drank some beer, then some more.

"You know, Speed, how can you be so calm when he may be signing his own death sentence with this? Violet's, too."

"I told him. I can't make him. He says he's got a plan."

"What's the plan?"

"He wouldn't say."

"Bullshit."

"Jamie, if I could think of something to do to stop all this, I would. Don't you know that?"

"Start with telling me how to find my daughter. You owe me that."

"I wish I could. You're not going to make anything better by going off like some vigilante on a mission."

"Where do you get off telling me what to do? I'm supposed to leave my little girl with some Negro bootlegger who's trying to get himself and her killed? You don't really know me. Tell me where his business is."

Cook's fists balled. He tried to control his voice. "Don't make this something between you and me. Listen to me. We're dealing with people who are fully grown. Don't push so hard that you make them go through with this craziness just to spite us. Joshua, he's just not the same now."

"What do I care how he is? He's ruining my daughter's life. That's what I care about. Where's his business? You know where that is."

"You gonna kidnap her? Fight a duel with sabers? This ain't something that's in your line. It's not in my line anymore, either. You won't even know where to start. Let's figure out what we can try to do, what's possible. You and me, we've been pretty good at that, a couple times before."

"Stop it, Speed. Answer me. Where's his goddamned business?"

"You're going to make things worse." Cook tried to relax his hands. Balled up like they were, they were starting to hurt. "If you're so hot to find your little girl, go find his business your own damned self."

Fraser stood abruptly, his hand crushing the brim of his hat. His chair fell backward with a clatter. Only a few drinkers looked over as he stalked away.

At the door Fraser pushed past three women in tight dresses, big smiles plastered across their faces. Right behind them was the Babe. "Watch it there, kid," Ruth said. "There's ladies coming through."

# Chapter 16

Her rule was that Joshua couldn't help, so he sat and watched, which he hated. The leg brace, with mean-looking leather straps and steel rods and buckles, had to weigh five pounds. Sometimes she called it her thighbone, since it made up for the one that never healed right. The first few times she put it on with him around, she tried to keep her skirt pulled down to her knees, then reach up under it.

"Just pull your skirt up, girl," he had said. She said it wasn't decent. "Not decent?" he said. "After what we just finished?" She flushed and sent him out of the room.

Now she pulled her skirt up to get it done. And she let him stay in the room. But she didn't let him help.

"Don't stare," she said, perspiration beaded on her upper lip. "I hate it."

"I love that leg, sweet girl, and every other part. Let me help."

"Nope," she grunted, straining at a buckle. She gasped when the prong went through the eye and the tension on the brace relaxed to a level of steady discomfort. "There. Brooklyn's favorite gimp is ready for a day of hobbling around."

"You don't need to talk like that." He rolled over and knelt at the edge of the bed facing her, placing his hands on either side of her waist and pulling her to him. He could feel her muscles. Every other part of her was strong, making up for the leg.

"Talk like what?"

"Making fun of yourself. I'd punch anyone who talked like that about you."

"And what would that fix, mighty warrior? I'd still be a gimp." He laid his cheek against her torso, his arms around her now, the fabric of her slip rustling in his ear. She dug her fingers into the tight curls of his hair. What did she think of how it crimped close to his skull? Or of his caramel skin? She had puzzled over the palms of his hands, so much paler than the rest, not much different from hers. He had been less surprised by her whiteness, after the women in France, but still could wonder at blue veins in her wrists, her breasts, the red flush of feeling on her cheeks.

Talcum powder motes tickled his nose. He reached under her skirt and slid his hands up to the asymmetry of her thighs. Under the heavy brace, the injured leg had narrowed. No matter how many exercises she did or how much she walked, the leg remained thin, vulnerable. When Violet thought he was looking at it, she would say that at least it wasn't getting worse.

Joshua smiled. The hunger was building again. He slid his hands further up her leg. He rose and kissed her lips.

"Say, buster," she said softly. "The brace."

He kissed her again. "No time. We'll work around it."

In just a few weeks, he'd grown addicted to the feel of her, the smell of her. Even the talcum. He was surprised, after the first couple of times, how she took her pleasure. Some of the French women had done that. He learned to like that, their response, to wait for it. But where did this sheltered American girl learn about it? When he asked her, she smiled. She said maybe she was a natural. That smile, that attitude that she knew more than he did—at first it could make him nervous. Then he started to like it, too. He stopped thinking about how she was bound to come to her senses, realize she had no business being with the likes of him. He steered her back onto the bed and fell onto his elbows, then into her. He couldn't get enough.

Afterward, they lay in a dozy haze. The morning light dazzled. Her head rested on his shoulder, fingertips tracing a rib, back and forth. The buckles on her brace bit into his upper thigh, just as they had to be biting into hers. He couldn't remember feeling so complete. Until now, the idea of heaven never made any sense to him. Bliss was a word without meaning. What could that be—endless ice cream on sunny days? Now he knew what those poets had been talking about, or should have been talking about. The part about having it forever, though, that still didn't make sense.

"I hope I remember this," she said, "when I'm old and fat." She had raised up to stare into his eyes, inches from his face.

He smiled. "You won't need to remember anything. We'll still be doing it."

She lay back and rested her head on the pillow, then leaned over to kiss his ear. "You like fat white women?"

"My favorite." He kissed her eyelid.

"Joan says we're going to hell, living like this."

"What do you think?"

She didn't answer.

"What do you think?"

"I wish my only remaining friend didn't talk like that."

"Violet—that's superstition. You know that? Some of the guys on the line over in France used to talk that way. 'Course, heaven and hell weren't any crazier than what happened to us every day."

She was quiet, not wanting to say something wrong about the war, still trying to figure out that part of Joshua. She knew he didn't sleep right. Once she woke up in the night to find him lying next to her staring at the ceiling. Another time she found him smoking out in the other room. A couple of times she found his hand squeezing her arm or her leg, grunting and moaning. He could have his eyes wide open but not be awake. What happened in France was never far from him. When she asked about it, he put her off. He said it was getting better. She hoped it was, that it would keep getting better, even that she could help him with it.

"Anyway," he said, "you don't need to take that sort of talk from her."

"It's not what she says, the sin and hell part. But it's being by ourselves so much. Knowing that just by being together we make people angry. I try not to go out on the street around here. The women, the colored ones, they give me hard looks."

"You just give 'em hard looks right back."

"At least they don't spit at me, curse me out, like those longshoremen did, that time we were over near the river."

She could feel his heart speed up with the memory. She pulled her head up. "We can't fight them all, Josh. Where would you start?"

"I know it. I know it, but I can't help wanting to."

She dropped her head onto the pillow and rested her fingertips against his cheek. "It makes me sad. It's our happiness that makes them angry."

Joshua sat up and swung his legs to the floor. He stood and reached for his underdrawers. "That ain't it."

"No?"

"They don't care if we're happy or miserable. It's that we *are*, that we exist. A pretty yaller-haired girl and some ignorant nigger buck."

"I don't like it when *you* talk like *that*."

"Us not saying the words won't stop them from saying them, from thinking them."

Violet sat up, her forearm holding the sheet across her breasts. She watched him catch his big toe on the waistband of his shorts. His foot went through cleanly on a second try. He sat on the bed.

"Say it, Violet. Whatever's eating at you."

"Well, there's my parents and your parents, and our happiness makes them unhappy, too."

"We can't live our lives to make other people happy. Not even our own folks."

She nodded her head. "I keep thinking that if we talked to them, if we showed them how much we loved each other, they'd stop feeling that way. Then they'd know how right this all is."

He gave her a tight smile. "Don't you worry about it, sweet girl. It's out of your hands. I'm never giving you up. Not ever."

Violet pivoted carefully on her bottom until her legs touched the floor on the side opposite from Joshua. Her hand automatically tugged the skin where the brace pinched. Facing the wall, she let her face clench, squeezed her eyes tight. The moment passed. She ran both hands through her hair and took a breath. She had to get up, get moving. "Can you face more scrambled eggs?"

"Didn't your mama teach you how to fix nothing else?"

"How to mix a sidecar?" She reached for the cane. It was a bright morning. A breeze moved the curtains over the back window.

"That's dinner, not breakfast," he said as he stood. "Remember, Cecil's coming." They met at the foot of the bed. He grabbed her and lifted her off her feet with a hug. She held on as tight as she could, before he started packing.

* * *

Violet couldn't deny it. The tiny kitchen—an alcove, really—was just plain dirty. She started the coffee and let her eyes play over the counter, the hot plate, the sink. There was no excuse for it, even if they'd be moving out soon. She couldn't leave the place looking like this. As soon as Joshua left for Saratoga, she would wash each of their mismatched plates and cups. She would wash them twice. And the few pots. Then she would scrub down the table that the hot plate sat on, then the walls and the floor. At least twice.

The sourness of the apartment was weighing her down. No one came to that neighborhood, the Fort Greene section of Brooklyn, unless they lived in one of the ramshackle buildings that were carved up into too many apartments with too many people in them. She could hear conversations through walls, plus every footstep on the floor above. A door slam across the street could startle her. Their neighbors were almost all colored, but only a few were like Joshua. A lot seemed beaten down, defeated. Some she had trouble understanding when they spoke, almost like in a foreign language. She felt conspicuous around here, and then there was her limp.

The leg. It was part of her, sure, but it didn't always feel that way. It had its own moods. Sometimes it wanted to hurt because she had done too much, or moved the wrong way without thinking. Sometimes it wanted to hurt because it wanted to hurt. And sometimes it didn't. Always, though, she had to take it into account. Before moving, she had to think. What was the best way for this shift? How should she distribute her weight? How could she stay steady? If she didn't check in with the leg, it imposed its own punishments. It might be satisfied with a quick jolt of pain. Or it might drop her heavily to the floor, inflicting humiliation as well as pain. She could get off the floor on her own now, using the cane, but it was a spectacle, pathetic and graceless and grunting.

"Why, Miss Violet!" Cecil's voice, with an overlay of put-on southern accent, snapped her out of it. He strode toward her ahead of Joshua and offered a formal bow. "Honey chile, I'm just hoping there's some scrambled eggs in my future."

She put on a smile and offered a shallow curtsy. "Sir Cecil, I do hope it's to your liking. And a cookbook will be on today's shopping list." Both men laughed, then crowded in to pour themselves coffee.

When they left her alone before the skillet, Violet found herself remembering that day. She was wearing a blue crepe dress with a drop waist. Her mother said that no woman over forty could wear that. She topped it off with a pale blue cloche hat with gold ribbon and flowers. She thought her hair peeked becomingly out of its low brim.

The bank seemed dark when she entered. A tall guard offered to help her. She had to tilt her head back to see his face. After Griff was summoned to greet her, he left her in a sitting area near the back. He had to finish a meeting. The roar from the street seemed to tilt the building. Something knocked her down. Then she was looking up at Joshua's face, ghostly with clinging dust. She couldn't make sense of it, not then. It should have been Griff, but it was Joshua. And it had been Joshua ever since.

"Violet!" Joshua's voice came from the sitting room.

"Oh, goodness." She yanked the pan off the burner and scraped the eggs onto a plate. She pulled the charred parts out with a fork. She could eat those parts, or maybe make do with the toast.

"The butter's turned," she said as she placed the plates on the table, "so it's jam only."

Joshua told her to sit and he'd get her coffee. He came back with the salt and sprinkled it liberally on his eggs.

"We really should be the ones making with the pots and pans," Cecil said, "what with your leg and all, standing there. This here man of yours was a wizard at opening cans of vittles in France."

"That's sweet," Violet said, "but I need to be on my feet. And standing's easier than walking. I need to do it all. To get stronger."

"Will Joan come today?" Joshua asked.

"No, she's on at the clinic. She's coming tomorrow, after you boys leave for Saratoga." She turned to Cecil. "Joan comes all the way out here to Fort Greene to work with me on her day off. Only a real friend would do that."

"Hey, hey," Joshua put in, "we're paying her. The Cooks pay their way."

Ready to change the subject, Violet said, "I thought I heard you talking about that Brotherhood that you two used to be part of. The African thing."

Joshua cleared his throat. "Cecil has news." Violet turned.

"Well," Cecil started, visibly calculating how to frame the news. "You know about the investigation of that bombing where you got hurt, how it's been going nowhere? It's been in the papers. They can't figure out who the hell did it, or why, or how."

"We do know how," she said. "They blew up a bomb."

Cecil smiled. "Okay, but how did it get there? Anyway, now they've started sniffing around the Brotherhood, trying to connect it to the bombing."

"Was the Brotherhood that radical? Did they bomb places?" She looked at Joshua.

"I don't know of anything like that," he said, shrugging. "But there were some angry men there. Real angry. Some big talk, you know."

"What does this matter to us?" she asked. "Do they think you two placed the bomb?"

Cecil grinned. "No, no, nothing like that. Just something for us to know about. Keep an eye on, you know? We deal with the police some, in our business."

"And"—Joshua placed his cup down—"we got to get going. Off for Saratoga tomorrow to start the big changes, remake that business." He made to stand up. "Cecil, why don't you warm up the car. I'll be down in a sec."

After Cecil left, Joshua reached over and took Violet's hands. "We'll be up there maybe four days, maybe five. Not more than that. You'll be okay getting ready for Montreal?"

She nodded. "Sure. You go off for the racing season with all the rich people and I'll scrub down the kitchen. Maybe go back to the library and find something to improve my mind even more."

"Not even more! I'll never catch up." When she didn't smile, he leaned over to look into her face. "If I'm going to sell this business, I have to go where the big shots hang out. We'll have our meetings, figure out the best deal we can get, then I'll head out and meet you in Montreal. Then it's next stop, London."

They stood and met in an embrace. "We shouldn't have to live like this," she said. "Nervous. Hidden away."

"Not much longer. In September—you can write this down—in September we'll be in London, with a new life. Our life together. A better one. It's going to happen. I promise you."

"And the captain will marry us on the ship?"

"He will, or he'll answer to me."

They looked at each other some more. They were out of words. He was out of promises. He kissed her again and left.

The dark bar of the Jubilee Club was quiet, the only noise the ballad being sung by the crooner in the next room. Babe, a straight-up Manhattan in front of him, was feeling tip-top. Nothing like banging out two home runs against the first-place Indians to pick up a fellow's spirits. He'd been on championship clubs before and this Yankee squad was starting to get that feel, that strut. They thought they were good and, hell, they were good. Only a couple of games back in the standings. He thought they'd run down those Indians sooner or later and knock them off. So did the other guys.

He wasn't sure what time it was, but that was definitely the third show of the night in the next room. As soon as it ended, it would be time for that cute blond number in the chorus. He was looking forward to the next part of the evening.

"Babe," a large man said as he straddled the stool next to him. He called to the bartender for a double bourbon. Babe was as convivial as the next guy, maybe more so, but this guy could've taken a stool a little farther down the bar. Just give them both a little space, you know, especially when you're big, like both of them were. Glancing out the corner of his eye, Babe thought the guy looked familiar. This time of night, a lot of guys look familiar.

"Remember me?" the man said.

Babe shrugged.

"We met in Shreveport, spring training. John Slaughter." John Slaughter extended his hand.

Babe didn't move a muscle. He remembered this son of a bitch. "Ain't that someone calling you from the other room?" He turned back to his drink.

"So it's like that."

"What'd you expect, you start trying to mess up a man's life, his livelihood? You and that prick commissioner." Babe finished the drink and signaled for another. Damn. He'd been in a good mood.

"You know, Babe, we're just protecting you, protecting all the ballplayers. You know, the integrity of the game."

"Listen, you dumb-ass sonofabitch. Who do you think pays your salary to run around the country 'protecting the integrity of the game'? Me"—Babe thumped himself in the chest—"little old me, the man who puts those rear ends in the seats. So where the hell do you get off investigating me? Aren't you satisfied with screwing those eight saps out in Chicago?"

Slaughter looked into the mirror over the bar like it might hold the answer to Babe's tirade. He threw back his drink. Babe could feel how good it would be to give this guy a quick shot to the kisser. That's what the old man always said. Get the first punch in. Then the rest is easy. But this guy wasn't worth it, and hitting a cop was always a dumb move, even if he was a funny sort of half cop. Babe didn't need Slaughter to get even more interested in investigating him. "Hey, pal, there's that voice again, the one in the next room, calling you." Babe said. "You need to leave."

The big man looked back at Babe. His face was like stone. "First, I came here to tell you something. Something that may surprise you."

"Great. Surprise me."

Slaughter pulled out one side of his suit coat to show folded up papers in the inside pocket. "See these? They're blank subpoenas. You know what they are?"

"Sure. Everyone does. Something legal."

"I can use them to get records, papers, any damned thing I ask for from anybody I want. All I got to do is fill in the names. Judge Landis, he's a shrewd bastard. Made some kind of deal with the local prosecutor here, guy who's running for election now. You know him?"

Babe grunted. He'd probably met the guy, but he had better things to do than follow all the goddamned lowlife politicians in the world.

"Well, the judge, he wants me to use these to find dirt, dirt on that 1918 World Series of yours."

"I didn't do nothing wrong with that Series. We won the sucker, you know." The bartender delivered his drink. It glowed in the bar's half-light, tawny with promise. Babe let it sit on the bar. He needed to listen, maybe think.

"We just go where the evidence leads us, Babe. There's a few things I'm gonna need to figure out."

"So?"

"So, if you know about something laying around, something

you don't want me to see . . . Well, now you know I'm gonna come looking."

It was Babe's turn to look into the bar mirror. He looked back at Slaughter's dead features. "Why you telling me this?"

"Maybe you're not the only one who thinks those eight saps in Chicago got screwed." Slaughter reached for his wallet while he slid off his stool.

Babe put his hand out. "On my tab."

"I pay my own way," Slaughter said.

Babe watched him walk out. His stomach didn't feel right. That goddamned paper that Rothstein had. He was going to have to take care of that. He thought about that Speed Cook guy. Maybe he could take care of it.

Then the blond number came sashaying in wearing a silver dress. Just looking at how she moved, Babe's stomach stopped bothering him.

# Chapter 17

Babe was with a tall, well-dressed man as he approached Cook in the Ansonia's lobby. He looked more than a bit off his feed.

"Late night?" Cook asked.

"Don't ask," came the muttered reply.

The well-dressed man nodded at Cook. "Christy Walsh," he said.

"Yeah, yeah," Babe said. He worked a toothpick into his rear molars, then looked at the toothpick to gauge his success. "Christy helps with business stuff. He and Ruppert, you know, they talk the same lingo." He waved the toothpick vaguely. "Let's get this show on the road."

On the sidewalk, a shiny doorman held out a key for Babe while Walsh let out a low whistle. A cream-colored coupe with black trim sat at the curb. Its top down, the roadster sparkled in the sunlight. Walsh stepped slowly down the car's length, stopping to touch the winged hood ornament.

"I've heard about the Duesenberg," Walsh said. "She's something else. Smart how they made it so you need a key to start it.

It'd be a hell of a temptation to hop into this baby and find some empty road."

Babe beamed at the car. A fat stogie had replaced the toothpick in his hand. "Brand new—on loan for as long as I want. Pile in and lemme show you what she can do. It's a straight eight, power coming out of its ears."

Cook had mixed feelings as he folded himself into the backseat. He'd heard about Ruth's driving. Wrecks and cops followed him like fire dogs.

As they pulled into traffic, Walsh started in. "Babe, you need to tell me why we're doing this. Colonel Ruppert's got no reason to get into this Black Sox business, not with Judge Landis hogging the limelight on it. You can't win with that man. You know what happens when you wrestle with a pig?"

Ruth didn't look over.

"You get filthy," Walsh said, "and the pig has fun." He leaned closer to Babe. "We should be saving all our chits with Ruppert to get you more money, juice up your income. Any time we ask for a favor like this, he's gonna turn that against you when we go in on your salary."

"Listen," Babe called while swerving onto Seventy-ninth Street, headed east, "this has got to get taken care of. That's my last word. Now you need to listen to this man." He nodded toward the rear seat, then resumed weaving between delivery wagons, trucks, cars, and people. He hit the horn to punish an indecisive driver. He laughed out loud. "Jesus, great car, ain't it?"

Walsh raised an eyebrow over his shoulder.

"First," Cook started, "we're asking Ruppert to do something that's actually in his interest, not against it. Nothing should be more important to him than protecting Babe. Babe is baseball, pure and simple, certainly for the Yanks. Second, this is real important for Babe. That investigation by the commissioner needs to stop. If it goes on and on, that could end up costing him lots of money, not to mention peace of mind. And what's important for Babe should be important for Ruppert."

"How's it important to Babe? Not that old stuff about the 1918 Series? He and the Sox won the damned Series."

"Stop thinking so much!" Babe shouted without removing the cigar from his mouth. He plunged the Duesenberg into the twisty road through Central Park. "We need to get these guys off my back. Play it the way the man here says."

Looking exasperated, Walsh called over, "But I still don't get it."

"You don't need to, kid."

The Ruppert mansion glowered from the corner of Ninety-third and Fifth, an ill-tempered pile of mismatched Gothic gewgaws hemmed in with ornamental ironwork and topped with a weird corner spire. Just looking at it made Cook uncomfortable. What kind of person would build that monstrosity, or choose to live in it? Come to think of it, either might be better than living across the street and having to look at it every day.

Babe left the Duesenberg at a NO PARKING sign and led them up the front steps. A tuxedoed servant deposited them in a rear room, fusty and cluttered with bookcases.

Babe dropped into one of the wingback chairs that flanked a massive fireplace. Cook and Walsh drifted along the shelves, which held gleaming beer steins made of ceramic and pewter. A few glass steins sparkled with inlaid patterns of delicate silver filigree. Walsh stopped at a glass-covered case of porcelains and jade, while Cook lingered over a scale model of a baseball stadium that stood on a corner table.

"You have found my pride and joy!" A medium-sized man entered. In a trim three-piece suit with a compact bow tie and slicked-back hair, Ruppert was all aerodynamic efficiency. "We may have to put it in the godforsaken Bronx, but that still qualifies as New York City. The New York Yankees—Babe Ruth's

Yankees—must have their own home, a stadium built for baseball. Not that foolish Polo Grounds."

Cook extended his hand and gave his name. Ruppert reciprocated, with a crisp bow from the waist but ignored Cook's hand. He took the chair that faced Babe and pulled out cigars for both of them. "It's a beautiful morning for a cigar, is it not?"

Ruppert and Ruth enacted the rituals of tip-clipping, match-striking, and savoring the first puffs. Babe blew three smoke rings, close to perfect ones. "At least no one's made cigars illegal yet," he said with a big smile.

Ruppert rose to the bait. "Ach, this liquor law is such madness, madness I say, and I say it until my face is blue. Trying to stand between Americans and a product as full of nutrition as beer. Why, without beer this country might never have been founded. The settlers, the pioneers, they drank beer to stay alive. The water was terrible, like poison!"

"I still feel that way," Walsh put in with a smile. He and Cook had settled on a stiff couch that faced the fireplace. "Who knows what's in the water? Especially in this town."

"Exactly. That is exactly my point. This country must come to its senses. And, my God, no one wants to drink this near beer. Have you tried it?"

Ruth offered a grunt and a look of disgust.

"Colonel," Walsh said, "I thought you were shifting your brewery over to other products. How's that going?"

"Hopeless. Utterly hopeless." Ruppert held his hands out in mock surrender. "The workers, they cannot figure out anything that does not ferment. Then it involves a whole new system of shipping, often to very different stores. It is a nightmare."

"I heard," Walsh said, "I heard some brewers are looking to make malt syrup and then sell that. The theory is that, hey, if the malt syrup happens to end up in the hands of bootleggers who make beer from it, how could the brewers be expected to know what they were going to do with it? Seems like maybe that's legal."

Ruppert, abandoning his broad gestures, offered his first smile of the conversation. "You are well informed. It is an interesting idea. Very interesting. We are looking into it." He turned. "Well, Babe, what brings you here with such a distinguished delegation?" He gestured with his cigar at Cook. "Don't tell me—you're considering a jump to the colored leagues, eh? The Lincoln Giants have the need of an outfielder?"

Ruth and Walsh laughed at the gibe. To Cook's taste, they laughed a bit too much. When the hilarity subsided, Ruppert put the cigar back in his mouth. "Time is money. Who's speaking for you here?"

Babe pointed to Cook. Cook made the pitch the way he planned to, laying out why everyone's interests would be served if Judge Landis kept his nose the hell out of the 1918 Series. Investigating beyond the Black Sox would be bad for the game, bad for the Yanks, bad for the Babe. Most of all, bad for Colonel Ruppert.

Ruppert heard him out, then took a long, luxurious pull on his cigar. He blew the smoke skyward with gusto, then shrugged. "You know, Mr.—" He arched his eyebrows.

"Cook. Speedwell Cook."

"It would be an acute pleasure—a schadenfreude, if you know the German word—to watch Judge Landis strip Harry Frazee and the Red Sox of that championship of 1918. It would serve that silly bounder right. He's certainly got it coming. He has no more business owning a ball club than does . . ." Ruppert started to gesture toward Cook, but the movement stalled out in midair. "The man in the moon."

"But look who also would get hurt," Cook said, ignoring Ruppert's gesture. "The game can't take it, nor can the Yankees. That new stadium, I'm afraid it might just go poof." Cook spread his fingers to pantomime an explosion.

"But the Babe didn't throw that Series," Ruppert objected. "The Red Sox won."

"Colonel"—Cook leaned forward—"there's more to this story, which I can describe only in the strictest confidence." Cook waited a few beats. When Ruppert said nothing, Cook picked up again. "Babe's in hock to the guys who . . . guys who have been fingered as fixing the Series with the White Sox in 1919. Babe had nothing to do with fixing any Series, of course, so his debt hasn't come to light in the Black Sox mess. But if Landis keeps going after whether the other Series was fixed, and there's anything to it, those same men are certainly the ones who did it. It's what they do. That makes it a real risk that the Babe's connection to these people will come up. Even if he had nothing to do with the Series, no one's going to notice that. You can see the headlines: *BABE IN CAHOOTS WITH GAMBLERS!* And that, Colonel, wouldn't be good for anyone."

Ruppert gave Cook a flat look. "I take it that this debt isn't just a few bucks."

"We wouldn't be here if it was."

"What was it for?" Ruppert looked back at Ruth. So did Cook. He thought he knew, but it was up to Ruth to say.

"It's a private matter," Babe said in a low voice. "There's other people involved."

Ruppert sank back in his chair. "My, that's certainly intriguing," he said, staring into the cold fireplace. He turned back. "Mr. Cook, how do you come to be involved in this? A suspicious man might even think you were acting on behalf of those mysterious fellows who fixed the Series. Or were somehow involved in this mysterious debt."

Babe guffawed. "A jig like him? You don't know those guys if you think they'd send him to handle this."

Ruppert took a deep breath. "Babe, it's no secret that it's hard to do anything about Hizzoner Judge Landis. That man is full of himself and getting fuller all the time. We can't fire him.

I can't even say bad words about him in public. That's in his blasted contract!" He turned to Walsh. "Did you see he's making Charlie Stoneham of the Giants sell the racetrack he just bought. Making him sell it outright!" Walsh shook his head in shared dismay.

"Colonel," Cook said, "even Judge Landis has to recognize that the Babe's different. He's the whole game right now. You know that. Look at how the newspapers are following his home run totals. Will he hit sixty? Seventy? A hundred? No one in baseball can afford to have his reputation at risk. Even Landis has to appreciate that."

The room grew silent again. The silence expanded. Ruppert stood. "I will look for a way. I will be in Chicago with the judge soon. But I make no promises. He is a tough nut. And I want you to understand that if he takes the bait and does what we want, we may pay a hell of a price for that down the road. The next time he has the chance, he may unload on the Babe or the Yankees. The judge, let me assure you, is a man who enjoys holding grudges. They give him a reason to get out of bed in the morning."

Ruppert shook hands with Ruth and nodded at Cook. He asked Walsh to stay behind to discuss another matter. The other two walked down the front hall and out to the street.

Babe, donning his hat, wheeled on Cook. "You don't like this," he said. "I could hear it in your voice."

"Don't like what?"

"Any part of this, this situation." Babe waved his hand. His broad face showed confusion. "Listen, you were a ballplayer. I heard you were pretty good. You should know. It's the greatest game in the world. There's a million ways to win and a million ways to lose. You play with everything—your arms, your legs, your head. When you got the hitter facing the pitcher, both looking for that edge, trying to figure out what the other guy thinks his edge is, what the other guy thinks you think his edge is, fielders trying to figure out where to be, base runners dancing . . . Jesus, it never gets old."

"The ballplayers do," Cook said. He jammed his left hand into his pants pocket. It had hurt like blazes all morning.

"I'm talking about baseball, about what happens when bums like Rothstein and Attell and Judge Landis, who don't know nothing about the game, and they . . . they take a crap all over it. You don't want to touch it when they're done." He looked directly into Cook's eyes. "They make it their game, and if you want to play baseball you've got only one choice—you play their game."

"Don't break my heart, Babe. They threw me out of that wonderful game of yours because my skin is dark."

"Yeah, yeah, I heard. Some guys, you know . . ." He shook his head and looked off toward the park on the other side of the avenue. "Walsh tells me just to shut up and hit homers."

"Yeah. I bet he does."

Babe stared down Fifth Avenue. "I've gotten worse advice."

"I bet you have."

Babe straightened to his full height. He expanded his chest to fill out his double-breasted jacket. It was white with blue chalk stripes, making him look like an oversized snowman. Then Ruth stepped close to Cook, no longer a snowman but simply a large, grim man.

"We need to close this thing out with Attell and his crowd," Babe said. He pointed a forefinger at Cook but kept his voice low. "I got my reasons, good ones. You need to tell those guys what we did here, today, how we brought Ruppert around. He's going to deliver the message to Landis, tell him he should shut down the investigation. Nothing on the 1918 Series. We delivered."

"I'll pass on the word, of course. But I don't know. If I was Attell—or his crowd—I might want to wait to see how it plays out. Maybe Ruppert doesn't follow through. Maybe Landis doesn't care what Ruppert says, goes ahead anyway."

"Exactly. That's why we gotta finish the deal now. If we wait, who knows how many ways they'll figure out how to welsh? That's what those sons-a-bitches do. Lie, cheat, steal. I did what I said I'd do. You testify to that. I put it on the line for them. They need to do what they said."

Cook found himself nodding. The Babe who stood in front of him wasn't the high-spirited kid whose parents put him in an orphanage because he was running wild through the streets of Baltimore. This Babe had the force to make that kid into a national colossus, more famous than the president. Certainly better liked. Sure, Babe had that great swing, that amazing body, he had all that. But other guys had great talent. Babe had something hard inside, something most people never saw, a will that gave him the discipline and the drive to become great. He was no freak, no accident.

"Sure, Babe, sure. Word is the smart guys're all going up to Saratoga. Racing season. I can go up there and look for them, you want me to."

"I'll pay for you to go, just don't go playing the horses all day." He gave a slight smile, then looked over at the entrance to Ruppert's gaudy mansion. "What the hell's keeping them? I didn't get any breakfast. Christ, I'm hungry."

They climbed into the Duesenberg to wait. Babe started the engine and let it idle. In the backseat, the doubt tugged at Cook's mind. What else did Rothstein have on the Babe, something that wasn't whether the 1918 World Series was fixed? Not knowing the full story, that might make this job a lot more complicated.

# Chapter 18

Fraser drummed his fingers on the steering wheel. He was trying to keep his eyes on the two-story house that slumped wearily toward Lafayette Avenue in Fort Greene. A nondescript Ford sat in front of the building's ragged paneling and faded paint. A colored man from the house had just climbed behind the wheel. He began reading a newspaper, in no rush to go anywhere or do anything. Over the last thirty minutes, a few Negroes had walked down the street in the morning sun, their errands as opaque to Fraser as their dark complexions and their scruffy neighborhood. It was frustrating to sit here, knowing that Violet was right inside. He and Eliza wanted to talk to Violet alone, not with Joshua around, so they waited.

Occasionally, Fraser's eyes drifted over to the royal blue Cadillac at the curb in the next block of Lafayette. That car had no business on this street. Neither did the driver, a white man with a pointed Vandyke beard who was as out of place here as Fraser and Eliza were. He had driven the Caddy up, stepped out, then sauntered out of Fraser's view.

"Are you sure about this address?" Eliza's voice was tight.

Tugging on the bill of his snap-brim cap, Fraser tried to control his tension. "I'm not an old hand at finding bootleggers, but this is where the detective said they were. Neighborhood looks right. That man in the Ford could be a partner or something."

Eliza sucked her breath in. Fraser laid a hand on her forearm. "We need to wait," he said.

Just then, Joshua Cook stepped out the front door, dapper in a light blue suit and maroon tie. He checked the street in both directions, then trotted down the half flight of stairs and climbed into the car. The driver fired the engine and pulled out. When it turned down Portland Street, Eliza said, "I'm going in."

"Just another minute," Fraser said. "Let's be sure he hasn't forgotten anything."

They heard another car start up. It was the blue Cadillac, the man with the Vandyke beard behind the wheel. It crossed in front of Joshua and Violet's building, then followed down Portland Street. Fraser's stomach churned. That didn't feel good.

He said nothing about the Cadillac to Eliza. Maybe she didn't notice it, didn't realize that Joshua seemed to be drawing more attention than he should. She didn't need something more to worry about. Neither of them had been sleeping much. When they started getting over the shock, had eased up on the recriminations and self-recriminations, they were left with the hard edge of loss, an edge that Fraser felt every minute. Years before, he had lost a child, a boy, with his first wife, and then he'd lost her, too. He wasn't going to lose another child.

He said that to Eliza the night before, after telling her the detective's news—that Eliza and Joshua were living in the same apartment. Her eyes flared over that news. Her hand went to her mouth. He told her straight, didn't beat around the bush. He didn't care about scandal or what was proper or not. And he didn't care about pride. And he sure as hell didn't care about race. He wasn't—they weren't—going to lose Violet. He wasn't going to lose another child. Because that would kill him.

Eliza had stared at him for the longest time. Then she sagged and looked down in a way he couldn't remember seeing before. "Okay," she said. "You're right." Even with that decided, he still didn't sleep much, keyed up at the prospect of seeing Violet, wondering if Eliza really meant what she had said.

After the street was quiet for another minute, he nodded to her. They stepped out onto the street.

The front door wasn't locked. The floorboards creaked as they walked back to 1B, in the back on the left. After knocking, Fraser recognized Violet's uneven gait, the pop of the cane on the floor. When the door swung open, she stood in the blue kimono that Eliza had bought her for the hospital. She froze, eyes wide. She seemed ready to bolt. Eliza rushed in and hugged her hard, saying Violet's name over and over. Violet didn't return the embrace. Eliza smoothed Violet's hair out of her face and leaned back. "We've been so worried," she said.

"Mother," Violet said sharply. "I don't have time for this. I have a trip to get ready for." A steamer trunk stood open in the main room. Clothes draped the furniture but couldn't conceal upholstery that was split at the seams, wooden surfaces marked with scars and divots.

"We just want to see you, to talk with you," Fraser said. "A trip where?"

Eliza stepped in front of him. "We'll help you pack, if that helps, dear. But you can't just go off without a word." Violet backed two steps into the room, still not looking at her mother. "I won't say anything like I did the other day," Eliza went on. "I was surprised then. I shouldn't have been angry. That was stupid of me. And wrong." Eliza stepped into the room and sat uncertainly on a chair. "We love you and want nothing but good for you. That's all we've ever wanted."

Violet was quiet for seconds more, then turned to her mother.

Eliza tried again. "I can see you're well. You're taking care of yourself." Eliza steeled herself for the next part. "I can see that you and Joshua are happy." At this, Violet also sat, perching on the edge of the divan. Eliza reached over and took her hand. "Can you tell us what you're planning? Where are you and Joshua going?"

The younger woman took a careful breath, then said, "I'm taking a train to Montreal, where Joshua will join me in a few days." They waited. "He's going separately by car to Saratoga—he's got business there, he's been setting it up for a while. Then we'll go on to London."

"London!" Panic passed through Eliza. Fraser, standing behind her, gripped her shoulder.

"Why London?" he asked.

Violet leaned back in her seat, but her eyes were still wary. "Joshua's business . . . , well, you know what he does. He says he can get into the legitimate end of it in Europe. There he can be an exporter, not take so many risks. We may end up in France, he's not sure. But he says we can live, you know, like normal people there. Live openly, as man and wife." Eliza sucked in her breath. "No, we're not married yet, but we will be. It won't be like here. He says that during the war, it was better over there."

"Violet," Fraser said. "Violet."

She shook her head and set her jaw. "We've gone over and over it. We could marry here. It'd be legal here in New York, not like some states, but he doesn't want to deal with the clerk's office, with all of the issues, everything that would come up if we did it here. And we can't live here, not together, not the way people would be about it. I never really knew how people are. How it is to be colored."

"Violet," he said. "When is the baby due?"

Eliza twisted to look at him. "What?"

When Violet didn't answer, he gave her a small smile. "Honey, I'm an old country doctor. Let us help."

Violet's face crumpled for a moment, then swiftly recomposed. "How can you be sure? I haven't been. Sure, that is."

"I wasn't entirely until just now."

She covered her face with her hands. Eliza knelt next to her chair, her head pressed against Violet's. In whispers, she repeated her daughter's name. Fraser cleared a place near them on the couch. He sat heavily.

After a minute, Eliza moved back to the chair, still gripping Violet's hands. "Does he know?"

Violet shook her head and took a stuttering breath. "I don't know what to do about it. I don't want that to be why, why he chooses me. I'm such a burden."

"You must tell him."

Violet looked helpless. Fraser sat forward, his forearms on his knees. "Violet, why are you leaving in such a hurry? There's something else, isn't there?"

"Oh, Daddy, I don't know. Joshua says it's nothing, but maybe it isn't." She looked down. "The police may be looking for him."

He looked surprised. "For bootlegging? It's not that easy to get arrested for that."

"It's about the bombing, the one I was in. Somehow they may suspect him of being involved."

"That's crazy," Eliza said. "He was hurt, too. He saved you."

"He and his partner, Cecil," Violet said, "they were in some radical groups, after they came back from France. Not any more. He swears to that. And that they had nothing to do with the bombing. He couldn't have. I know him." She looked intently at each parent, then cast her eyes down again. "But, you know, the investigation's been going on so long and they've never found out who was behind it. And he was there. Somehow they may know that."

"They're looking for him?" Fraser asked.

Violet nodded. "He just heard."

"So," he said pensively, "the cops think maybe he just blew himself up a little bit, by mistake." He shrugged. "I suppose that could happen with a bomber who didn't know his business."

"He says he's the perfect pigeon for the police—a Negro, a radical past, a bootlegger, with army training. He thinks we need to go right away. He says he won't ever let anyone put him in prison again. I think he means that."

The silence was thick. Fraser thought back to the Cadillac. It was wrong for a police car, much too nice. And the man with the trim beard didn't strike him like a cop. No need to talk about all that now. Not with Violet's condition, not with how edgy she was already. "So," Fraser said, "you're planning to sail to London from Montreal. Why not from here?"

"Joshua's business in Saratoga, it's partway there. Also, he says it'll be easier for him to get across the border into Canada and then leave through Montreal. He's afraid the police might be watching for him at the shipping lines here in New York."

Fraser nodded. "That makes sense. He's been making careful plans, I can see that. But have you really thought about this? He's got so many problems, Violet. And the government has ways to bring people back from foreign countries if they want to."

"You don't have to do all this, not by yourself," Eliza said, nodding at the clothes littering the room. "We can help with these things, with legal problems and lawyers, with the baby. We want to help."

"No, Mother, I have to do this. We chose these problems because we chose each other." She looked off for a moment. "Yes, I'm afraid, too. Of course I am. I know you both think I'm just being some empty-headed girl, carried away by a forbidden love, but I'm not."

Fraser had leaned back on the divan. He fingered a seam on

the armrest. He was bursting to speak out, to explain the plain logic: Violet needed to forget this whole adventure; being with Joshua could never bring her what she wanted from life. Her life would shrink. She would end up hating the man who shrank it. But Eliza had said those things and had failed. And now he would lose not only Violet, but her baby. Plain logic could drive Violet to more dangerous mistakes.

"Thank you," Violet said, looking from Eliza to Fraser and back. "Thank you for not being angry."

"Violet," Fraser said without rising. "We have to think about these things. For your welfare, and for the baby. Please hear me out." Eliza's eyes were full of warning, but he went on. "We can't know for sure, but Joshua's business in Saratoga, right in the middle of racing season—that makes me nervous. I know Joshua's a capable young man, but that town's full of all the big-time gamblers now, hoodlums from everywhere. And we know his business can be, well, a rough one. He doesn't want you there now, which I entirely agree with, but his business there may well be risky."

"You think he's in danger?"

"I don't know. But his business has danger, that's why he's trying to change it." He sat forward with his elbows on his knees. "I just don't think you want to be waiting alone in Montreal for him, not knowing when he'll get there. It would be lonely, hard. And I don't think you should be traveling with him when there's any risk, any risk at all, that the police might swoop down on him. Not in your condition. You have to think of that, of more than just yourself, or even the two of you. What about your mother and you going to London straight from here? Then Joshua can join you there from Montreal. The police won't be looking for you. Not yet, anyway. You can travel without fear."

"Yes, honey," Eliza said. "That would spare you the trip to Montreal also. That's such a long ride, switching into a hotel, all of that. And I can be there to help with everything. Joshua can't object to that. He can go to Montreal as he planned and follow us over."

"How will he know where we've gone? I have no way to contact him in Saratoga. He could end up in Montreal thinking I had run out on him."

"I'll go to Saratoga and let him know," Fraser said. "It won't be hard to find a young man who dresses as well as he does." He could see her indecision. "Violet, I can't say we understand all of this. But no matter how much we may be afraid for you, this isn't a scheme to separate you two. We only want to look after you. Joshua should be glad about it."

Her small, sad smile nearly split him in two. She sniffled and nodded. "We were going to be married on the ship. By the captain."

Eliza, her eyes red and glassy, hugged her daughter. "I know that sounds romantic, Violet, but we would be so sad not to be there for your wedding."

Violet pulled back as her tears fell. She nodded and said quietly, "Yes. I know."

"Right," Eliza said briskly, straightening up. "Let's get you packed and get your trunk over to the Ansonia. We can make the arrangements from there, get the money and the tickets."

"Joshua's left me money."

"Good," Fraser said. "There can never be too much of that. Why don't you get dressed and we'll start getting this all sorted out?"

Violet stood deliberately, then walked, unevenly but steadily, into the next room. She closed the door behind her.

Fraser and Eliza looked at each other. "Look at these clothes of hers," Eliza said, spinning a half circle on her heel, "they're all brand new. She took almost nothing with her from the Ansonia. He's throwing money at her."

"Yes, well, I suppose he loves her."

Eliza looked at him. "Oh, Jamie."

He couldn't answer any of the questions that lay within those changeable eyes, now as dark as he had ever seen them. "Not now, Eliza. I can't, we can't . . . we can't lose her." He made himself think of the practical questions. "You can leave your business like this? It could be months."

"How can you even ask?"

"All right. I'll go to the bank in the morning, arrange for drafts you can take."

"Yes." She put her hand on him. "Jamie. What will he be? The baby?" She could see he didn't understand. "Will he be colored? Or white? Something in between?"

"I don't think you can tell." He held her with both hands. "I don't know much genetics. Except that he'll be Violet's baby, and our grandchild."

"Yes." She moved her lips without speaking, then managed, "I know she's a sensible girl, underneath all this. We have to believe that. My God, she's going to be a mother. She's a child herself." She looked up at him. "We just have to swallow Joshua, this whole business. So we will." She looked around again. "What else? What else?"

"We'll go over it all when we're back home. We'll think more clearly there. I'll have to arrange to go to Saratoga and find Joshua. Maybe I can be of use somehow. Anyway, I'll wire you whenever there's news. Maybe I'll follow you over to England." Eliza was chewing her lip. "What?"

"You should get his father to go with you to Saratoga." When Fraser didn't answer, she added, "This is no time to be resentful, Jamie. You're the one who's forever saying that Speed Cook's a useful man in a tight spot. Well, Joshua's in a tight spot."

# *Chapter 19*

Out of town cars lined the back street where Fraser's rooming house rose in semirespectable shabbiness. The cool morning tingled with the possibilities of Saratoga's high season. The resort promised mild breezes, mineral baths, luxury lodging, and posh dining, plus sporting from racing to gambling to golf to the more intimate type. Pleasure seekers from New York and Boston and Philadelphia, fleeing the August heat, clogged local roads and incoming trains.

Fraser headed for the massive Grand Union Hotel, which filled nearly a square block of the small town. He and Eliza once came to the summer mecca during August racing season. She had hated the crowds and ostentatious displays of wealth. He wasn't sure why Saratoga's crowds and crass wealth offended her more than those at Broadway theaters, but they had dropped Saratoga in favor of ocean-side cottages on Long Island. After spending his first thirty-five years in Ohio, Fraser could never get enough of the seashore.

The Grand Union, its five square towers crowned with triumphant flags, dominated the town. Its sandstone walls were a smart backdrop for the pastel finery of the racing crowd, on display even early in the morning. Fraser was looking for either of the Cooks, father or son—he had learned from Aurelia Cook that Speed was in Saratoga on his own business.

As a man of science, Fraser had noted with interest that both Cooks were in Saratoga at the same time. It could be a coincidence. That was possible. Speed could be here to deal with Attell and his crowd, that job he was doing for Ruth. But other explanations might apply. Speed might be here on Joshua's trail himself, or might even be part of his son's schemes. Fraser didn't know what to think. The world was moving way too fast for him. He still struggled to understand Violet's romance, not to mention Joshua's dangerous business and Speed's connection with Eliza and Babe Ruth.

Weaving through morning strollers, Fraser settled into a rocking chair on the hotel's front porch. The chair, with its traditional Adirondack design, was a good size for him. He pulled yesterday's newspaper from his jacket pocket, then a pair of reading spectacles from the inside pocket. He pantomimed interest in the paper, turning a page every few minutes. His attention focused on the racing fans and vacationers who passed into, out of, and around the hotel. After forty-five minutes, he noticed the distinctive bulk of Speed Cook approaching from the direction of the racetrack.

Cook moved nimbly for a large man, his rumpled suit well below Saratoga's standards for haberdashery. Rather than hail his friend, Fraser followed him into the lobby. Inside, Fraser lingered near a voluble group to the side of the entrance, standing close enough to imply a connection but far enough away to avoid having to speak with them. Approaching the front desk, Cook gave a bellhop a slip of paper, then moved to the other side of the lobby entrance. He was evidently trying to be inconspicuous, a hopeless task here for a colored man of his dimensions. Fraser sidled to a wall, using his open newspaper to shield his face, again feigning interest in yesterday's headlines.

A small form emerging from an elevator looked like Abe Attell. When the form made a beeline for Cook, Fraser was certain. It was Attell's walk, up on the balls of his feet. Like he was keeping balanced in case he had to throw a jab or a quick one-two. The two men spoke briefly, no handshakes or greeting. Attell left while Cook was still speaking. Cook's face and posture betrayed no irritation over the rudeness. Fraser followed him out the front door, relieved that his suspicions had been wrong. Cook was here on his own business, not as part of Joshua's.

Halfway down the front walk, Fraser called out. Cook spun and grimaced. "I'm in the middle of something. What do you want?"

"Are you in the middle of something that involves fooling around with Abe Attell?"

"I asked first."

"Where's Joshua?"

Cook rolled his eyes. "How the hell do I know?" He turned toward the street.

"Really? That's the best you can do?"

"What, you think he's up here?" When Fraser nodded, Cook started to look curious. "Really?"

"Let's go for a walk."

"I've got things to do," Cook objected.

"You'll be glad you did. And sorry if you don't." Fraser nodded down the road to the racetrack.

They skipped the small talk, both preferring silence. When they reached the end of the town and turned onto the Avenue of the Pines, other foot traffic disappeared. They reached a lush-looking golf course. Graceful elms leaned softly over the roadway.

Fraser told him about Joshua and Violet. He left nothing out. Cook didn't interrupt but repeatedly looked over, his eyes searching Fraser's face.

When Fraser finished, they stopped and faced each other. "So, you're telling me"—Cook ticked off the points on the fingers of one hand—"that the cops are after Joshua for a bombing that nearly blew him to kingdom come, that Joshua and Violet are moving to Europe to get married, that they're having a baby, and that Joshua's here in Saratoga on some mystery mission that you're afraid may get him killed. And maybe some angry bootleggers are after him, on top of that. That about it?" Fraser nodded. "Well, I surely appreciate the news, but what the hell do you want from me? Did you simply want to see the look on my face when I heard all this?"

"Simmer down, Speed. We're way past the stage where you and I can get angry about this stuff. I know I threw a fit before, but not now. You said we worked together okay before. That's right. We need to again, whether we want to or not. I need help. I need your help with this." Cook put his hands in his pockets and dropped his chin. "First off, I need to find Joshua and tell him that Violet will meet him in London. Eliza's taking her over on a ship that leaves tomorrow. He doesn't know about that. He thought they'd meet in Montreal and sail from there. He needs to know the change in plans."

Cook didn't move, so Fraser kept going. "Look, I'm guessing that, whatever his business is here in Saratoga, it doesn't include being easy to find. You'd be a lot better at finding him than I would. At least that's the sort of thing you've always said."

"What else? There's more."

Fraser leaned in. "Aren't you curious why Joshua's got to come to Saratoga before leaving the country, going to start a new business overseas with a new wife? Doesn't that suggest something to you, something about a man who's been stealing other people's liquor shipments for more than half a year?"

"He's been stealing from other bootleggers?" Cook wore a disbelieving look.

"That's what my detective reports. I suppose it keeps the profits up."

Cook scratched the side of his head. "All right, just say it, Jamie."

"I'm not saying for sure. I don't know anything for sure any more. I'm just saying I'm worried. Worried a lot. During race season, there's more cash in this town than on Wall Street. Dice games on every street corner, high-dollar poker in all the hotels. Not to mention side bets on every race, on whether that mosquito flying by will land on my wrist or your elbow. Right?"

"Sure. So you think Joshua's planning on finishing up his career as a criminal by knocking over some major gambling joint?"

"Can you rule that out? Speed, look. He's decided to come here instead of getting the hell out of the country when the cops may be looking for him, not to mention that other bootleggers may be looking for him. Most times, those would be very good reasons *not* to go to Saratoga. I don't mean to be butting into your family business, but now it's my family business, too. Somehow my daughter is in love with him. Can't say I'm thrilled about it, and I don't know what the hell I think about any of this. If I'd known this is where we were going to end up, I might've turned my back on you when you came by back in Cadiz twenty years ago." Cook shook his head and looked up at Fraser. "But I don't want to see Violet's heart broken. I don't want my grandchild never to know a father. So if there's something I can do to prevent those from happening, I want to."

Cook walked away a few paces, then leaned against a tree. He kept his eyes fixed across the road. After a deep breath, he spoke. "You know, Joshua never gave us a lick of trouble when he was young. He was the finest young man you ever wanted to see. I was proud that someone like me could produce someone like him. Now it seems like he was saving up all the ways he could make me crazy. That boy's more than I can figure."

"How do we find him?"

"I've been here two days getting nothing done and haven't seen hide or hair of him. 'Course, I haven't been looking for him. If he's planning what you think, he's not hanging out with the parlor snakes at the swank hotels. He's off in the shadows, not being noticed. The stables might be a good place. That's probably where I'd go. Negroes wouldn't stand out there. Lots work as grooms and stable boys, behind the scenes, you know, cleaning up."

"Does he know anything about horses?"

"What'd he know about bootlegging before he took that up? God help us, he picks things up quick."

"So what's he here for?"

Cook plucked a long blade of timothy grass and stripped off the leaves at its base. He climbed a slope that rose between the path and the golf course. The two men dropped onto the crest, looking over a lush fairway. Cook started chewing on the grass stalk like any Ohio farmer. "Okay," he said, "he ain't up here bootlegging or stealing liquor."

"Why not?"

Cook shook his head impatiently. "No customers around here to sell liquor to. Also, all the good stuff—and that's what he handles, not the bathtub rotgut—it comes off the ships off Long Island. He's got no reason to come to Saratoga for bootlegging or for grabbing liquor."

"Something important pulled him here," Fraser said. "It's business, and it won't take him long, since he's heading to Europe in a few days. Only thing that makes sense is that he's getting money to set him and Violet up in England, start their new life. I suppose he could be collecting on debts."

"It's money, all right, but not collecting debts. Can't anybody owe him money except some small-time distributors and the speakeasy owners, and they're all back down in the city. No need to come to Saratoga to collect on them."

"So he's going to steal it?"

Cook didn't answer for a few beats, then spat out the grass blade. "Yup. Damned stupid. And I bet I know who he's planning to steal from." Fraser waited. "Damned stupid. And reckless."

"You going to say who?"

"Don't know for sure. I'm afraid it's Arnold Rothstein."

"Come on, Speed. That'd be crazy, and Joshua isn't crazy."

"Think about it, Jamie. He needs one last score before he heads to a new country. Who's got the most money, carries it around with him, not in any safe but right out in the open?" Cook looked at Fraser.

"Okay."

"And what do the cops and the government care if Rothstein gets robbed? Hell, he won't even report it missing. He's a crook. Crooks complaining that somebody robbed them? It doesn't get a lot of sympathy. Joshua's got to get through customs to get out of the country, start clean somewhere else, and he's already got that bombing business over his head. So he needs to steal from a crook, not from a bank or a business."

"But it's crazy. He'll get himself killed."

"That's the hard part, not getting killed. Maybe he figures Rothstein's got so much money he won't miss some."

"That's crazy, too."

"Yup."

"We need to find him. Keep him from going through with this."

"Come on, Jamie. You dealt with him in Paris. You really think you're going to talk him out of anything?"

"So what do we do? Help him out? Sticking up criminals isn't something I know much about."

Cook gave him a half smile. "There's always time to learn."

"You're kidding."

"Yeah." Cook shrugged. "Maybe not entirely. Maybe there's some ways we can help him. He's probably here with his partner, Cecil Washington." Cook sighed. "This is going to mess up my real business up here, mess it up big time."

Fraser remembered his first question, back at the hotel, the one that Cook never answered. "Speed, what are you doing with Abe Attell?"

"That's got nothing to do with Joshua. Or Violet. That's my deal."

Fraser kept staring at him.

"Really." He shook his head. "It's business, something for Babe Ruth, if you can believe that. Your missus knows all about it. I talked to her about it a couple days ago. It's important, something I need to see through, but you and I don't need to worry about it. Nothing to do with Joshua."

"How can you say that? Attell is Rothstein's boy. It's all connected. What do we do about that?"

Cook looked evenly at Fraser. "Listen to yourself. 'We.' How the hell did you and I end up joined at the hip?"

"Let's not start talking about getting joined at the hip."

Cook winced. "Didn't mean it like that."

Fraser pushed up from the ground. "Anyway, no time to worry that one out. What about that guy I saw outside Joshua's house in Brooklyn? Have you noticed anyone looking suspicious, or like a cop pretending not to be a cop? Or even just someone watching out for other people, like maybe Joshua?"

"Come on, Jamie, half the people in Saratoga look suspicious. That's why everyone comes here, for the thrill of rubbing elbows with suspicious-looking people. Back at that hotel I could point out a dozen men who meet that description. You want to keep an eye on all of them?"

"I'm trying to figure how to help Joshua without getting him or us killed."

When Cook stood, he made a point of not groaning. The left knee was killing him, but he wouldn't limp. That made him look like some old coot. He jammed his hands in his trouser pockets. "All right. I'm thinking a couple of things. We probably should split up. Like we did back at the beginning, you know. You work the white folks. I take care of the colored."

# *Chapter 20*

Clover Farms sprawled over a thousand acres on both sides of the road to Ballston. For much of the year, its four whitewashed, green-trimmed stables stood half empty, but racing season changed everything. Summer trains brought thoroughbreds from Pennsylvania, Maryland, Kentucky, as far away as Florida and California. With at least three handlers for each horse, plus the dozen extra hands it took to maintain the place when it was at capacity, the segregated dormitories were bursting for the season's six weeks. Joshua had pegged it as a good place to lie low, but hadn't appreciated how much work the strategy would require—mucking out stables, hauling water, loading and unloading high-strung animals, rubbing them down, polishing leather. The work started at sunup and lasted until sundown.

Perched on a hay bale, he leaned back against the barn in the cool early twilight. His work clothes were stiff with dried sweat and dirt. A cigarette smoldered between two fingers. He had no energy to smoke. He drank from a bottle of vile near beer. Its only virtues were that it was legal and it was wet. Cecil was checking on the second car they'd stashed the night before, maybe halfway to Glens Falls. He wasn't late yet, but getting there.

Joshua was too weary to get fired up about the night in front of him. That was good. No point being nervous. He used to think that being on edge ensured he was on top of things. France taught him that wasn't so. Nerves didn't help, might even make you think worse. You had to be sharp, sure, but not nervous. Tonight would be just him and Cecil, doing the sort of thing they'd been doing for a while. Years, actually. Getting through it.

Cecil dropped onto the bale next to him and nodded. That meant the second car was still safe, hidden from view, both cars gassed up and ready. Joshua handed him a bottle of near beer.

Cecil took a long pull and screwed up his face. The expression passed and he stretched out on his back. "What the hell were we thinking?" he said up to the darkening sky, "back when we followed Brother Briggs and all? Talking about the inherent worth and dignity of labor, of the majesty of rolling up your sleeves and taking pride in performing the most menial task."

Joshua snorted. He started to massage his left calf. It had cramped up on him twice that afternoon.

"Nothing but hard damned work," Cecil kept on. He rose onto his elbows. "Now, labor, you know how they talk about 'labor'? Labor doesn't sound half bad. Sounds like there's something about the public good laying around in it, you know. Like you're making the world better, and it'll make you better to be part of it. You know—liberty, fraternity, labor, like that. But then you get out here"—he swept an arm in front of them—"and it's just work, nothing but goddamned work all day long, which is exactly like what it sounds like."

"We got soft, that's all." Joshua smiled. He gave up rubbing his leg. "We turned into capitalists, so we've got the sorts of muscles that capitalists have. Muscles for stealing."

"You think we qualify as robber barons yet?"

Joshua laughed. "No problem on the robber part. Maybe a ways to go on that 'baron' part. You want to be 'Sir Cecil'? Baron Washington?"

"Either's good." He took a swallow and made another face. "Just like the setup we got tonight. I doubted you. I admit it. I doubted you. But your man Rothstein went and won fifty grand on that sixth race today—it was so goddamned obvious the race was fixed even I could tell, and I'm still working on which end the manure comes out." Joshua smiled. "You never said how you knew he was going to win that big."

Joshua's grin got wider. He laid a finger beside his nose. "It's good to have friends, Cecil, then you just keep your ears open. Ain't any secrets around these barns." The night air felt soft against his skin. He stubbed out his cigarette on the sole of his shoe and flicked the butt far away. Didn't need to go burning down the joint, not tonight. "You remember the drill?"

"'Course I do. We ain't talked about nothing but the drill for three days now. I've been dreaming about the drill."

"Good. Good. Let's go over it again."

"Evening, son."

Cecil started at the voice, deep and quiet, coming out of the gloom beyond the barn's lights. Joshua didn't start. He knew the voice and the outlines of the thick figure.

"What're you doing here, Daddy?"

"I suppose that's the question I've got for you. I had no idea you were interested in the horse business."

The younger men rose from the hay bale. Both brushed off their pants. Cecil shook hands with Cook. "Maybe," Cecil said, "maybe I'll go clean up. Change my clothes." He headed to the colored men's dormitory.

"I'll be along soon," Joshua called after him.

When they were alone, Cook spoke. "You don't seem real glad to see me."

"Not the best time, Daddy. Something's going on."

Cook regarded his son for a moment. "Well then, let's get right to it. First, Violet's not going to meet you in Montreal."

"What? What're you saying? What'd you do?" The words came quickly. "You've always got to go horning in and messing everything up."

"I didn't do a goddamned thing, young man. Get a grip on yourself. She's going straight to London with her mother, going to wait for you there."

"With her mother? Oh, Lord, now you got the Frasers to stick their noses into what isn't their business."

"It turns out they think that anything involving their daughter and their grandchild is their business. I had a hard time disagreeing with them."

Joshua's brow creased. "Grandchild?"

"Her father's a doctor. He could tell right off, it seems, even if you didn't have enough sense to. I imagine Violet had an inkling, too."

"A baby." Joshua looked off toward the woods across the warm-up track. "When? When?"

"February. Maybe early March. That's what Jamie said."

Joshua walked a few steps to the side, then back. "Jeez. I can't have this on my mind tonight. Not tonight."

"Son, it's going to be on your mind for as long as you live. Take my word for it. It's never going away."

Joshua stared at his father, then looked down. "Right. Right." He looked back at his father. "Okay, I got it. Message received. Hey, I've got to go."

"I've got a second message."

"Don't even try to start that now. Violet and me, we're doing what we're doing and we're going to make it right. I'm going to make it right. The best way I can."

Cook put up his hand. "It's not what you think." He took a second. "I want you to use me tonight, any way you can. Knocking over Arnold Rothstein's card game's a damned crazy thing to do, but I know you. I figure you've gone to some trouble to set it up. You're not a child. Haven't been for a while. You saved our tails over in France, Jamie and me, at a bad time. So I'm not here to stop you. I'm here to be useful. I'm old and I'm slow. No one knows that more than me. But I'm smarter than most and still stronger than lots. Look, I found you here, and that wasn't so easy."

Joshua shook his head. "I can't, Daddy. Cecil and me, we know what we're doing. We work together. We can read each other. Whatever comes at us, we know what the other'll do. You'd be something new, something different. Something we didn't know. It'd mess us up. We can't have that."

"Use me or I'll just get in the way."

"No, sir. I appreciate the offer. I do. But we've got it worked out. No way to change it now. That's how mistakes happen." He held his hands out. "Daddy, don't get in the way. That'll just get someone hurt when they don't need to. Maybe you. Maybe me."

Cook couldn't think of anything smart to say. He'd do what he thought was right and so would his son. Words weren't going to change that. A question popped into his mind. "One thing. Do you know why a fellow with one of those goat beards—you know, the pointy ones—would be following you?"

"A goatee?"

"Don't get all French on me. He drives a blue car, a Cadillac."

Joshua smiled. "Yeah, I do. That's Ferguson. He's a vet I got to know. He does odd jobs for me, business things. Watches out for me some of the time. You know, an extra pair of eyes?"

"He's on your side?"

"Yes, sir. When I pay him."

"You paying him to be in Saratoga?"

"No, he's not here for me. Could be working on something separate from us, or could be up here to take the waters." When

Cook didn't respond right off, Joshua asked, "Have you seen him around here?"

"No, not up here. It's probably nothing."

"Even if he was, we can't turn back."

After Joshua left, Cook stood in the near dark for a moment, feeling the night's dew on his skin. The hay's sweet smell mingled with the tang of manure. He rubbed the back of his neck and moaned softly. He'd be watching tonight, just watching. Not doing a damned thing. That was the hardest. But he knew why Joshua had turned him down and knew that the reasons were pretty good ones. He'd got old and fat and wouldn't be much good. He hated that, too.

He didn't know the plan, but the idea, robbing the biggest hoodlum in Saratoga? It was one of those ideas. It was either brilliant or crazy. Brilliant because Rothstein was so powerful, so big, that no one—least of all Rothstein—expected someone to take a run at him. Like robbing Fort Knox. Rothstein'd have protection, lots of it, but it might be sleepy protection, overconfident. And, from what Cook had heard about the day's racing, the man must have a bankroll on him that a bold man would think was worth the trouble of trying.

It was crazy, though, for pretty much the same reasons. You had to figure there would be six or eight poker players, each with a gun. Add, what, two or three coat holders or bodyguards? Hard to know. At least three. Then a couple on the front door and a couple outside. So, fifteen or so men, most of them armed, some of them good at their jobs. Not all of them would be stupid, though some would. Maybe most. Cook had never been real impressed with the reasoning powers of the criminal class. On the other side, there would be Cecil and Joshua, plus the element of surprise and what better be one hell of a clever plan.

Joshua's plan was likely to make it tougher for Cook to look after Babe's business. If Rothstein ever suspected it was Joshua

Cook stealing his money, he wasn't going to do any business with Joshua's father over Babe's IOU.

The hell with Babe. Cook would figure out some way to help Joshua—not getting in the way, but helping. He couldn't sit this one out. Might as well get Jamie in, too, if he wanted in. He had just as much right. Actually, Cook thought, it'd be good to get Jamie in. Ever since that day, twenty years ago if it was a day, when he asked Jamie to doctor to Aurelia's aunt, life kept throwing them together. It wasn't like they'd been best friends from the start. Or ever since. But he knew that twice now, when things looked bad, they'd answered the bell for each other. He also knew that this time mattered most of all, for both them.

Yeah, Jamie would be in.

He rubbed his neck again and started walking back to his car. That left hand hurt like hell. He should ask Jamie if there was something could be done for it. Ought to get some advantage from having a doctor in the family.

# Chapter 21

Through an afternoon and evening of shadowing Abe Attell around Saratoga, Fraser's frustration had grown and grown. The little man was busy. He stopped at a newsstand, at a florist, in a gift shop. Everywhere he went, his derby at a jaunty angle, he ran into people. Were they chance encounters or was he passing messages, doing business? Was he running errands for Rothstein? For himself? Fraser didn't know. Watching Attell from fifty feet away raised more questions than answers.

Fraser almost lost him at the racetrack. The festival atmosphere was infectious, the colors kaleidoscopic. Flags flapped from poles in the infield. Wide-rumped horses twitched by, bored jockeys perched like pilotfish in bright silks. Women in flowing dresses and floppy hats fluttered close to natty gents wielding flasks that glinted in the sun. The occasional hard type in the crowd, someone with scuffed shoes and dirty fingernails whose next meal turned on the next race, couldn't dampen the gaiety of the fortunate.

At the end of the sixth race, the one where a swaybacked roan came from nowhere to win by a head and pay out at 30–1, the crowd's elation engulfed Fraser. Thousands cheered for the perennial dream of instant riches won by shrewd betting or dumb luck. When Fraser came back to himself, he looked over at the box where Attell had been. It was vacant, suddenly stripped of touts and hangers-on. Fraser's heart thudded as he hustled back inside the clubhouse. No sign of him.

Fraser hurried behind the grandstand where cars stood in a field in uneven rows. Still no Attell, but, damn, there was that man with a Vandyke beard. He was climbing into a blue Cadillac. Had to be the one from Brooklyn, from outside Joshua and Violet's house.

Fraser decided quickly. He rushed to an idling taxi and ordered it back to town. The slow crawl of cars kept the blue Cadillac in sight. The taxi's flawed suspension reminded Fraser of wooden-wheeled journeys over the rutted roads of Harrison County, Ohio, when he might ride a couple of hours to deliver a baby or patch up some unlucky farmer. He knew nowhere near as much medicine then, but he knew a lot more folks. New York, with all those people, could make you feel empty.

Back in town, Fraser caught sight of Attell, still sharp in a beige three-piece suit, walking down a side street. Fraser ditched the taxi, letting the blue Cadillac get away, and headed after Attell. Fraser felt too large for this job, that he lacked the subtlety to track Attell. It would be a miracle if the little man didn't notice him galumphing around in his wake. But Fraser was supposed to follow Attell, so he would.

The prizefighter stopped at a bland-looking clapboard house. From across the street, Fraser resumed his newspaper reading. The traffic in and out of the house was surprising. It must be a speakeasy. Attell emerged after about ten minutes, looking no worse for wear. Fraser doubted that Attell was much of a drinker.

Attell continued through the neighborhood that bordered the center of town, stopping twice more at equally anonymous houses. These had to be business calls, Fraser decided, not social visits. Was Attell collecting shakedown money, a percent of the take? That made sense. Businesses he had an interest in.

Attell's fourth stop was the dining room of the United States Hotel and its casino, where he joined a table of celebrants who were midway through a large meal. Fraser gratefully made his way to a seat at a side table. He longed to free his feet from his shoes or at least put them up on the chair across from him. All he could do, though, was extend his legs under the table while ordering a sarsaparilla and bowl of soup. He had to be ready to bolt whenever Attell started for the door.

After thirty minutes, the small man donned his derby and bounced out of the dining room. Fraser resumed his pursuit down side streets until Attell reached a large Tudor-style house, well-maintained, that stood apart from the neighborhood. Fraser set up his viewpoint from a half block away on the street's far side, lounging against a tree and testing how much of yesterday's news he had memorized. After twenty minutes, he began to get suspicious. A couple of men had entered or left, but not Attell. Until now, Attell hadn't been much for long visits. Also, gathering dusk was making newspaper reading a pretty thin pretext.

"Aren't you the shy one."

Fraser looked up. The young woman was small, her head barely to his shoulder. Brown hair curled from under an ivory hat with a shallow crown, wide brim, and blue velvet bow. She smiled, holding a small bag in both hands.

Fraser reached to tip his hat. "Excuse me?"

"We noticed you standing over here, you know. We keep an eye on the neighborhood." Fraser nodded, unable to dredge up anything useful to say. "Lots of fellas get shy," she said, giving her shoulders a flirty twist. "The neighbors don't much like it, having fellas on the street. So it's better if you either come in—we don't bite, not unless that's what you want—or else you go on your way."

"Uh, no—sorry—no. Really, I wasn't planning to come in. I was, you know, waiting for somebody. I guess he's been delayed." Fraser conspicuously checked his watch. He gave the young woman a perfunctory grin. "I certainly don't want to cause trouble with your neighbors. I'll look for my friend around town." He tipped his hat again, then put his newspaper under his arm. "Sorry for any inconvenience."

"You *are* a shy one." She giggled softly as Fraser moved off, stumbling on a level stretch of pavement. He hurried toward Broadway. Had Attell slipped out the back door? Fraser gritted his teeth over the waste of his time, half a day spent learning nothing. Then he remembered the bearded man. He had learned one thing.

At Broadway, Fraser ran through the alternatives he'd worked out with Cook. He had insisted on a backup plan if he lost track of Attell.

"Where can I try to pick him up again?" he had asked.

"The Brook," Cook had answered, no hesitation. "It's the swankiest joint, casino, what have you, way out in the country. One that the New York smart guys set up. I think Rothstein owns most of it now. It's the place to go for high-end card games that'll skin you quicker'n you can say 'Jack Robinson.' " Cook told him how to get there.

Fraser headed for his boardinghouse, where he fired up the Stutz. He didn't much care for the car, a brute that had to be wrestled with more than driven, but Eliza insisted on it. She took comfort from its weight and density. After getting flipped from the Babe's car the summer before, she preferred a car like a dreadnought. Fraser tried to argue that it was the driver that mattered, not the car, but they still had the Stutz.

He eased it under a tree, giving himself a view of the big lot behind the Grand Union, one the hotel used for its guests' cars. He was playing a hunch, and it paid off fast. After only a few minutes, Attell strutted down the sidewalk, spats flashing. He climbed into a bland-looking Olds and set off in the direction of the Brook. Fraser made no effort to hurry or follow closely. He figured he knew where Attell was going.

The ride took only twenty minutes. Fraser killed his headlights when he realized the lights up on the left came from the Brook. The casino presented a wide porch to the road, then reached back in two perpendicular wings. The second story glowed with yellow light and dangerous secrets.

Fraser drove by slowly. After the road curved away, he nosed the big car in front of a large bush. People coming from the direction of the casino wouldn't see the Stutz until they were almost past it. If then. He killed the engine.

With no moon, the stars stretched like diamond chips almost to the western horizon, where the sun left a silver glow. His head filled with the scrapings of crickets and katydids. He fought down a surge of fear. There were a lot of men with guns at the Brook, and Joshua was going in there to take their money.

Fraser couldn't remember ever feeling brave. A few times, pushed hard by events and by Speed Cook, he had done things that might have seemed brave. But it wasn't his nature. Right now he felt old and afraid. The night could be violent. No way around it.

He clenched his teeth and stared back toward the Brook.

# Chapter 22

Two tall figures entered the woods behind Clover Farms. Each carried a canvas sack. Without a moon or a flashlight, they walked gingerly, protecting their tuxedoes from branches on all sides and from mud underfoot. If they were going to pass, even for a few moments, as waiters at a deluxe joint like the Brook, they couldn't look like they'd crawled through the wilderness to get there.

Joshua had spent the last two nights in this forest, finding a good path and confirming that Rothstein's gunmen, like Cecil, were city men who preferred pavement to woods. They patrolled the Brook's open grounds without ever venturing into the trees behind them. Most of the people they were guarding against, Joshua figured, were city men, too, also uncomfortable in the woods. On both nights, Joshua had reached the back wall of the casino without being challenged. He had looked in a few windows to confirm what he had learned from a drawing of the building's layout that he had paid one of the Brook's workers to draw. The price had probably been half the worker's monthly pay, but the sketch had the detail they needed, showing doors, stairs, the dining rooms, the high-stakes card room, main casino, even the closets and serving areas. No one knows a building like the people who clean it.

Joshua had heard stories about the Brook—about the luxury, the steaks, the cigars, the shows, the women. Rothstein and his partners provided every comfort that might distract the customers from the crooked gambling. Or at least soften the pain of their inevitable losses.

After twenty minutes, Joshua and Cecil stood where the woods ended. The building lay across a hundred feet of lawn. Two storage sheds provided cover for the perilous trip across.

Quietly, they set their sacks on the ground. Each man tucked a small towel into his shirt collar, then began to apply black makeup to his face, neck, and ears. In the weak light, they checked each other to make sure all exposed skin was covered, then traced on the other the white Sambo smile favored by blackface performers. They tossed the makeup and towels aside and drew long-nosed Mausers from the sacks. The pistols, their streamlined design expressing their lethal purpose, went into the rear of their waistbands, under their jackets. Cecil had so admired Joshua's pistol that he bought one from another veteran. Joshua nodded at Cecil, then led off.

Crouching, the sack in one hand, he started across the open ground. When dog barks erupted, he crouched lower and froze.

"What's that?" The voice carried in the moist night air. It came from Joshua's left, toward the road.

"Ah, probably a damned squirrel," another voice said. "That cur barks at the wind." The second voice came from the same direction. The guards had patrolled separately the last two nights, but these two were together.

When the dog quieted, Joshua moved again, pausing behind each shed in turn, then reaching a shadowed stretch of the casino's rear wall. Looking back at Cecil, Joshua was surprised how the painted ivory smile reflected the light from the casino's windows. Joshua hadn't thought of that. He angled his face down while he waited. When Cecil arrived, his breathing was steady, his eyes steady, too. Joshua pointed at the light from a window above them. They both stared at it so they wouldn't be dazzled when they stepped in from the darkness.

A man came out of a door about twenty feet away. He strained to haul a metal trash bin against his right hip. As he had the last two nights, he left the door open behind him and headed back to one of the sheds. Joshua and Cecil stepped inside, their sacks at their sides, heads down to shield their garish makeup. They moved past the kitchen, still bustling at 1 AM. They stopped at a closet, opened its door to conceal themselves. Each took a silver tray from his sack, along with a wig and gloves.

They had used this blackface stunt before, not only for the irony of it. It worked like a jujitsu move, turning the victims' race attitudes in favor of Joshua and Cecil. If the robbers were in blackface, they had to be white men, right? Colored men didn't put on blackface and wigs. So that was the description that would travel from the robbery.

Joshua felt his heart begin to race. He slowed his breathing and emptied his mind. His whole life turned on the next twenty minutes. If the plan worked, then he'd be in London with Violet in a week, get married, start his business, and wait for the baby. If the plan failed . . . no point thinking about that. He'd thought through some of the dozens of ways things could go wrong and how to deal with each. But they weren't going to go wrong.

He led Cecil down a side passage. "Hey, buddy," a voice came from a room they passed, "how's about a fresh drink?" Joshua and Cecil kept walking, hoping the man was so drunk he hadn't noticed the makeup and wigs.

They stole up a service staircase and entered the upstairs corridor, advancing on their toes. A colored maid carrying towels came out of a room. She gasped and stared, wide-eyed. Joshua held a finger to his lips. She scurried back into the room and closed the door behind her. They paused at the end of the hall. Joshua peered around a corner.

The man sitting next to the door of suite 201 was studying the *Daily Racing Form*. His cigarette smoldered in one hand. Joshua took Cecil's tray from him and put it under his arm with his own. He nodded. After three running strides, Cecil had the barrel of his pistol against the guard's cheek. Staring at two armed men in blackface, the man froze as the newspaper slid off his lap. Cecil used his free hand to haul him up by the front of his suit.

Joshua reached for the doorknob.

The wind filled Fraser's ears. It was strong enough to tilt the cornstalks, heavy with ripe ears. Feeling itchy, wondering where Speed was, he got out and walked up the road toward the Brook. He and Speed hadn't set up any specific rendezvous. He couldn't think of anything to do except poke around, trying not to be seen by any of Rothstein's men. When an engine approached from behind, he ducked into the tall corn. The car curved past the Brook. Fraser resumed his exploration, crossing to the casino side of the road.

Reaching the edge of the curve, where the front lawn of the casino began, he knelt down to take in the scene. The Brook wasn't all that impressive from this angle. Fraser decided it must extend away from the road. A low social hum carried through the wind. Cars came and left, all in the direction of Saratoga, though it was past midnight. A porch light showed two men loitering in languid poses, cigarette smoke curling around them. In France, Fraser had heard from the soldiers that the quiet men often were the most violent, the bloodiest fighters.

"You fixing to make yourself a target?" Cook's low voice came from behind him, from the far side of the road. Fraser couldn't see him. "In the ditch," came the further hiss. "Where you should be."

Fraser did as directed. The grass in the ditch was wet. "Atell's in there. What's going on?" he asked.

"They're doing it tonight."

"Jiminy Cricket."

Cook smiled into the night. "No cause to go blaspheming."

"What're we doing?"

"Not sure. The boy wouldn't tell me much." A car pulled down the long drive from the Brook and turned toward Saratoga. They flattened against the side of the ditch until it was gone. "How far's your car away?"

"A couple hundred yards that way." Fraser pointed.

"That's good. Right direction." After a moment's pause, he started again. "For getting away, they must have a car stashed, be planning to head straight north to Canada. On the getaway, that's when they'll be vulnerable. The surprise'll wear off. Rothstein's probably got a dozen gunsels around here. They'll be angry, hot to show the boss how good they are. When our boys take off, heading up to Canada, that's where you and me maybe can help."

# Chapter 23

Joshua burst through the door, throwing the trays against the wall to make maximum noise, their cymbal-like clatter both jarring and confusing. Cecil pushed the guard to the floor, then spun on another who sat inside the door, hitting him flush in the face with the pistol barrel. That one fell, deadweight. Joshua's voice rang out: "Hands on the table, chilluns!"

The cardplayers looked into the barrels of two German pistols. Cecil strode to the table, while Joshua announced, "My friend here'll take your guns. If you sit nice and quiet, I won't shoot you." Cecil held out his sack. Some grudgingly, some quickly, the gamblers gave up their guns. Cecil carried the nearly full sack over to Joshua. He lifted the guns from the guards on the floor and added those to the sack, then left it at the door.

"Now the cash," Joshua called out. "Don't make us wait. My friend gets very impatient! Ain't nothing in your pockets worth dying over. Don't sweat the jewelry. Just cash."

Cecil grabbed the bills on the table and stuffed them into a second sack. Then he circled the table demanding wallets.

"I don't know who you are," Rothstein snarled, color flooding his usually pallid face, "but you're going to be one sorry son of a bitch."

"Wait, massah—I almost forgots. Y'all need to stand up now. Just you." He waggled the gun at Rothstein and adopted a singsong tone. "Now, please, suh, would you step back from the table, maybe three giant steps." Rothstein retreated about half the prescribed distance. Joshua nodded. Cecil pulled up the carpet under the gambling boss's chair. Rothstein's complexion neared purple while Cecil opened a compartment in the floor and scooped up a newly revealed wad of bills. That casino worker had told Joshua about Rothstein's hidey-hole.

Cecil backed toward the doorway, gun in one hand and money sack in the other. Joshua picked up the bag of guns and said, "Y'all's gonna want to count to one hundred before doing anything, seeing how our partner is directly outside this door, holding two guns. He sho' 'nuf has bullets aplenty to shoot anyone's coming out this room, leastways the first fourteen of 'em. If you wants to stay healthy, I suggest you be the fifteenth."

The two men backed out and closed the door behind them. Joshua turned the lock with the key from inside the door. They dashed to an open window at the end of the short hall. Joshua tossed out the sack of guns. Each man dropped from the window frame to the ground. Cecil never let go of the bag of money.

They sprinted across the lawn to the trees, skirting lighted areas. Angry voices burst from the building.

From the ditch across the road, Cook heard the shouts. The men on the front porch pulled out their weapons and jumped into the night. Gunshots and muzzle flashes showed their progress across the lawn. The chances of hitting a running form in the dark were close to zero. "They're cutting through the woods," Cook said to Fraser, pulling him up by the arm. "Let's go."

Cook and Fraser jog-trotted around the curve toward the Stutz. They heard an engine roar in the woods on their left. "That's them," Cook said. A large car broke from the trees and veered their way. Cook pulled Fraser into the ditch. He didn't want to spook the boys, draw their fire as they sped past. Then Fraser and Cook climbed up on the road. Both were gasping when they got to the car and got it running. Cook hopped in as Fraser started in the direction the boys were going—north toward Canada.

"Follow them," Cook said, "but not fast."

"You're sure it's them?"

"Who else?" Cook craned his neck to look for the pursuit. "Get in the middle of the road." Fraser did. "Weave back and forth, not regular. You're drunk. We both are." He pulled out a flask and splashed liquor on both of them.

The next seconds, while Fraser wobbled the Stutz down the road, keeping his speed low, seemed to take forever. How could professional hoodlums be so slow? Finally, they heard a car engine. No, several engines. "Okay now," Cook said. "We're still drunk."

A car roared up and tried to pass on the left. Fraser swung left to block it, then jerked right, as though recovering from a surprise swerve, then turned back left before the car behind could pass. The driver behind hit the horn, hard. Then again. Fraser turned the wheel in response, as if startled, but still held the center of the road.

When the trailing car pulled right, Fraser slid that way. The honking became more frantic. A second horn joined. Fraser jerked the wheel from side to side, in no rhythm, as if in panic. "Good," Cook said. "Hang on."

Fraser veered left to block the second car, which had pulled out to pass both the Stutz and the first car. For a moment, the two pursuing cars advanced side by side. The second car fell back, no longer honking. More seconds passed. Then Fraser heard tires squeal. An engine roared to its limit.

One of the cars smashed into the Stutz's rear and kept accelerating, heaving Fraser into the windshield. He didn't register the smack of skull against glass—it was the steering wheel in his chest that took his breath, then hurt like blazes. Then his brain didn't work so well. He snapped back into his seat, fingers holding the steering wheel but controlling nothing. The Stutz leaned right, then jammed itself into the roadside ditch with another lurch that sent Fraser back against the windshield.

Dazed, Fraser saw a thought float by, wondered what it was. Yes, that's it, cars explode in crashes. He should get out. He pawed his door, wondering where the handle had gone, then heard noises behind him. He swiveled his head to see, a motion that sent a stab of pain through his neck and head. He groaned. Men were jumping out of cars on the road. One was a blue Cadillac. The men had pistols. They ran toward the Stutz.

"Don't shoot! Don't shoot!" he tried to say, but his voice was weak. He lifted his arms in surrender.

Another car engine blasted. A shouted voice surged, indistinct, then faded after the car passed. A flashlight blinded him. More shouts came from behind it.

Squinting against the glare, Fraser asked, "What's going on?" Cotton batting circled his head. The world was slow. Noises muffled. "We, we . . ." The words were in his head. He had to catch up to them. "My friend," he got out, "my friend and I, we, you know, were in town." No one answered. "I'm a doctor," he said. Why did he say that? Some sort of general claim on the goodwill of the universe?

A man leaned down and screamed something at him. Fraser still couldn't make out any words. When the flashlight moved off his face, he looked through flaring circles. Then a face loomed up. It had a Vandyke beard. Maybe it did. Fraser couldn't be sure. There was a metallic taste in his mouth.

The shouts separated into words. "Stop screwing around! Get after those guys!"

Two gunmen turned and started back to their car. A third jammed a gun barrel into Fraser's chest. Yes, definitely a Vandyke beard. "Fucking dumb civilians. You and your friend, count yourselves lucky we don't shoot you and leave you here to die. Goddamned lushes." He waved the gun at Cook. "Your nigger friend's gone way over his limit."

Fraser looked over. Cook had been quiet the whole time. That wasn't usual. He wasn't moving. Cracks spiderwebbed the windshield on that side. Cook's head must have hit it hard.

"Hey," Fraser said, "he's hurt." He looked over at the beard. "Help us! Please! He needs a hospital."

"This is your friend's lucky day, Doc. I'm not shooting him and you're a doctor."

# Chapter 24

Cecil pulled the sleek touring car into the farm lot and stopped behind a large willow. A worn-looking Chevrolet stood there, next to an unhitched plow. He and Joshua wiped the makeup off their faces. They changed into worn overalls they had bought from a Brooklyn church that ran clothing drives for the poor. They threw their blackened towels and clothes into a small stream that ran behind the lot.

Joshua pulled a bottle of moonshine from the old Chevy. They took turns rinsing their mouths out with the bad liquor. "Don't go lighting any cigarettes around me," Cecil said with a smile, their first words since fleeing the poker room.

"Tell you what, brother," Cecil continued. "This is looking okay. Don't mean to jinx it, but did you see their faces? Those were some surprised badmen. It was a treat to see them scared."

Cecil climbed into the Chevy. Joshua froze holding the door handle.

Cecil leaned over. "We got to move."

"Who was in that car behind us?"

"The one pulled out after we took off?"

"Yeah. It was a big one."

"Don't know. I wasn't calling the roll. Innocent bystanders, I guess. Come on. We got to go."

Joshua didn't move. "Innocent bystanders don't hang around outside the Brook after midnight." He hit the car roof with his open palm. "Dammit. I bet it was my father." He leaned into the car. "Listen, he could be hurt."

"Josh, we've already spent too long talking. Going back? That's the worst idea you ever had. We just cleaned out Rothstein. We made his boys look stupid. They're coming now, lots of 'em, and they're loaded for bear. You got a sweet little girl to worry about, a baby coming, all our plans."

Joshua still didn't move. "Come on!" Cecil called. "Even if that was your daddy—and you don't know that—he's a volunteer. He picked his poison. Anyway, he's a rough tough character, didn't you tell me that enough times?"

When Joshua remained where he was, Cecil raised his voice. "Get in the damned car. We need to make tracks, right now. We're some country Negroes drank too much and can't seem to find Glens Falls, hard as we try."

Joshua got into the car. Cecil had them on the road before the door was closed. He started driving slowly and unsteadily north.

Cook was slumped against the door of Fraser's Stutz. Fraser tried to open the passenger-side door to get to him, but it was stuck. To get at Cook from his own seat, Fraser stretched on his side, the steering wheel jammed into his back, legs hanging out the door. He tried to look Cook over in the darkness.

Cook's breathing was shallow, his pupils dilated. Fraser could feel swelling at the top of Cook's forehead, where his hairline had once started. Cook must have leaned over to brace himself, then got thrown straight into the windshield, unable to break the momentum with his hands.

Cook's torso began to spasm. He vomited yellow, oily-looking liquid onto his shirt. Fraser squirmed to reach his handkerchief. He tried to mop up. An acrid stench filled the car. Nothing from inside the human body smelled very good. Fraser wriggled out of the car and took off his jacket. He knelt on the driver's seat and draped the jacket over Cook.

He fought to clear his head. They were stuck in the middle of nowhere, yet way too close to the Brook. He'd have to flag down a passing car, but it was a lonesome stretch of road at a lonesome time of night. Also, anyone driving by could be connected to Rothstein.

Cook groaned. His eyelids flickered. "Where?" he mumbled. "Where am I?"

Fraser leaned over to look into Cook's eyes. "A few miles toward Glens Falls," he said. "We got run off the road by Rothstein's thugs. You hit your head."

Cook groaned again. "Not such a great plan, eh?"

"Not for us, but maybe we helped Joshua. No sign yet they've caught him."

Cook's eyes fell closed. He panted for a few seconds. "Hope so." After a couple of more breaths, he winced as he tried to sit up straighter, but couldn't. "I'm done, Jamie."

"You're not gonna cash in your chips in a boring old car crash. That's nowhere near glorious enough for Speedwell Cook." He gripped Cook's shoulder, meaning to be reassuring. "I'll flag down a car and get us to a hospital. Maybe there's a farmhouse around here where I can get help."

Fraser tried to help Cook get more comfortable, pulling him from the gap between the seat and the door. "Better?" he asked.

Cook nodded. Then he seemed to black out again. His breathing got shallower. Fraser couldn't make up his mind. Wandering around the countryside in search of a friendly farmer meant leaving Cook in pretty shaky shape. He couldn't see any lights, any sign of nearby people. It had to be three or four miles back to the Brook, but he could hardly go there. A passing car, that was their best chance. But there hadn't been any. Not yet, anyway. And Rothstein's men might come by from either direction.

Cook grunted and started awake, eyes wide. "Speed," Fraser said, "I'm here."

Cook tried to take a deep breath but it broke up halfway. He looked right at Fraser. "Something I didn't do, what I came to Saratoga for. Need to get an IOU from Attell and Rothstein. It's Babe's. That's the job for Babe. I told your wife about it."

"Come on, Speed. Babe's got plenty of money. Why doesn't he just pay it off?"

Cook pulled down his mouth at the edges. "Won't let him. Ran the interest so it's more'n even he can cover. They . . . they want him on the string. Bad for the Babe. Bad for baseball." He stopped and licked his lips, his eyes drifting closed. He opened them. "There's something else, too. Some other hold, other thing they got. He won't say, not to me, but I think so."

"What do you care? Aren't you the guy they threw out of baseball, the one who thinks they should all go to hell?"

Cook grabbed Fraser's arm with his old catcher's hand, still powerful. "I took this on. It's important for Babe, for the game. For me. You get it back. He'll pay you." Cook relaxed his grip. "Give the money to the baby."

Fraser's eyes blurred. "Sure. I'll do what I can."

Cook gave a half smile. "Don't do what you can. Get it."

Fraser nodded. "Yeah, okay."

Time passed, not that much. Cook grunted. "What is it?" Fraser asked.

Cook still had the half smile on his face. "Could be a funny-looking baby, if it looks like you or me."

"The baby'll be perfect. You'll see."

* * *

By the time a car came by, Cook had been dead for a while. Fraser didn't try to wave it down. He stayed in his seat, next to his friend.

They sat together until morning light, when a passing truck driver stopped to see what was wrong.

# Chapter 25

A man in a loose brown suit pointed Fraser to a church down the block. The stone structure of Abyssinian Baptist, topped by four spires and a pyramid crest, announced respectability. Fraser squinted against the high white sky as his eye followed the spires up. Except in the shade, the day was warm.

Inside the church, balconies circled three sides of a broad worship space. A choir loft rose behind the altar, a bank of stained glass windows beyond. White lilies swanned next to the pulpit. Joshua had sent a wire asking Fraser to arrange for flowers. He wired money to pay for everything. He couldn't come, of course. Rothstein's men might be watching. Joshua's telegram to his mother had been awful. "The sins of the son," it said, "visited upon the father. I'm so sorry."

Fraser wondered if Speed had ever been in this building. They had never exchanged a religious word. One of a thousand subjects he and Speed never talked about. What would be a better place for this service? The Catholic Protectory Oval up in the Bronx? Anyway, funerals were for the living, not the dead. Aurelia picked the church, probably for what it would say about Speed. That he was a man of substance. A serious man. Not the full picture, but part of it.

"You're here for the Cook service?"

Fraser pivoted to the soft southern accent. He took a hand extended by a man nearly his height. "Adam Powell. I'm pastor here."

"Mr. Powell, how do you do." Fraser was off balance. Surely this Harlem church had a Negro minister, but Mr. Powell wasn't any more Negro than Fraser was.

"How are you, sir? You didn't suffer any injuries from the crash?"

"Nothing serious, no." The pastor's eyes told him that the question came from kindness, but Fraser felt the accusation behind it. Speed Cook died and the white man lived. An old story.

"Such a shame that Brother Cook's son can't be here."

"Yes," Fraser said. "Yes. He's in Europe. Business. He's very regretful."

Pastor Powell showed Fraser to a reception room off the altar. Fraser shook hands with colored men in somber suits, white shirts, dark ties. Every one of them respectable, even the ones who looked like baseball men.

Fraser thought one was Cannonball Dick Redding, who had pitched against the Babe, but he let it go. Not the time or the place. The same for the small, balding fellow with a close-clipped beard, Doctor Du Bois, who had made Cook so angry when they were in Paris two years back. Fraser didn't feel like paying court to a great man.

He went to Aurelia. She sat near the coffin in a red plush chair. Leaning over, Fraser grasped her arms gently and spoke empty words of comfort, the ones he always used. Ones he had probably said to her before over the last few days. Her eyes flickered up, registered who he was, then went back to the middle distance. He and Aurelia had rarely spoken until five days ago, when he placed a scratchy call from Saratoga Springs that took three operators and ten minutes to set up. They had since stumbled through this bad dream together. Speed's younger brother had showed up a couple of days before, but he wasn't much help. He was taking the loss hard.

Fraser, the survivor, had dealt with the shoals of policemen, the coroner, arranging to bring Speed to New York and then to this church. What would go on inside the church, that was all Aurelia. She and her daughter never showed Fraser anything other than firm self-possession. Their grief was their grief, not anyone else's. Certainly not his.

Fraser could no longer avoid the gleaming walnut box. It was too small for the man Fraser knew, but there he was, eyes closed, a serene expression molded onto his dark face. Fraser would have preferred an angry glare, maybe an ironic twist to the mouth or the intense gaze Speed got when he was planning something. But this expression, not one Fraser could remember seeing, made the point that Speed was gone. It wasn't him.

Aurelia had rejected the undertaker's suggestion that Speed be buried in a new suit. His black suit was brushed and pressed but still old and worn. She chose the music, the prayers, the speakers, declaring that they were what he would have wanted.

"Doctor Fraser." It was the pastor again. "We have refreshments." He gestured to a small table covered with cakes and cookies. "You might fortify yourself. The service will be long. There's much to remember about Brother Cook."

Fraser nodded. He chose a sugar cookie. The sweetness flooded his mouth. Did Speed like sugar cookies? He had no idea. Fraser felt like an impostor, portraying the trusted friend in whose arms Speed Cook died.

It turned out that Pastor Powell knew his business. The service stretched on and on, numbing Fraser with endless words and heart-churning music. He recognized some of the songs—"Swing Low, Sweet Chariot," "Just a Closer Walk with Thee"—though he didn't join in. He liked those songs in variety shows, but they were different here, no longer pleasing tunes. Here they pulled him down.

Seated with the other honorary pallbearers, Fraser felt conspicuous, surrounded by faces that ranged from beige to purple black. He imagined himself an anthropologist adrift in a new culture, one no less foreign than the tribes of the Kalahari. A handsome gray-haired man with a deep, sonorous voice delivered the eulogy. He described someone Fraser didn't know. A generous, openhanded man who was never too busy to help others, who felt every injury and indignity suffered by his race and fought to stop them. Was the eulogist tidying up the furious and sarcastic and always competent man that Fraser knew? Or had Speed shown only one part of himself to Fraser across the barrier of race? Or was that all that Fraser could see?

Moving down the center aisle behind the actual pallbearers, Fraser felt even more conspicuous, a clumsy goose among sleek ravens. On the street, a phalanx of Negroes stood in crisp military uniforms. Two, probably in charge, sported plumed hats from the age of Lord Nelson. Sunlight glinted off gold epaulets and brass buttons. Scabbards hung from their belts.

A man wearing an armband gestured him to an open car. Fraser wedged in between two beefy gents who seemed like former ballplayers. Another sat in the front, next to the driver. It was hot in their suits, in the sun, waiting for the miserable ride to the cemetery.

The man on Fraser's left turned his head and spoke. "I understand you were with Speed," he said. "At the end."

Fraser nodded, noticing that the fellow was older than he had first thought. He was about Fraser's age. "Yes," he said.

"I'm glad he wasn't alone."

"Did you play with him? With Speed?"

The man shook his head. "Don't know anyone who played *with* Speed Cook. You played *for* that man." He leaned ahead to look across Fraser. "Isn't that right, Jerome?"

"Amen," the other said.

"So," Fraser said, "he was your manager? Or the team owner?"

"Hell, no," the man smiled. "Just a teammate. Too long ago. But I played for him just the same. Isn't that right, Jerome?"

"Uh-huh."

Fraser leaned back in his seat and introduced himself. Pete Johnson, the man on his left, had played outfield in Detroit and Cleveland. Jerome Hill had pitched. Both lived in Philadelphia now.

"I'm curious," Fraser said, turning his head from one to the other. "What kind of ballplayer was he?"

The conversation lasted all the way to Queens, then after, when Fraser and his two new friends got something to eat and to drink. They talked into the evening.

The empty feeling had Fraser in its grip. Everything had come at him so fast, and then he was completely alone—Speed dead, Joshua and Violet and Eliza on the other side of the ocean. He was waiting for Eliza to send word for him to join them, or that she'd be coming back, but she never said. She must not know yet. They had made no real plans for themselves after Violet turned their world upside down. He didn't know if Eliza would stay in England until the baby was born, or maybe she would bring Violet home if Joshua . . . didn't work out. Maybe Fraser would join them for a while in England. Or not. Or maybe they would all stay in England forever and ever after.

He went to the institute and saw patients. He tried with them. But the research part of his day, he didn't even try with that. He avoided his colleagues, a course that drew no real notice. Antisocial behavior among medical researchers was hardly worthy of notice. Eliza had recruited Uncle Wilfred to look after her theatrical agency during her absence. Though Wilfred seemed a dubious choice, Fraser would have been a far worse one, so he followed his longtime practice of leaving such matters alone.

His spirits rose when each letter from Eliza arrived. In one, she reported cheerfully about the wedding, a civil ceremony that almost didn't happen when a British official demanded to see the groom's passport. After traveling through Canada under an alias, Joshua had no passport to offer. A hurried trip to the American consulate established that the Englishman was wrong. America's passport requirement had expired with the war. On the following day, armed with an explanation on official USA letterhead, the couple was married. It made Fraser sad that he hadn't been there. Eliza mentioned no problem over the races of the bride and groom. None of her letters mentioned race. Fraser didn't know if that meant there were no problems, that England was proving everything that Joshua had hoped it would be. He allowed himself to hope so.

The three of them had taken a furnished flat in an unfashionable neighborhood. Joshua wanted to live frugally until the liquor-exporting business was up and running, though Fraser knew he must be sitting on a great deal of Rothstein's cash. It probably was best not to flash that around, draw attention from the wrong sort. The women spent most days sightseeing while Joshua scouted for office space and worked out purchasing and shipping arrangements. Many nights they went to shows in complimentary seats provided by Eliza's London theater connections.

Beyond Joshua's frugality, Eliza didn't mention money problems. It seemed that Joshua had gotten away with it. Fraser hoped that he and Speed had helped. Did that make him a criminal, too? Was it a crime to help someone steal from criminals? The questions didn't interest him much. He had done it for Violet. That was enough.

Was the money worth Speed's life? Speed might think so, but then he had some funny ideas. Knowing how the question haunted Joshua, Fraser wrote directly to him about his father's death, so he would know the truth. And so he would understand that Speed always chose what he did, no one could stop him, and that in this case he would do it again.

Joshua's note back was short, nearly curt. Fraser tried not to mind. Haunting questions, guilty ones about those closest to you, didn't yield to logic. Fraser still hated how oblivious he had been as a boy during his father's final illness, how inept he was when he lost Ginny and their baby in a single terrible night back in Ohio. The logical explanations—that he had been a small boy, that he did his best during Ginny's childbirth—cut no ice with his accuser. Himself.

Eliza's letters said nothing about when they might come home. Nor did she urge him to join them. She must be waiting for things with Violet and Joshua to settle, for her own mind to settle. He envied her. At least she was with the others. After reading each letter, he felt more alone than when he opened it. He tried to keep that feeling out of his letters back, but it must have seeped in. His were much shorter. He had less news.

Fraser started going for nighttime walks along the Hudson, trying to quiet his mind so he could fall asleep. He had strolled those piers with Eliza when he first came to New York. He seemed to pass more toughs there now, men left behind in the mad race to get rich, but they didn't bother him. He had picked up the New York walk, the one that told would-be criminals you would be too much trouble, they should try someone else.

Even after the riverside strolls he slept poorly, waking up every hour or two, chasing some anxious thought about Speed, or Eliza, or Violet, or the baby. If it was 4 AM or later, he went ahead and started his day. Sometimes he walked in the early morning, too.

About two weeks after the funeral, Fraser stopped at a corner on a dawn walk. He looked down. He wore the pants of one suit with the jacket from another. He turned back and watched morning spread over Manhattan like a laundered sheet. The light came gradually, striking a different window as each moment passed, revealing another building he hadn't noticed before. The buildings turned colors, starting in blueblack murk, then finding gray, then revealing their true colors as the sun breached the horizon and forced him to shade his eyes.

Fraser kicked at a stone on the pavement. It went a few feet. He stepped and swung his leg again. The stone skittered down the walkway. He thought for the thirtieth time about what Cook had asked him at the end, the business with the Babe Ruth IOU. Speed had cared about it. He said that it might save baseball. That sounded so melodramatic, not much like Speed, who wore his cynicism like armor, the better to shield his dreams.

No matter how many times Fraser shoved the Babe's IOU from his mind, it came back. He felt paralyzed about it, not knowing where to start. Talk to Abe Attell? To Rothstein? Where would he find them? What would he say? Why would they talk to him? Speed would have known answers to those questions, or at least would have made some damned good guesses. Also, he wouldn't have been so gutless.

Fraser started walking toward his building. Babe, he realized, was the place to start. Speed made the deal with Babe. The ballplayer knew Attell and Rothstein well enough to land up to his armpits in debt to them. And Babe was a neighbor at the Ansonia. Fraser would stake out the lobby until the Babe showed up. Nothing easier.

# Chapter 26

The air felt cool, like autumn, at least it did when the breeze carried away the cigar smoke of the grandstand. The beginning of a change in season matched Fraser's change in strategy for buttonholing the Babe. He had sat for three nights in the Ansonia's lobby without even a sighting of the baseball star. The building's staff, generally indulgent of its high-paying tenants, was growing wary of one who spent his nights in a lobby chair, reading and dozing. So now Fraser was trying to track the Babe down at the ballpark. That was the one time and the one place he could be sure to find Babe Ruth.

The Saturday doubleheader had sounded like a good idea, but was turning out to be a whole lot of baseball. Fraser's rear end ached. His scorecard lay on the concrete floor, wedged against the metal leg of the seat in front of him, untouched since the second inning of the second game. Six times he had climbed over the men seated between him and the aisle in order to stretch his legs and salve his restlessness. Ballpark etiquette barred another such expedition for at least two more innings.

Absentmindedly, he fingered the note to Ruth in his pocket.

He had composed it before the doubleheader started. It said that a relative of Speed Cook's wanted to report on Cook's work for Ruth. Fraser planned to give it to a clubhouse worker when the second game finally ended. He hoped Babe would be intrigued enough to see him.

Nothing in these games with the Philadelphia Athletics held much baseball significance. The Yankees had clinched the American League pennant and were going to the World Series. They held a six-run lead in this game. A trickle of homeward bound fans began in the fifth inning and grew at the end of each half inning. It was a lot of baseball. In the top of the eighth, a buzz started among the remaining few. Men nudged their neighbors and pointed. Fraser sat forward. The Babe was walking out to the pitcher's mound, coming in as a relief pitcher. He had hardly pitched all year. Fraser had never seen the star slugger during his pitching days.

From the mound, Ruth's powerful frame loomed over home plate, a mere sixty feet, six inches away. His windup was spare but his demeanor was downright frisky. Smiling, he shouted to the first batter as he stepped up to the plate. The crowd's mood rose with the Babe's. This was going to be fun!

But it wasn't. The Athletics hadn't scored for seven innings, but they found Babe's pitches irresistible. Line drives flew off their bats in every direction. Runners flashed from base to base and started to cross the plate. Ruth's smile turned to a scowl. He muttered and kicked the pitcher's mound after every hit. The score narrowed to 6–3, then 6–5. Why didn't Yankee Manager Huggins put another pitcher in? The big man clearly had no magic in his left arm that day. Huggins made no move. The cavalry never came. Babe finally got the third out, but not until the Athletics tied the game, 6–6.

The manager showed no mercy for the game's greatest home-run hitter, sending Ruth out to pitch the ninth inning, too. Ruth's demeanor was all business this time. He got three outs before any Philadelphias could score, hanging on to the tie score. Ruth shut them down again in the tenth and the eleventh. In the bottom of that inning, the Yanks finally pushed the winning run across the plate. Heading for the exits, smiling fans chattered to each other. They knew they might have seen the last game Babe Ruth would ever pitch.

When the clubhouse man reported that Ruth would see him, Fraser found the star on a folding chair in the clubhouse, a stormy expression on his face and an unlit stogie in his mouth.

"Say, kid," he snarled at Fraser, "what is this? You don't look like no relative of Speed Cook."

Fraser held out his hands in a calming gesture. They'd met before, more than once. Ruth's way—treating everyone like he knew them—made it hard to know if he actually did know you. "It's a long story, Babe. You heard that Speed died?"

"Yeah," Ruth said, "I heard. Tough luck."

"I was there, when it happened." Ruth looked up. "The last thing he said was about a job he was doing for you, getting something back for you. It seemed important to him."

"Yeah," Babe said, leaning back and eyeing Fraser. "So?"

"Do you still need it?"

The Babe grimaced and looked Fraser up and down. "No offense, kid, but you ain't exactly the type for the job he was doing. I got places to be." Ruth turned away and then turned back. "Say, that wasn't why that coon got killed, was it? Doing the job for me?"

"That wasn't it," Fraser said. "It was a car accident."

Babe nodded. "That's good. I mean, not good, but I wouldn't want to be why he croaked."

Fraser decided to try again. "Listen, I worked with Speed on other jobs. Don't get fooled by the suit."

Ruth shook his head. "What do you think you can do about it?"

"You'll still pay for what he was trying to get?"

"Sure, sure, kid." Ruth stood and started unbuttoning his jersey. The clubhouse was emptying fast. "Do you know *why* I needed him to get it?"

"Speed didn't say, but I'm guessing it has something to do with you not wanting to be involved with certain people, with the baseball commissioner and the Black Sox business."

"Who would?"

"My other guess is that there's something more behind it, something more than just gambling."

Ruth stopped in his undressing. "Don't hurt yourself guessing. It won't help anything." He reached for matches and started to light his cigar. When it was burning, he narrowed his eyes. "Do I know you?"

"No, not really." Fraser stepped closer to Ruth and lowered his voice. "If I get it, what you want, I want the money to go to Cook's family."

"Sure, kid. Once the money's out of my pocket, it can go to Old Mother Hubbard, all I care."

"Where do I find these people, the ones you need to get it from?"

Babe gave him a disgusted look. "Listen, if you don't know where to find them, you definitely ain't the man for the job." He turned his back and shrugged out of the shirt, dropping it on the floor. Fraser thought for a moment.

"Who else is working on this problem for you?"

"Doc, these guys aren't your strong suit. No fooling."

The "Doc" showed that Babe was starting to remember him. Fraser decided to push. "I'm thinking you've got nothing here. I'm bidding against nothing. You're just sitting around with your eyes closed, hoping nothing bad happens. Speed was your only move, and now he's gone. Let me make that move for you. If I come up empty, what've you lost? Just get me started. Where do I find them?"

Ruth took a silk shirt off a hanger and pulled it over his thick shoulders. “All right. It could be your funeral. Remember I told you.” Fraser nodded. “You know Lefty’s, on Broadway, right there at Times Square?”

“I’ve been there.”

“Rear booth, on the left. Every morning of the year, as long as he’s in town.”

“Just walk in the front door?”

“Best way I know to get inside. You may not get real long to talk. He’s not a patient guy. You should know what you want to say.”

# Chapter 27

Turning sideways past waitresses and customers, Fraser worked down the left-hand side of Lefty's. He held his furled umbrella next to his leg so it wouldn't drip on anyone. Halfway down the aisle, he caught a glimpse of a man in the last booth. That had to be Rothstein. Fraser stopped to shake out his umbrella again, using the pause to get a better look at his quarry.

Reputation, not appearance, drew his eye to the gambling king. Neither large nor small, Rothstein had a high forehead, bland features, a small mouth. The short hair was combed carefully. His dark-colored bow tie was knotted tight. His suit was equally dull. He stared impassively at two men across from him, not saying anything. He could have been an accountant preparing for a day reviewing receivables.

When Fraser began to move, a hulking figure who badly needed a shave stepped from a side booth. This domesticated gorilla placed a palm against Fraser's chest. "Hey, pal," he said. His voice sounded like it was scraped over a cheese grater. "Where ya think you're going?"

Meeting the gorilla's gaze, Fraser said, "I have a matter with

Mr. Rothstein." He moved to get by. The other man shifted to block him. His hands were large and blunt, perfect for clenching into fists.

"Who are you?"

"Doctor James Fraser." Medical credentials might not help here, but what could they hurt?

"Does he know you?" The gorilla disdainfully looked Fraser over.

"I'm a friend of Speed Cook."

Fraser said the name as though the gorilla should recognize it, but he couldn't tell if it registered or not. The other man nodded at an empty booth. "Try the coffee. I'll see if the boss wants to see you."

Fraser sat so he retained his view of Rothstein. At regular intervals, the people facing the gambler were replaced by new supplicants. They never stayed long. Slightly reassured to be in the great man's waiting room, he ordered a coffee and a cruller. The pastry, with a generous dusting of powdered sugar, tasted good going down but then sat in his stomach like a stone. He tried to act nonchalant as the petitioners continued the parade to the rear booth. What were all those conversations about? Inside tips on races and prizefights? Sure. Schemes for cheating and stealing from an employer? Maybe. Gambling debts that couldn't be met for a few more days, or longer? Definitely.

The gorilla nodded at Fraser. Brushing powdered sugar off his vest and pants, Fraser rose. He gathered himself. He intended to be all dignity and self-possession, unfazed by the humiliating wait for a few precious moments with the Great Rothstein.

Not two steps from his booth, Fraser froze. Rothstein was leaving through a back corridor, presumably headed to an alleyway exit. What gave? Fraser's temper began to rise. This was a step down from humiliation to full-fledged mortification.

Abe Attell emerged from the same corridor that had swallowed Rothstein. He gestured for Fraser to join him in Rothstein's booth. Fraser, uncertain, sat. Attell waved for the waitress and ordered a coffee. Fraser passed.

Attell rearranged the sugar bowl and cream pitcher, pushing them to the side. "You got a lot of nerve, brother."

"What?"

"You coming in here to talk about Speed Cook? We ain't stupid, pal. We figured out it was Cook's nigger kid up in Saratoga. That kid's got bad habits, likes to take stuff that ain't his. The way I think, we got no business with you but to tip you upside down and shake till the money falls out. But the boss, he's cooler than me. He says I should hear you out. I figure there's always time for you to learn your lesson."

Fraser fought for his footing. He had intended to talk to Rothstein, not Attell. And he expected a business conversation, not threats. Attell wouldn't have talked to Speed this way. Fraser decided to act like Attell hadn't said anything. "Cook was talking to you about a debt from the Babe."

Attell cocked his head and smirked. "You know, I don't got a lot of time to spend on the problems of dead niggers, much less ones whose kids are thieves."

"Mr. Rothstein wanted you to hear me out."

"Okay, you got ninety seconds." He wagged an index finger. "Start with the part where we get paid back, both the note that Niggerlips signed and the money that got stole."

"Speed Cook and I had nothing to do with any stealing. Nothing."

"Cook kicking the bucket three miles from the scene of the crime kinda blows a hole in that one. You're down to seventy-five seconds."

"What does Babe owe on the note?"

"We'd take seventy-five grand from the big ox, *plus* the money that got stole."

Fraser looked away from the table. That was why the problem was so big, why Babe called on Speed. Even Babe couldn't pay that much. The job—first for Cook and now for Fraser—was to get the IOU back without paying Rothstein's price. What was Speed thinking when he took it on? "How'd it get that big? That's nowhere close to what I heard."

Attell pulled out a pack of Lucky Strikes and lit one."Forty seconds. Babe knew the terms, what the interest was. What it always is. And he knows that this wasn't just money. It's what he was using it for, which no one's ever heard about. We held up our end on that. Nobody's ever heard. And that big ox knows we held up our end. His end is to pay up, not change the deal. Tell him that."

Attell puffed on his cigarette. He picked up the Luckies and matchbook. "Time's up. Lesson's next."

Fraser had come with only one card to play. "I'm thinking we can work a trade."

Attell let his eyelids droop and sat back. "Thirty seconds more, Doc."

"I'm a doctor, you know. . . ."

"That why they call you Doc?" Attell was having way too much fun.

"What about inside information on the medical condition of the Yanks, of the Babe? Wouldn't that be valuable to someone in your line of work?"

Attell smiled and shook his head. "What is it with you? You think you're dealing with children? We get the lowdown on the Yanks, on everyone."

Fraser waved a hand dismissively. "From clubhouse boys, towel jockeys, sportswriters. Even the players, even the Babe, they can't tell you what you can learn from a doctor who's on the inside, one from the Rockefeller Institute, who's seeing the players close up." He leaned forward. "Listen. You've got the World Series coming up, the Giants against the Yanks. Every game right here in New York, every New York fan crazy to get a bet down on his team. Business is going to be brisk. They'll bet on everything, on how many times the Babe takes his cap off. The sort of information I'm talking about would be very useful. I have the expertise, and I have the access. There's nobody else can offer you both."

Attell took a drag on his smoke, then stubbed it out in Fraser's coffee cup. He shrugged. "Maybe no lesson today. How do I get word to you?"

"Leave a message at the Ansonia. You know it? Also"—Fraser held up a finger—"I'm trading for Cook's son, too."

Attell grinned, the sort of grin a wolf gives to a small lamb that's been separated from the flock. "Jesus, Doc, you got brass ones. Tell you what. You make us enough money to pay back for both, maybe we'll think about it."

Fraser smiled back.

He needed to talk to Babe. What the hell had he just done?

"What the hell do you think you're doing? Trying to get me on the hook for fixing another Series?"

Ruth looked exhausted at six in the morning. He had just stumbled into the Ansonia's lobby, where Fraser had been waiting for too many hours. The Babe's fedora was askew. His necktie hung in two limp lines. His suit begged for dry cleaning. It was hard to believe that this shambling wreck would lead the Yankees into the first game of the World Series in nine hours.

"You don't need to do anything, Babe. Nothing. Nothing involves you, even breathes on you. I'm the one who's in touch with these people. And nobody's talking about you throwing a game, throwing an out, or a single pitch. I'm simply going to trade information. Accurate information. The deal may not smell too great, but that's because of who I'm trading with and why. It shouldn't be illegal. Nothing like what the Black Sox did."

Babe scratched his cheek and yawned. Sensing indecision, Fraser pressed his point. "Look, you want to get something valuable back from some hard guys who know it's valuable. And you don't want to pay for it."

"I don't have the money!"

"Well, we've got to give them something. So this is something. And it doesn't cost you a dime."

Babe yawned again and stood. "Okay, Doc. Just don't fuck me up, okay?"

Fraser rose to be on Ruth's level. "Don't worry about that. But listen, to do this thing right, I need to be in and out of the clubhouse during the Series. I need to be *seen* getting in, you know what I mean? Seen by the smart guys. And they need to see me watching you during warm-ups, out on the field. Even during the games. So I need to be real visible out at the Polo Grounds."

The Babe started walking toward the elevator. "Okay?" Fraser called after him.

"Yeah, fine," Ruth said without turning his head. "Come to the clubhouse before the game."

# Chapter 28

By the second game of the Series, Fraser was starting to relax around the team. He arrived at the Polo Grounds hours before the first pitch. He sat by while players griped about their muscle pulls and bruises, helping out where he could. When it was time to warm up on the field, he followed them out. He took up a spot near the Yanks' dugout, arms folded, leaning against the railing. He kept his eyes nailed on the Babe.

The slugger got ready his own way. He shagged a few fly balls and played catch to warm up his arm, swapping tales with teammates about the night before. He was all business when it was his turn for batting practice. The whole park stopped to watch. Ruth usually aimed for the fences. When he tagged one, caught it full on the barrel of the bat, he held the corkscrew pose at the end of his swing and admired the ball's flight, its brave defiance of gravity.

Fraser liked the way the small manager, Huggins, kept his players on their toes. The man wasn't real warm. Pretty frosty, really. But he didn't miss much on a baseball field. Fraser also took a shine to the starting pitcher for the second game, Waite

Hoyt, a strapping kid from Brooklyn who couldn't be much older than Violet. His open face reflected every emotion that passed through him, beginning with the thrill of pitching in the World Series. The boy was just about jumping out of his skin.

And so were the fans. This Series was for the championship, sure, but it also was a class war, a battle for civic dominance. Giants fans affected the hauteur of aristocracy. After all, their team had been winning championships since the 1880s. In 1904, the Giants refused to play in the World Series because, they sniffed, the newly formed American League wasn't worthy of the effort. The 1921 Series was their sixth since then, but there were cracks in the foundation of their arrogance. The Giants had won only one of those World Series, something that drove their manager crazy. That was feisty John McGraw, the reigning genius of the baseball world, a fierce apostle of scratch-and-claw baseball. A perfect inning for McGraw was for his leadoff man to earn a walk, steal second, take third on a bunt, and score on a sacrifice fly. No hits, two outs, one run. He despised the power game of Babe Ruth and the Yankees. Sitting around and waiting for a slugger to hit home runs was stupid, McGraw thought, and unreliable. He was eager to prove it by winning the Series.

The Yankees were the brash newcomers. They'd been around only half as long, and had been renamed the Yankees a mere eight years before. They'd never won anything, never been in the World Series. They didn't even have their own ballpark, making do as renters in the Giants' Polo Grounds. But they had turned baseball upside down with the Babe and his prodigious clouts, with a whole new way to play the game. The man had clobbered fifty-nine home runs that season. That was more home runs than eight entire teams hit. Even die-hard Giants fans thrilled to watch him, this magical manchild who was remaking the game right before their eyes.

When the game began, Fraser took his reserved seat behind

the dugout. He watched Ruth when the slugger was on the field, but so did everyone else. The fans shouted to him when he trotted out to left field. They screamed for home runs when he came up to bat. Everyone stood when he stepped into the batter's box, hoping to see this force of nature work his will on the game they loved. While John McGraw seethed in the Giants dugout, Ruth commanded the ballfield.

The Yankees had a 1–0 lead when they took the field in the fifth inning. Fraser had noticed Abe Attell sitting in a box about two sections over, right behind home plate. Attell's box was three up from the one where Commissioner Landis presided, his features set in a permanent frown under a shock of flyaway white hair. Vice and virtue, a hundred feet apart. Vice looked to be having a better time.

Fraser didn't wave to Attell or nod in his direction. He knew Attell would look for him. He wanted the gambler to appreciate Fraser's privileged position with the Yanks, and with the Babe. He was pretty sure Attell had.

In this game, McGraw plainly had resolved that he wouldn't let Babe beat him. The first time Ruth came to the plate, the pitcher walked him on four pitches. Next time, same story. McGraw was out to show baseball that you can't win the game with home runs if the slugger never gets a pitch he can hit.

When Babe's third at-bat also ended with a base on balls, his frustration got the better of him. He stole second base cleanly, not even bothering to slide. The Yankee fans whooped and hollered in delight. You might keep the Babe from hitting home runs, they told each other, but he'd beat you another way, sure he would. Then the big man, showing surprising grace and speed for his size, stole third base, too, sliding in just ahead of the catcher's throw. The crowd went wild, screaming their lungs out, exulting in his daring.

By the end of the game, Yankee pitcher Waite Hoyt had channeled his excitement into an overpowering performance, shutting the Giants out and giving the Yanks a 2–0 lead in the series. With three more wins—the Series was being played as a best-of-nine contest—the upstart team could win its first world championship ever.

Except Fraser had noticed something after Ruth slid into third base. His left arm, the way he carried it. He never rubbed it or showed any discomfort with it. But he held it out slightly from the rest of his body. Something, Fraser thought, was wrong.

Fraser found Babe in the clubhouse after the game, wearing only his victory cigar. But the arm was bad. The inside of his elbow looked like raw hamburger meat.

"We need to wash that," Fraser said. "Get some disinfectant on it."

Babe beamed, cigar clenched at a jaunty forty-five-degree angle. "Don't be an old lady. You're here to be seen by the smart guys, not to sweat over this stuff. I'm telling you, though, that field"—he took the cigar out of his mouth and shook his head—"it's a mess. All sorts of pebbles and crap on the base paths. Like a sandlot."

Fraser knew he should push the Babe on this. He was the doctor and the damned thing needed attention. Then again, he had already said that, and this was exactly the sort of information that might give Fraser the edge he needed with Rothstein and Attell, something he and they would know and others wouldn't.

Babe stood up. "I'll wash it off in the shower. Listen, I'm in a rush, need to see some people. Gonna cut loose. Two games to nothing, eh? If only they'd give me a goddamned pitch to hit. Then I'd show that bastard McGraw something to remember!"

Fraser held his tongue as the slugger strutted off, towel in one hand and cigar in the other. He knew he should demand that Babe at least put some iodine on the wound. Well, he had tried, sort of. It was the Babe who had pushed him away.

When Fraser reached the Ansonia, the desk clerk handed over a message. Part of him hoped it was from Ruth, asking him to clean and dress his arm.

Inside the creamy Ansonia envelope was a torn-off scrap of paper. There was writing on one side that made no sense. The other side read: "8 pm, George's, Fifty-third and Eighth." It was signed "AA."

Fraser smiled. He had a nibble. A definite nibble.

Attell was waiting for him at George's on Fifty-third. Another good sign. The little prizefighter was eager.

They went through the motions of looking at the food-stained menu, the cardboard soft from use. George's was a greasy spoon that had earned the label.

"Order the scrapple," the little man said. "It's terrific here. Stick to your ribs. They serve it twenty-four hours." Attell seemed to be in high good humor, which Fraser hadn't expected. He feared the gambler would resent having to deal with someone he held in contempt, like Fraser, or else he would be on edge to make a deal. Instead, Attell seemed almost joyful. He must think Fraser was a patsy. It was insulting, but understandable.

Fraser ordered a grilled cheese sandwich, guessing that the cook couldn't do much harm to that, but he was wrong. The bread was limp and the cheese carried a worrisome aroma. Fraser elected to make do with coffee while Attell inhaled an intimidating brick of scrapple. Conversation was impossible while the gambler shoveled the gelatinous substance into his face. Wiping his mouth with a daintiness that contrasted with his other table manners, Attell gestured at Fraser's plate. "You going to finish that?"

Fraser pushed the dish over. Attell was equal to the challenge. Fraser tried to recall the symptoms of tapeworm.

Attell sat back with a sigh.

"You could order another," Fraser said.

Attell held his hand up, palm out to Fraser. "Don't tempt me. Honest food, you know?" He made a feeble effort at stifling a belch, then surrendered completely to the next one. "So," he said, a satisfied look on his face. "How bad is it?"

"The arm?"

Attell nodded.

"I won't know until I see it tomorrow afternoon. But it's his throwing arm, so it'll be hard to protect it. Pretty much impossible."

Attell sat forward and spoke softly. "You know, if the Babe's hurt—you know, really hurt—it raises some possibilities. For a betting man, that is. The Yanks are up 2–0, so the action's running their way. But if the Babe has a bad wing, and if we're the only ones who know how bad . . ." He shrugged. "That could be very interesting. Very interesting." Attell's eyes narrowed.

Fraser's heart rate picked up. This felt too easy. He made himself wait. He gave Attell time to like the situation more. And more.

"So," Fraser said, "I take it we have a deal? A trade? For Babe's IOU and for putting Speed's kid in the clear."

"Not so fast, Doc," Attell said. "We have an idea of a deal. It's just a little baby idea. See, first we gotta see if this really helps us with the betting line tomorrow. And if it works good, then maybe the idea starts to grow up a bit, maybe we can move on to have a grown-up deal."

Fraser stared at him, trying to let the silence get uncomfortable. "Why would I do that? That way you hold all the cards. No matter what happens, you get to say that the information from me didn't help."

"Hey, you know you can trust us. We're businessmen. We can't stay in business if we don't keep our word. It's the same as paying off bets. Ask anyone. We always pay off. It's only good business."

“Trust isn’t so easy to come by in this situation.”

“Hey, for us, too. We’re taking the chances here, remember? We’re covering the bets, putting up good money, which we gotta pay off if you’re wrong. Which reminds me. If we act on the information you give us, you’d damned well better be right. Being wrong—hell, I don’t need any help from you to be wrong. I can do that all by myself.”

“Tell you what, Abe. I’ve got an idea how we can do this.”

# Chapter 29

Fraser was groggy with another dream when he opened his eyes in the sunlit train car. He was chasing someone. Or someone was chasing him. Maybe it was because of the jouncing ride of the early express back from Philadelphia. The patchy track bed delivered random jolts into the steady pulse of steel wheels on steel rails, all of which tortured Fraser's spine.

He used a handkerchief to wipe sweat from his forehead. This was it. He had made his deal with Attell. Now he had made his deal with Pete Johnson and Jerome Hill in Philadelphia. After hurrying home to clean up, he had to get the bank to wire funds to them, then recruit Uncle Wilfred. Then back to the Babe and then Attell and Rothstein again.

He let his head rest against the window. New Jersey rushed by as the morning light slanted higher. He imagined packing his clothes, heading to the piers, and walking onto the first ship to England. After six days, maybe five, he would see Eliza, see Violet. He wouldn't have to pretend he had the nerve to face down New York gangsters. He had wondered a few times in the past if Speed would ruin him somehow, even get him killed.

Eliza liked to predict that he would. Fraser never imagined it could happen after Speed was gone.

By the time he climbed out of a taxi for game three at the Polo Grounds, Fraser was thinking about the lives that were built around baseball. Instead of tromping down hospital corridors that reeked of disinfectant to see people he didn't often help, a baseball man lived his life in the sunshine, under an open sky. His brain was filled with nothing more vexing than whether the third-baseman was playing too far off the foul line. So what if you were wrong? Nobody suffered for your mistake, not really suffered. Maybe he could be a sportswriter—that looked soft. Even an usher, or a trainer for the players—he might be qualified for that.

He pushed out of his mind the arrangements he'd been making since he left George's Diner with its twenty-five strains of botulism. There were too many moving parts to the deal. Any one of them, starting with Uncle Wilfred, could fail. It was a risk to involve the old fellow, but Fraser needed someone he could trust. Speed was gone and the rest of his family was in London, which left Wilfred. At least he was enthusiastic. Also he had no competing obligations. As Eliza had predicted, Wilfred's new show had folded after only eight performances in August. The old fellow would respect the role Fraser had given him to play today. At least Fraser hoped he would. Fraser had to play his own role.

Fraser found Ruth lacing his shoes, already dressed in the pin-striped uniform and short-visored cap.

"Hey, Doc," the big man greeted him, a grin on his face, "how's your old man?"

"More to the point, how's your elbow?"

Babe shrugged. "Feels great. Just had a three-hour nap. I'm feeling tip-top."

"Let me take a look." Ruth held out his arm. Fraser pulled up the sleeve and peeled off an amateurish bandage. He rotated the elbow to pick up the light. He didn't need a lot of time to see that it was bad, but he took a little extra time anyway. That delay usually made patients uncomfortable, got their attention better. "It's not looking good, Babe. It's getting infected. See here?" He pointed to a swelling.

"Doesn't feel so bad."

"It will." Fraser let more seconds slip by as he bent to look more closely. "That needs to be drained." He waved at the small black bag he had carried in. "I've got the instruments with me. It won't take long and then I'll bandage it up."

"Can I play after you do that?"

"Probably not today. It'll hurt, but I bet it already does. I'll have to cut into the elbow. You'll have to be careful not to re-open the wound so it doesn't get reinfected."

"Tell you what, Doc. Let's skip it, wait a day. Maybe it'll clear up."

"Infections don't usually just reverse themselves. They run their course, which can be very damaging."

"What can a day hurt? If we win today, we're up 3–0. It won't be so bad if I miss a game."

Fraser knew in his bones that it was a mistake. He should insist. But he let it go. Ruth held his arm out. "Bandage it up, but not too much. I don't want the Giants thinking I'm really hurt. They'll go after the elbow if they do. Fucking McGraw's a killer."

Instead of following Babe out to the field, Fraser headed for the street door. From the sidewalk, he waved to Wilfred, who sat in a taxi pointed west, toward the pickup spot. When the cab pulled away, Fraser turned back to the stadium. Now three things had to go right. First, the Yanks had to start losing because of Babe's bad arm. Second, Attell had to keep his word. And Wilfred had to get it right.

From his vantage point next to the Yankees' dugout, Fraser could see that Babe was being careful with his arm while trying to conceal the injury. He showed no restraint during batting practice. The swings still looked titanic, and the ball still flew off his bat. Even if the arm held up for a while, Fraser told himself, it was going to give out.

When the Giants took the field to start the game—they were designated the home team for this one—Fraser stood to encourage the Yanks. He looked over to Attell's box. The little man was there. Fraser took off his hat, waved it out at the field. That was the signal.

By the third inning, Fraser was a wreck, his leg jiggling madly. The Yankees had a 4–0 lead. Babe had hit a single that drove in two runs. Had Fraser called it wrong? Was Babe that good, playing through the pain and stiffness of that ugly elbow? Was he beyond the limitations that applied to mere mortals? Or was he just better with one arm than everyone else was with two?

The scoreboard mocked Fraser. The Giants hadn't scored yet in the Series. Not once in twenty innings. Even John McGraw's brand of low-scoring baseball required at least one run to win a game. How could they possibly overcome a four-run deficit? McGraw was showing his own nerves. He had already brought in a relief pitcher to stop the Yankees as soon as possible. Preferably now.

Babe looked cocky taking his lead off first base, chatting with the first-baseman. He yelled over as the pitcher started his windup. After each pitch, Babe trotted back, toed the bag, and winked at the fans seated behind the foul line. After the third pitch, with a count of two balls and one strike, Babe took off his cap and carefully placed it back on. Everyone in the stadium could see his grin. Fraser couldn't help but envy his mastery of the sport, how much he enjoyed that mastery. Fraser had underestimated Ruth's talent, and his spirit. Fraser was going to pay for that mistake. Attell and Rothstein would see to that.

As the pitcher delivered the next pitch, Babe broke for second base. Yankee fans shouted. The big galoot was going to swipe another base, grind these Giants into rubble all by himself. His slide set off a dust storm. The umpire crouched low to get the best view. "Out!" came the bellowed call. Yankee fans froze. The Giants' rooters roared to life.

Babe bounced up and started to trot off the field. He winced. His movements revealed the pain. No one could miss it. Fraser looked away. He knew he should be ashamed of himself, but his heart leapt with joy.

The Giants tied the game in the bottom of the inning, showing their first signs of life in the Series. The next time Ruth batted, he struck out. Even in the best of health, Babe was prone to strikeouts. His swing was so long and so powerful, he was bound to miss the ball some of the time. A lot of the time. But this time was different. He didn't look good. He was favoring the elbow, anyone could see it. Fraser's leg jiggle slowed down. The door was open. It was up to the Giants to walk through it.

It didn't happen until the bottom of the seventh. The Giants loaded the bases. Irish Meusel, a dangerous hitter, came to the plate. His younger brother Bob was playing right field for the Yankees. This time family seniority prevailed. Irish scorched a double past his brother and scored two runners. The Giants kept right on battering the Yankee pitchers, scoring six more times. When Babe led off the eighth, trailing 12–4, the Giants still weren't taking any chances. They walked him on four pitches. Manager Huggins wasn't taking any chances, either. He sent in a sub to run the bases for Babe. No more suicidal base-stealing by the big man.

Fraser took a deep breath. His leg wasn't jiggling at all.

Wilfred took the seat next to him before the ninth inning began. He was dressed for his part, a fair imitation of a racetrack tout in a checked suit and spats. He smelled like the third shift at a brewery. "What'd I miss?" he asked.

Smiling, Fraser said, "The longest damned ballgame I've ever sat through." He looked over at Wilfred. "Did you get it?"

Wilfred winked, a long, slow one. He reached into his jacket pocket and handed over a sheet folded into quarters. Fraser held it low, between his knees, opening it just a bit to peek in. It looked right. He refolded it and placed it in his trousers pocket. "Any trouble?" he asked.

"Nah. Once it came over the wire that the Giants scored all those runs, the guy showed up and handed it to me. Didn't say a word."

# Chapter 30

In the hushed clubhouse, Babe was a brooding presence on a folding chair. The other players gave him a wide berth. He glared at Fraser. "Don't say a goddamned word." He held his arm out. "Go ahead and drain this bastard. I can't move it right. Can't sleep with it."

The elbow was puffy, abloom with sickening yellow and red, green and purple.

Fraser found a side room that was the closest thing to an aseptic location. A man in a suit arrived and announced himself as the team doctor, though Fraser had never seen the man in the clubhouse before. He announced that Colonel Ruppert had instructed that he should take charge of Babe's care. Fraser wondered if the man had been hired that afternoon. The new man watched while Fraser washed and laid out his instruments, then lanced the wound. After draining it, he rinsed it and applied a tight dressing. Babe didn't make a sound, though he steadfastly averted his eyes. "I'll look at it again at game time tomorrow," Fraser said. "I'll try to rig up something smaller then."

Babe flexed his arm and grimaced. He walked off to his locker. Fraser didn't see how he could play the next game.

After cleaning his instruments, Fraser found the clubhouse empty except for one very sulky home-run hitter. "Say, Babe," he said, "want to see a little good news?"

Ruth, still silent, looked over. Fraser dug the paper from Wilfred out of his pants pocket. Babe glanced at it. Then he looked more closely. He balled it up and threw it at Fraser's face, catching him under the left eye.

"You dumb cluck," Babe said. "That ain't mine."

Next morning, Fraser bellied right up to the gorilla at Lefty's. "I need to see Rothstein," he muttered. "Now. No waiting. Or you and I have a problem." Fraser was committed to running this bluff. He wasn't even sure it was a bluff.

While a flicker of uncertainty crossed the gorilla's face, Abe Attell materialized, all smiles. "Hey, Doc. Thought we might see you. Let's grab a pew."

Fraser didn't order anything. Attell asked for coffee. As soon as the waitress left, Fraser said, "So, you made a big mistake. You gave my man the wrong IOU. At least I'm giving you the benefit of the doubt, that it was a mistake. Because you said you're such scrupulous businessmen. You remember that? I kept up my end of the deal. Men of your word, you said. My Aunt Fanny."

"Hey, hey, hey. No reason to use harsh language, Doc." Attell was enjoying himself again, which was just as infuriating as he meant it to be. "You should understand. The way Mr. Rothstein and I see it, you haven't actually kept up your end of the deal. Not yet."

Rage flashed through Fraser's muscles. He ached to throttle this two-bit punk. Attell smiled, his crooked nose almost glowing with high spirits. "Listen, Doc. Our deal is that you give us winning information about the Babe. You gave us half of that. We got the information. We did what we thought was right with it, what you'd expect. But"—he held up an index finger—"was it winning information? Nobody knows. Only time will tell, you know? The Giants came back, they won a game. Great. And that inside information you gave us? Well, now everyone knows it. Everyone saw Babe leave the field yesterday. Now the world knows he's hurt, so now our edge is gone. We had it for, what, less than twenty-four hours? So what we might win from this deal, that's based on all the bets that are already in play. Which is a lot of action, you better believe it. Still, the Giants gotta win four more before you've held up your end. Then we've got a deal."

"So why'd you pass along someone else's IOU? Just to make me look stupid?"

Attell sat back so the waitress could place his coffee on the table. "Doc, call it an education, no charge. You're an educated man, am I right? A doctor?" Fraser chose to seethe silently. "But now you know that you don't send some over-the-hill dandy to do business with us. Don't even think about that. And now you also know that you have to look at the paper, read it close, when you make a deal. Am I right?"

When Fraser still didn't speak, torn between fury and disgust with himself, Attell drank some coffee. "Look, Doc. The Giants win four more? Everything's jake, we tie up the deal." He drank some more coffee. "Just one question I had. Mr. Rothstein, he watches the betting pretty careful. Real careful. Everything shook out just like we expected yesterday, except for this one place, this one place where everyone seems to love the Giants. You don't know anything about some smart guys handling bets down in Philadelphia, do you?"

"A dumb guy like me? How could I know something like that?" Fraser left without waiting for a response. Attell smiled and finished his coffee.

* * *

Rain came that afternoon, giving both teams a rest. For Babe it was a little time to heal. Fraser went to the Polo Grounds anyway, in case the weather cleared. He passed the time feeling like a fool. Speed would never have blundered so badly.

Sunday was a perfect day for baseball. In the trainer's room, Ruth said nothing when the dressing came off his arm. Fraser drained more pus and cleaned it again. It still looked terrible. After taking longer than he needed to examine the wound, he looked up at a pair of angry eyes. He couldn't figure out the smart thing to say, or the right thing. Well, the right thing was to get Babe to sit this one out. Would that be best for his betting strategy, his Rothstein strategy? Say, the Yanks lose this one but Babe comes back stronger than ever and they take the Series. Wouldn't it be better for him to play at half speed and make the injury worse? Fraser stood up straight, disgusted by his own thinking.

"Don't play, Babe," he said. "You're going to aggravate it. And the Giants know you're hurt. You know what McGraw's like. They'll go after the arm. Sit this one out. You guys still lead the Series."

"Hey, kid." Ruth turned to the team doctor, a still silent presence. "Bandage this up for me, will you?"

"All right, all right," Fraser said, reaching for gauze. "Just try to be careful with it, will you? It must hurt like crazy."

Ruth didn't answer. He made a face when Fraser applied more iodine, then again when he taped the dressing tight. "I'm giving you as much motion as I can." Babe tried his arm. He tried it again. He left for warm-ups.

Fraser went through the motions of observing Ruth on the field, then took his seat. Babe played the whole game in left field. When he singled in the fourth, he didn't try to steal second.

The Yanks held a 1–0 lead, but the game turned in the Giants' half of the eighth inning. Centerfielder George Burns, a little guy, stepped to the plate against Carl Mays, the Yankee pitcher who had won twenty-seven games that year. Two men on base. Most hitters didn't like facing Mays, not since he killed Ray Chapman with an inside pitch the year before. They tended to get nervous. But Burns hung in and smacked a double, scoring two runs and giving the Giants the lead.

By the time Ruth came up to bat in the bottom of the ninth, the Yanks trailed 4–1. His arm had to be shrieking with pain. His broad face wasn't lit with the usual grin. He didn't razz the pitcher or the catcher. His eyes were stern, his blunt features drawn into themselves. He dug his heels into the batter's box. He swung so hard at the second pitch that he nearly fell onto the first-base line when he missed. Fraser couldn't imagine the waves of affliction that had to be coming from that arm.

With no change in expression, Babe dug in again. He pointed his bat at the pitcher, then swung again, starting his long stride before the pitcher let go of the ball, putting just as much force into it this time. The crash of bat on ball seemed to bludgeon the world into silence. A second later, a roar exploded like a wave hitting a beach. It was another huge Babe Ruth homer. Yankees fans and Giants fans shared the elation. Ruth trotted slowly around the bases. When he reached the dugout, he tipped his cap.

The heroic home run should have inspired his teammates to storm back and take the game, but it didn't. They meekly made the last outs of the game. The Giants had tied up the Series, 2–2.

In the next game, Ruth's elbow was killing him, plus a bum leg was acting up, too. The Giants weren't giving him free bases on balls any more, but Babe wasn't finished. Leading off the fourth inning of a tie game, he took several huge practice swings, notable even by his gargantuan standards. Then he stunned the crowd by dropping a perfect bunt down the third base line. In the Giants' dugout, John McGraw turned apoplectic over having his favorite tactics turned against him. He screamed at his infielders to wake the hell up. When the next batter doubled, Babe raced in to score. When he reached the Yankees' dugout, though, he passed out cold.

Fraser strained to see into the dugout from his seat. When he heard what happened from other fans, he tried to scramble over the fence to check on his patient. A bald usher with too few teeth grabbed him. "Where d'you think you're going, bub?" he asked. By the time Fraser sputtered his explanation, Ruth was staggering out to patrol left field. Huggins saw Fraser and walked over to him. He said they'd revived the Babe with spirits of ammonia. Then Huggins rolled his eyes and shook his head. "The big ape's got guts. Give him that."

Babe finished the game—a Yankee win that gave them a 3–2 lead in the Series. He had triggered the two-run rally that provided the winning margin. But he struck out feebly in his other times at bat. Fraser knew it. Everyone knew it. The Babe was too hurt to keep playing.

After the game, Fraser looked over the elbow with the team doctor. They agreed. The infection was dangerous. It could lead to blood poisoning, which might even mean amputation of the arm. Or it might just kill him. He had to stop playing. Ruth glared back. They prepared a public statement for the press. After leaving the Polo Grounds, Fraser sent a telegram to Philadelphia.

Next morning, he was back at Lefty's.

"You're absolutely sure now," Attell said. "There ain't gonna be no miracle cure, no ninth-inning grand slam? He's not playing possum?"

Fraser shook his head. "The torture he's in? It's incredible he played the last few games. Pain like that, it wears you out. And the public statement's right. This could kill him."

"Even a big strong guy like the Babe?"

"Yeah, even the Babe. He can't even drive a car. The Yanks hired him a driver. You know it's bad if he gives up driving."

"All right, then. After yesterday's game, we got another run of serious action on the Yanks. I'm telling you, the betting's been through the roof. But Mr. Rothstein won't be amused if you're wrong."

"Enough with the threats, all right?"

Despite having Babe sulking on the bench in civilian clothes in the next game, the Yanks took an early lead, but the Giants battled back to win. They took the next two games, each by a single run, beating Waite Hoyt in a heartbreaker to win the Series. John McGraw's scratch-and-claw baseball stood triumphant. In that last game, Babe came off the bench as a pinch hitter in the bottom of the ninth. It was a moment for the ages, the chance for the great slugger to trigger an epic comeback. Echoing Mighty Casey of the famous poem, he grounded out quietly.

After the game ended, Fraser sat for a while in the stands. He watched the Giants and their fans shout for joy and hug each other. Despite Prohibition, flasks were everywhere—mostly tipped upside down—while smiling police officers watched. Fraser felt his own elation. He and Rothstein and Attell had won. His elation was only slightly leavened by knowing Babe's disappointment.

Fraser decided not to stop by the clubhouse. It would be like a morgue in there, and he had logged enough funeral time recently. Babe wouldn't want to see him. Leaving the Polo Grounds, Fraser turned his mind to the problem that had never gone away. How could he make sure that Rothstein and Attell honored their side of the bargain?

# Chapter 31

The call came to Fraser's apartment that night. The voice said it was Christy Walsh. He described himself as Babe Ruth's business agent. He proposed they meet the next day in Ruth's apartment in the Ansonia. Not real early.

At around ten the next morning, the desk called to say that a man was waiting with a package for Fraser. He wouldn't leave it without seeing Fraser. Directed to the building's service entrance, Fraser found Pete Johnson in a gray suit with an orange tie. A large grip sat on the ground next to him.

"I didn't expect you so soon," Fraser said, shaking his hand.

Johnson smiled and lifted the bag. "No time like the present."

When they arrived in the Frasers' parlor, the guest declined food or drink. "This is business," he said, placing the grip on the coffee table with some authority. "This here's your share."

Fraser looked inside. Without thinking, he pulled out a wrapped packet of US currency. "How much is this?"

"That there's five thousand."

"How much is in here?"

"It's a hair under one hundred fifty thousand, including the ten grand you gave me to start with."

Fraser sank onto the couch. "Whoa, Nellie. How'd it get to be this much?"

Johnson sat in an armchair. "We bet the Giants, like we talked about, but we also got a lot of action on special bets—you know, how many home runs the Babe would hit, how many runs he'd score, all that sort of thing. People just wanted to bet on the Babe, even after he got hurt. Almost like they wanted to support him, you know, buck him up. And then he kept coming back after he was hurt, which made people think he'd make it through."

"Some of this is yours, yours and Mr. Hill's, for knowing how to place those bets."

Johnson smiled broadly. "Don't you worry about us, Doc. Jerome and I did just fine. Best week we've ever had. If you don't come around like you did, we'd probably have leaned toward the Yankees."

"There's something you should know. One of Rothstein's men said they were suspicious about some betting down in your city."

"He can be suspicious all night long. We played by the rules. Just like he did. You've got no idea how much that man made, all over the country."

"How much?"

"Millions, easy."

"No kidding?"

"No kidding. Also, you want to be careful how you handle this stuff." He pointed to the open valise. "Taxes is real high right now, after the war and all." He looked around the apartment. "I guess you do all right, so you know about that."

"Don't assume I know anything, Pete. Tell me how you would handle this amount of cash."

Fraser couldn't stop fingering the stack of bills while Pete talked, but he listened closely. By the time the man finished, Fraser knew what he would do with it.

"Didn't see you after the game." The Babe, wearing a red satin dressing gown over blue pajamas, was giving Fraser the fish-eye from across the room. He held his left elbow away from his body. The bandage bulged out his sleeve. Babe's apartment was three times the size of Fraser's. Red velvet cushions glowed from much of the furniture, set off by dark walnut wood. Henry VIII would have been comfortable there. A tall man in a navy blue suit sat in a gigantic chair. He had to be Walsh, the man who had telephoned.

"I figured you wouldn't want to see me," Fraser said. "I've been nothing but bad luck for you."

"I did want to see you. Wanted to punch you in the nose."

Fraser spread his feet. "Here I am."

The Babe walked over and picked up a cigar from a box on a side table. "I don't really do much fighting. Never did. My old man ran a bar. Didn't seem to be much percentage in fighting. Even the tough guys end up getting hurt, like the old man did." He lit the cigar. "Anyway, I got no gripe with you. All you did was tell me when my arm was bad. Which wasn't exactly news to the guy attached to it."

"Want me to look at it?"

"Nah, the club's got me seeing some doc over on Park Avenue. I'm due there this afternoon. What the hell, I figure. You ain't cured me, so I'll try someone else. Maybe he knows something you don't." Ruth gestured for Fraser to sit. "I got some barnstorming games to play pretty soon, so I need to be healed up soon."

Ruth sat down and nodded at Walsh, who cleared his throat. "Babe tells me you've been trying to pick up a job Speed Cook was supposed to do. With a certain businessman here in Manhattan."

Fraser didn't see any reason for euphemisms and circumlocutions. "Yeah, I've been trying to get Babe's IOU back from Rothstein."

"Right." Walsh was smoothing his tie, fingering the fat end. "We think—Babe and I, that is—we've been thinking about this situation. I didn't know about it until last night. We have an idea, a suggestion for how you might find it possible to approach this, ah, individual, in such a fashion that you might be able to work toward a more satisfactory conclusion of the matters that are unresolved."

"For the love of Pete, Christy." The Babe threw a leg over the arm of the chair. "Speak English." He turned to Fraser. "We got a scheme for making Rothstein cough it up. We don't want to mess up anything you got cooking, so we figured we should talk."

"Fine," Fraser said.

"Also," the Babe said, pausing to blow smoke rings, "I know what my handwriting looks like, so maybe this way you won't get fooled again."

"I've been going through Abe Attell," Fraser said, "but I don't know that you should be meeting with any of these people. If you're even seen with them, the commissioner's going to go off like a Roman candle."

"Yeah, sure, but Christy and me think it's riskier for those bums to have that piece of paper. So we're gonna have to take a chance or two to get it back."

"How?" Fraser asked.

Walsh, who had remained standing, stepped closer. "You go first. What was your plan?"

"I was going to go back to Attell and demand that he honor his promises. We had that deal, you know, that you weren't any part of—"

Ruth waved his hand. "Yeah, yeah, they wanted to fleece all

the suckers betting on the Series and you helped 'em do it. Start from there."

"Well, I kept up my end, and I know Rothstein did extremely well out of the deal. So he should honor his promises to me, which include giving me that paper."

"They're not his promises," Walsh said.

"What?" Fraser said.

"As I understand it, Rothstein didn't promise you anything. Attell did. Rothstein'll say he had no idea what the little guy was doing, but he sure didn't speak for me."

Fraser's scalp started to tingle. "But everyone knows that Attell works for Rothstein. That he speaks for him."

Babe broke in. "We're not talking about what everyone knows. We're talking about what a snake like Rothstein's gonna say and do. I personally think Christy could be right that Rothstein'll welsh on any promise made by Attell."

"Well, it did occur to me that they might not honor their promise, so I had an idea for a second angle." Ruth and Walsh looked interested. "Attell quoted me a price of seventy-five thousand for the paper. Based on some unexpected developments that I don't want to talk about, I'm in a position to pay that."

The other two men smiled. "Your heart's in the right place, Doc," Walsh said, "but you're not used to dealing with people like this. If you offer to pay, the price'll keep going up and up until they get to the price you can't pay."

"See"—Babe leaned forward—"they want to have this thing to hang over me, for whenever they need it. For when they don't have a doctor giving them the inside skinny on what's going on. So they can make me do what they want. They ain't giving that up for money, not after they made all the money you think you made for them."

"Why's their hold over you so strong? It's just an IOU—that's what Speed said. So the world finds out you got into debt and borrowed from the wrong people. Not smart, but not the worst thing in the world. Even Colonel Ruppert might be willing to pay it off for you, or front it for you."

The Babe and Walsh exchanged a look. Walsh shrugged. Babe said, "I can't take a chance on Landis getting wind that these guys were into me, with all that Black Sox mess. And, also . . ." He looked over at Walsh again.

"It's what it was for," Walsh broke in. "It was for a girl."

"So it was for a girl," Fraser said. "Most people think you like girls. They've seen your movie, at least a few have. You're a red-blooded American male. And everyone knows what can happen when boys and girls get together. Not necessarily a great thing when you're married, but so what?"

Ruth sighed, keeping his eyes on his cigar. "She looked a lot older, you know, older than she turned out to be."

"It was a setup, pure and simple," Walsh said.

"Yeah, they got me good." The Babe passed a hand over his mouth. "It looks bad. I don't even remember if she was a good kid or not. I guess she was. But we took care of her. She's fine now."

"There's photos," Walsh added. "They look bad. Not the sort of thing for a hero to be doing."

Fraser looked from one to the other and let the news sink in for a minute. "How young was young?"

Ruth didn't move.

"Too young," Walsh said.

"By a lot?"

Walsh nodded again. "And it was back before Babe was making enough dough where he might've handled a problem like this himself."

"And," Babe said, "I was dumb. Also scared."

Fraser made a face. "Did you ever tell Speed Cook about this?" Fraser thought he knew the answer, but he let the others sit through the uncomfortable silence. Speed had said there had to be something else going on, something more than money.

This met the description. Would Speed have walked out on Ruth if he'd known the truth? Or would he have finished the job? Fraser wasn't sure.

Was Fraser staying in or was he out? At least Babe was ashamed. Ashamed of what he did? Or of being dumb? Another thing Fraser wouldn't ever know. But it wasn't just the Babe and his career and baseball that hung in the balance. Also Joshua, and Fraser had a personal stake in that man now. That's what really mattered. "Okay," he said, "so how does this change what I planned to do?"

"Doesn't need to," Walsh said. "You can go right ahead with what you meant to do, though it probably won't work. It can't hurt. But I need to come along. You and I have an appointment tomorrow afternoon at Rothstein's office over on West Fifty-seventh. Babe won't come with us, but he'll be nearby in the office of a friend of mine. If we need him, I'll duck out and call him to come over."

Fraser thought for a moment. "Babe can't just saunter into the building that has Rothstein's office, walk right in off the street. Everyone would notice. He's Babe Ruth."

"He can come through an alley behind my friend's building that enters into the Rothstein building."

"Someone could see him in the lobby of Rothstein's building."

Ruth shrugged. "Like the man said, there's some risk, but I'm through tiptoeing around with these crumbs. It doesn't work, and I gotta get out from under them."

Fraser sat back, chewing on the inside of one cheek. "So," he finally said, "since you think my strategy's going to fail, what've you got in mind?"

The Babe, a broad smile making his face glow like the moon, stood up and stuck his hands in the dressing gown pockets. "Actually, it's two things, and they were my idea. Christy thinks they might work. I'm seeing a guy tonight about one of them. Then we'll be ready."

* * *

As suited a large man, John Slaughter had a seriously hollow leg. Babe was pretty near unconscious before the half cop finally began to run down. "What's there to celebrate?" Slaughter had asked when Babe found him at eight at the Downtown Club, which was nearly decent as those places go. "You guys lost the Series."

The Babe beamed at him. "There's always something to celebrate."

He led them on a downward tour through the layers of Manhattan society, moving on to the Renegade Room, then O'Malley's over on Tenth Avenue. Babe needed this guy to get sloppy, then feel overheated, then take off his jacket. That was the key. Babe aimed to lift one of those blank subpoenas out of the man's inside pocket. When Babe told Christy how Slaughter had been showing off those legal papers, Christy's eyes had narrowed. Like a flash he had a scheme for using one of them against Rothstein, but only the real McCoy. They couldn't fool Rothstein with a fake.

The thing was, Slaughter didn't seem to get sloppy or hot, at least not sloppy and hot enough to take off his coat. Babe finally drug him over to Francie's, a place where the liquor was free but the girls weren't. Babe had a word with Francie: he'd pick up the cost for one of her best girls to get Slaughter out of his goddamned suit coat. When that didn't work, he tried to set the man a good example, heading to the second floor with a doll of a brunette. Upon his return, after lighting up a cigar, Babe could see that Slaughter hadn't budged from his chair where he sat like some misplaced chunk of granite, mobile only when he knocked back another bourbon.

Babe had Francie send the twins over to work on Slaughter, but the big man didn't budge. He wasn't exactly a barrel of laughs. After he finished his cigar, Babe tried setting a good example for him a second time. No soap. Well, it wasn't exactly a waste of time, but it didn't move Slaughter.

Not until they reached the Red Hat down in Greenwich Village did Slaughter start to wobble. He hung on for three more rounds. Thank God the Red Hat never really closed. It was the sort of place that kept the lighting dim so the customers couldn't see each other, since it would depress them to see the people they were drinking with.

There wasn't any real warning. Slaughter swiveled his head slightly and cracked his first smile of the night. "Great night, Babe," he said. "I'll never forget it." Then he went down like a tree, with a sigh that ended in a crash. Babe could've sworn the guy's head bounced off the table, face sideways toward him, but Babe wasn't seeing things too crisp right then. The crack of skull on wood didn't attract attention. Another night at the Red Hat. Slaughter snored softly, a small pool of spittle spreading over two burn marks in the tabletop.

It took Babe a while—no way to be sure how long—to sort out the situation. The thing was, the bastard still had his damned suit jacket on. There were a couple of women in the joint. He could pay one to sidle up to Slaughter, get her hands inside that pocket and slip out the subpoenas. But when he looked at the women again, they looked too far gone to handle anything that complicated. He could take Slaughter back to his hotel room and pretend to get him ready for bed, grab the papers then. But Babe didn't really want to spend that kind of time with this guy. He didn't feel so hot himself. So that made it simple.

Babe threw a bill on the table to cover whatever damage they'd done to the liquor supply. He slid his chair next to the comatose Slaughter and put an arm around the half cop's shoulders. He tried to act like he was about to ease Slaughter out of the chair and get him moving toward the end of their evening. Levering Slaughter upright, Babe got the man's head off the table, then reached his free hand inside Slaughter's jacket.

Slaughter's hand clutched Babe's wrist long before the ballplayer could even consider a next move. Slaughter's eyes were open. They were directed at Babe's face, but Babe couldn't be sure how much the man was taking in.

"Easy now, buckaroo," Babe said. "We're all friends here."

Slaughter slowly relaxed his grip. His eyelids began to drop. So did his hand. Babe finished extracting the papers as he hauled Slaughter out of his seat. He stashed the papers in his back pocket, then started to move both of them toward the door.

# Chapter 32

Rothstein's office wasn't what Fraser expected, not for a man the newspapers called an underworld kingpin. It should have been an elegant hotel suite rented under a false name. Or a cluttered hole-in-the-wall in the back of a speakeasy littered with men wearing shoulder holsters, the atmosphere heavy with restless danger. Instead, it was a workaday office building, plain as mud, that fronted on Fifty-seventh Street west of Fifth Avenue. The nameplates in the lobby claimed the building was the home of insurance, real estate, and bail bond firms. A professional reserve permeated the top floor, the seventh, where the boss's office was. Conservatively dressed men and women spoke in measured tones and hunched over adding machines or typewriters. Not a pistol in sight.

Rothstein met them in a small conference room with a red and black oriental carpet. Bookshelves on one wall displayed pottery and other souvenirs of an ordinary life. It could have been the office of a local bank in Westchester County.

Rothstein's appearance was as disappointing as it had been at Lefty's. Wearing a high-buttoned business suit with a narrow bow tie, he received them politely but showed little personality. Behind the bland facade, though, intelligence lit his eyes. The man's demeanor seemed to mask a mind that was constantly making calculations and recalculations—where there might be gain, where risk. Nothing about Rothstein seemed genuine or spontaneous.

The meeting went much as Walsh predicted. Rothstein happily acknowledged that Abe Attell was an acquaintance, then professed bewilderment why anyone would think the two men shared business interests. "Gentlemen," he said drily, "I do a great deal of business, and I do it myself. As those who do business with me know, they may rely upon my word, but only *my* word, not the word of someone claiming to act for me. Did Mr. Attell present any proof that he could act on my behalf? Do you see him here in my office now?"

"You weren't twenty feet away from us at Lefty's," Fraser said as calmly as he could. "He agreed to cancel the Babe's debt in return for health information about the Yankees."

"Are you with the Yankees, Doctor Fraser?" Rothstein had picked up a pencil and was twirling it between his fingers, then passing it over his knuckles, one finger at a time.

"No, not officially, but I was caring for Babe at the time."

"You didn't make much of a job of it, near as I can tell. That poor fella's arm nearly fell off."

"If only I'd had the benefit of your medical expertise," Fraser said through clenched teeth, "things doubtless would've gone better." Walsh placed a hand on Fraser's forearm, then excused himself, saying he had a matter to attend to. "But I understand you made a magnificent profit from exactly that information about the Babe's arm."

"I'm not sure what you might be talking about. Perhaps it was more wild talk from Abe Attell. That fella can be a loose cannon. But I hope you're not implying that you made poor Babe's arm worse in order to cash in on betting against the

Yankees. Wouldn't something like that be against your professional duty as a doctor?" Rothstein leaned back in his chair and pointed the pencil at Fraser, signaling that he thought he had scored.

"So, you're saying you know nothing about an IOU from the Babe?"

"Mr. Walsh represents Mr. Ruth, I know that much. I don't see how you get into the picture here." Rothstein rose from his chair. "So, since you and I don't have any business together and never have, I wish you a good day."

The interior door to the room opened and a large man entered. Fraser recognized him. The domesticated gorilla from Lefty's, still forty-eight hours behind on his shaving. He strode next to Fraser and stood there, looking large, angry, and eager.

Fraser didn't budge. "I'm with Mr. Walsh, as you were told just a few minutes ago. We both represent Mr. Ruth. I ask my question again. Do you acknowledge that you hold an IOU from Mr. Ruth?"

"I'm not comfortable discussing Mr. Ruth's private business matters with you, Doctor Fraser, when I really don't know you. I have other appointments now. I've asked you politely to leave. I won't do that again." There was some force in Rothstein's tone. Fraser didn't care.

"Mr. Walsh and I haven't completed our business with you. I hear him coming right now."

The door to the conference room opened and Ruth's unmistakable outline loomed at the threshold. "Babe!" Rothstein said, putting a trace of startled warmth into his voice. "What a surprise."

Walsh followed Ruth in and closed the door. "Listen, Rothstein," the Babe said, ignoring the man's outstretched hand, "we need to get this business done, once and for all, you know?"

Rothstein gestured at the chairs around the table. Walsh took one, but Ruth leaned back against the bookshelves, his arms folded across his chest. The domesticated gorilla was caught in no-man's-land. Warily, he backed toward the door he'd used to enter and leaned against that.

Rothstein's eyes were cold again. He resumed his one-handed fiddling with the pencil. "Okay," he said quietly, "talk. I don't have all day."

"Jack Quinn," Ruth said.

"What of him?"

Ruth nodded at Walsh, who explained. "The commissioner has heard from a witness who claims you paid Carl Mays to groove the pitch to George Burns in the seventh inning of game four, the one he hit for a double that started the Giants' comeback."

Rothstein allowed himself a small smile. "I heard that fairy tale. It's bullshit."

"The commissioner won't think so when the Babe backs it up."

Rothstein's mouth turned up in an effort at a smile. "Don't make me laugh. The Babe doesn't know shit about anything like that. He can't say any such thing."

"The thing is, I can," Ruth said. "You remember where you were on that Saturday night before game four?"

"I had a social engagement."

"At the Broadway Central Hotel?"

"Yes."

"So did I."

"I didn't see you there."

"Funny. I saw you." The Babe unfolded his arms and pointed at the gambler. "I saw you when we shared an elevator up to the sixth floor where your social engagement was. That's where it was, right?"

Rothstein just stared at him.

"And you told me that I shouldn't worry about my arm being hurt for the next game, because you'd bought Carl Mays, so it didn't matter what I did. Mays would let in as many runs as it would take to lose the game."

"Bullshit," Rothstein said, raising his voice. "You know that's bullshit. You were injured, not out on the town that night."

The Babe grinned. "Really? You think anyone in New York's gonna think I stayed home at night because of a sore arm?"

"I didn't see you. You're telling me I rode in an elevator with a big goof like you and didn't even notice? Who'd believe that? And I never said any such thing. Nobody thinks I'm that stupid. And I never paid that gonif Mays a dime, which he'll back me up on."

Now Walsh started to smile. "Based on what the commissioner did with Joe Jackson and the rest of those White Sox," he said, "or should I say Black Sox, he doesn't put a lot of stock in guys who say they didn't throw a game."

"Why would he believe Babe?"

"Mr. Rothstein. I shouldn't have to spell this out for you. Babe is the Babe. Mays is the son of a bitch who killed Ray Chapman. And you, hell, you're the guy who fixed the Black Sox Series. Who do you think he's going to believe?"

"Why would the Babe say something like that, that Mays was bought? It would just bring out all those rumors about the 1918 Series."

"Who survives the fallout better—you or Babe?" Walsh said. He looked back at Ruth, who nodded. "Time to decide, Mr. Rothstein. Judge Landis is still here in New York, so we can get in to see him this afternoon."

"It's a game try, Walsh, but what do I have to be afraid of from Judge Landis? He's got no power over me. I've got no connection to organized baseball."

"How about the Manhattan district attorney? Does he have power over you?" When Rothstein didn't answer, Walsh leaned forward on his elbows. "I don't mean the old DA, the one you owned. I mean the new one, the one who's facing the voters in just a couple of weeks, who needs some headlines about how tough he is on crime."

Rothstein resumed his pencil play, passing the thin wood quickly between each pair of fingers, then back again. He gave a shrug, more with his eyes than his shoulders. "Show 'em if you got 'em, Walsh."

Babe stepped forward and drew a single paper out of his inside jacket pocket. He placed it in front of the gambler. Rothstein used his fingertips to move the paper in front of him and stared down at it for a long time, still passing the pencil through the fingers of his other hand.

"You see," Walsh said, "they want Babe to testify before the grand jury here in New York. Tomorrow, isn't that what it says? And it'll be hard for him not to mention that Jack Quinn business."

A crack startled the room. The gambler had snapped his pencil between two fingers. He leaned forward and looked up at the Babe. "But not impossible, am I right?"

It was Babe's turn to shrug. "I can be forgetful. I drink a lot."

"Talk to me."

Ruth nodded at Walsh. "You give us Babe's paper," Walsh said. "Doctor Fraser here is willing to pay for it, just like he proposed a little while back but which you said you'd think about, and now you've decided to accept. And this nigger kid, Speed Cook's kid—you pass the word that he's okay so long as he stays out of New York, which we guarantee he will."

Rothstein turned to the Babe. "What do I get?"

"Hell, kid," Babe said, "seventy-five grand ain't a bad day's pay, even for you. On top of which you don't go to jail over this Carl Mays business."

Rothstein's eyes darted around the room. He sank back into his chair, tapping the table with one of the pencil halves. "Wait here," he said.

He returned with a single sheet of paper, two photos, and

two negatives. Without a flicker of feeling on his face, he handed them to the Babe. Ruth looked at the paper closely. He placed it in an ashtray, then struck a match. He picked up the paper and lit a corner of it. All four men watched the paper flare, curl, and blacken. When the flame approached the Babe's fingertips, he dropped the residue into the ashtray. He pocketed the other items.

Rothstein's eyes landed on Fraser. "Attell will pick up the money from you."

"Have him do it today," Fraser said. "I'm leaving on a long trip, right away."

The three visitors left. They remained silent in the elevator and while walking to the Babe's Duesenberg, which gleamed at a Sixth Avenue curb around the corner. Fraser stopped them short of the car.

"I think I'll walk, gentlemen," he said. "It's a nice day."

"Enjoy the victory," Walsh said as he shook Fraser's hand. "And thanks for helping Babe out."

"Don't forget," Fraser said to Ruth. "You said you'd pay Speed Cook's widow what you were going to pay Speed."

"Sure, kid," the Babe said. "Just get the address to Christy here." He took Fraser's hand, too. "So I hear your daughter's married to Cook's kid, the nigger?"

"He's colored, Babe. Not a nigger."

"Yeah, sure. And they're having a kid?"

"Yeah, in a few months. That's where I'm going. To them."

"Yeah. Well. How about that?"

# Chapter 33

Fraser forced himself to lie in his second-class berth until sunrise. The *Aquitania*'s crossing, through choppy seas and swirling fog, had taken seven days. He spent at least three seasick nights wishing he was somewhere else, but here he was.

Impatience got the upper hand. He dressed and took up his usual spot on the ship's rail, on the starboard side in front of the main saloon. He had spent quite a few hours at that spot, turning over the events of the past year. It all started with that terrible movie, *Headin' Home.* Fraser felt the contradiction in his own journey: he was heading home to his family, but to a foreign land. And his family was changing. Or had changed. A couple of other passengers paused to chat. He was civil but not welcoming.

The late October chill sliced into him while dawn washed out the twinkling lights of Southampton. Low, grainy clouds spread over the sky. Sunbeams rushed through a single cloud break, blessing a patch of the dim land. Fog festered to the east but didn't obstruct Fraser's view. Three tugs steamed out from the harbor, coming to harry the ocean liner to its pier.

When the *Aquitania* was tied up, Fraser was almost to the end of the gangplank before he saw Violet. He stopped in wonder. Her long coat hung open to accommodate her swelling middle, not yet large but insistent. A woman walked into him from behind, then maneuvered around when he still didn't move. He smiled and waved. Eliza reached him first and held him. "You're safe," she said. "You're safe."

Joshua hung back from the reunion. When the giddiness of the moment receded, he shook Fraser's hand somewhat formally. His offer to collect the luggage started a wave of suggestions from all four of them, which ended as a plan for the men to lasso the bags while the women acquired a taxi.

Fraser watched Eliza and Violet depart. "Joshua," he said, "am I imagining it or is her limp really better? How's her balance, with the baby?"

"I can't say, Doctor Fraser. I don't really see a limp." He shrugged slightly. "Maybe a little, when she's tired."

They dodged through the crowd on the pier and joined the line for retrieving luggage. What should Joshua call him? The problem hadn't occurred to Fraser. Not "Father" or "Dad." Too ridiculous. "Doctor Fraser" was pretty stiff. Fraser decided to wait to see what Joshua called Eliza. They must have worked something out.

And there was something more important to say, even on this crowded dock, shuffling forward in the queue. "I feel terrible about your father. It seemed so impossible, with all his strength, to lose him like that."

"I know. I still don't quite believe it. And I'm completely responsible."

"You couldn't have kept him away that night. He had to be there."

Joshua looked away. "I could have done a lot of things different." His voice was husky. "I just have to live with that, sir. And try to be the man he expected me to be."

"You know, Joshua, I teased him once that he'd used up all his luck and mine, too, the chances he took. He just smiled and said he'd been playing with the house's money for a long time."

Joshua cleared his throat and nodded. "It's been hard, not being with my mother and sister, not with anyone who really knew him."

The stevedore shouted, "Next!" Fraser fumbled for his luggage receipt. Overcoat pockets, jacket pockets, trouser pockets, shirt pocket. He started over. They were in his right overcoat pocket, the first one he had tried. He pointed out the bags that were his. He had brought a lot of things. He might be in London a long time.

Eliza had rented rooms just for the two of them. They looked out on Clapham Common, a flat expanse without much distinction beyond the vibrant green of English grass. When Fraser's things were stashed and he had distributed the gifts sent by Joshua's mother and sister, Joshua opened champagne to toast the occasion. They drank to marriage, the baby, the World Series, and Speed Cook. They were near the end of a second bottle when Fraser pushed the conversation into territory the others had avoided.

"I'm still new to all of this. How's it going? Your marriage, being in England, and all that."

"You mean that I'm colored," Joshua broke in.

Fraser nodded. "Yes, but maybe not in the way you mean. I know you were thinking England would be better for you, for the two of you." His eyes went from Joshua to Violet and back. Both of them looked tense, despite the champagne. "Is it?"

"It's not everything I'd hoped," Joshua said. "Not paradise. When we're together in public we sometimes get dirty looks, even remarks."

"The good part," Violet broke in with a nervous smile, "is

that between the slang and the accents, I don't understand most of them."

Joshua's gaze rested on her, then came back to Fraser. "We know what they're saying. When I got here we looked into moving to Liverpool, which would be good for the shipping business. But it turns out they had race riots there a couple of years ago." He shook his head. "Not here in London, though. I guess there's not enough colored people here to riot over." He stood to offer the last of the champagne to Eliza, who held out her glass to receive it. He sat again.

"So we'll stay here. We don't hold hands in public, touch each other, things that might rile people up. But mostly we feel safe. Safer than New York. It's hard on Violet and Eliza. They're not used to it."

"We'll make it work, Father," Violet said. Fraser closed his eyes for a second. He couldn't find his voice.

Joshua, intent on opening another bottle of champagne, said, "Eliza has told us her Babe Ruth stories." So, it was to be first names, "Eliza" and "Jamie." Fraser supposed he could get used to it. "But you must have some Babe Ruth stories of your own now."

Fraser smiled as he reached his glass out for a refill. "Indeed. Indeed I do."

# *Author's Note*

Any history writer must take a deep breath before straying into the field of baseball history, where meticulous record keeping dwells alongside festering prejudices, massive legends, and scores that cry out to be settled. The challenges are even more pronounced when the subject is Babe Ruth, the greatest legendary figure of the game. Let me start with the records.

I have tried to follow faithfully the facts we know about the major league games, the players, and the manager portrayed in *The Babe Ruth Deception.* Both the box scores and play-by-play accounts of the 1920 and 1921 World Series are available online at www.baseball-reference.com. That Web site also has box scores (though not play-by-play accounts) for regular season games during those seasons. Plus, you can watch all of Babe Ruth's 1920 feature film, *Headin' Home,* at www.archive.org or www.youtube.com. It's a wonderful opportunity to see the Babe when he was young (twenty-four) and vigorous, not the older, potbellied fellow more often depicted tiptoeing around the bases after a late-career home run. Yes, Babe did film the movie in Haverstraw, New York, on mornings during the 1920 season and then had to dash down to the Polo Grounds for 3 PM game times, sometimes taking the field with his mascara still on. As an actor, the Babe was a great home-run hitter. Babe's injury, courage, and ultimate failure in the 1921 World Series are all true.

Far more murky is the question whether gamblers "fixed" the 1918 World Series between the Chicago Cubs and the Babe's Boston Red Sox. Eddie Cicotte—one of the infamous Black Sox players banned from baseball for fixing the 1919 Series—thought they did, and you can read his statement online at the Web site of the Chicago History Museum. Baseball historians still argue over Cicotte's claim. Sean Deveney's *The Original Curse* is inclined to believe it, while Allan Wood's *Babe Ruth and the 1918 Red Sox* finds the evidence suggestive but not conclusive. In 2011, baseball historian John Thorn told the *New York Times* that he thought it likely that the 1918 Series was rigged by gamblers. When I sifted the known facts, I concluded the allegation was fair game for a writer of historical fiction, though *The Babe Ruth Deception* doesn't pretend to settle the question.

Arnold Rothstein, gambling kingpin and all-around force of darkness in America in 1920, is examined thoroughly in David Pietrusza's *Rothstein: The Life, Times, and Murder of the Criminal Genius Who Fixed the 1919 World Series.* Fans of the television series *Boardwalk Empire* will remember him from that program. I did not have to invent Abe Attell, "the Little Hebrew," who was featherweight champion of the world from 1906 to 1912. After his boxing career, Attell fell into show business and gambling. He actually was a major investor in Babe Ruth's feature movie, *Headin' Home* (I couldn't make that up!), and is reputed to have been the man who delivered the bribe money to the White Sox players who threw the 1919 World Series. He was indicted with the Black Sox players, but the Chicago trial judge threw out the charges against him.

The Wall Street bombing at J. P. Morgan Bank in September 1920 killed forty people and wounded more than two hundred. Though widely attributed to radical or anarchist groups, it was never solved. Visitors to downtown Manhattan can still see some of the damage the bomb did to the Morgan building. A full treatment of the bombing appears in Beverly Gage's *The Day Wall Street Exploded: A Story of America in Its First Age of Terror.* There are many examinations of Prohibition, America's failed experiment in social virtue. A good one is Daniel Okrent's *Last Call: The Rise and Fall of Prohibition.*

When I grew weary of book and online research, I turned for ideas and information to my friend and neighbor Paul Dickson, who has written authoritatively on baseball history, on all matters involving alcoholic beverages, and on dozens of other subjects. Insightful comments on an early draft of the manuscript came from Ron Liebman and Gerry Hogan, friends and outstanding writers. Moral support and morale boosting came from the monthly lunches of the Hamlet Group. You know who you are.

This is my third novel with Kensington Books, which has brought me under the wise care of editor John Scognamiglio and publicist Vida Engstrand. More excellent good fortune. Great thanks to my master agent, Will Lippincott, who has willingly ventured with me into the thickets of fiction publishing.

My greatest debt, as ever, remains to Nancy, my love of so many years.